Project

Beth Button

D1153685

Dedication

For survivors of domestic violence and for the family members
and loved ones of those who did not survive
domestic violence.

CHAPTER ORDER

Introduction

On Friday night, September 19, 1997, Natasha Emily Hillshaw was found dead. Her ex-husband, Jacob Charles Grazen, now faces the death penalty, after being convicted of murdering her. Her body was found at his house, they had argued earlier that day, and domestic violence had dominated their marriage. However, to many of the people who have been following this case, it is not an open and shut one.

There are many suspicions and questions about what happened that night and what led up to it. Was the correct decision made by the jury in this trial? The victim had suffered from depression for years. Jake Grazen had been in therapy since the divorce and was diagnosed as not being a threat to anyone. Suicide is therefore the actual cause, some believe. In which case, an innocent man is going to die for a crime he did not commit.

I'm a third-year graduate student, in Journalism, at Arizona State University West. Last spring, I chose the topic of abusive relationships for my next project. I turned my attention to the Grazen trial, because I recognized it as an important opportunity. By interviewing people in the midst of their experiences, I could bring a real depth to my project.

The initial atmosphere in Phoenix seemed to be one of constant public debate. Some members of the press and domestic violence advocates focused on the abusive relationship and Jake's standing in the community. Should a well-known, influential man's

violence create any more or less concern and outrage
than the violence being committed in countless
households on a daily basis? Friends and families to
the victim, on the other hand, were just trying to get a
handle on their grief and confusion, while battling
with the strong media presence. And Jacob Grazen
and his supporters were concerned with his fate.

I didn't have the delusion that I would come up
with some great resolution, answering everyone's
questions and ending the problem of domestic
violence by discovering some crucial truth. However,
I thought that by focusing on the individual feelings
and reactions of the people who had direct
connections with the case, I could address the specific
issues in a more productive and real way.

I contacted several different people with ties,
personal and/or professional, to this case and asked
them to contribute a candid and thorough reaction to
each aspect of the case affecting them. I offered the
choice of an interview format or written descriptions.
Kristin Hillshaw chose an interview and helped me
edit her answers, adding some of her own questions.
The others opted for written contributions, which they
wrote at various points in the trial. (Only four people
declined to participate.)

Some of the participants wanted to discuss the
project at different points in their writing process and
I did meet with them, but I didn't offer much editing
beyond a spell check because I wanted to preserve the
exact tone of each piece. I sent out a packet to each
participant, with everyone's submissions before the

final version was compiled, so that they could respond to the other accounts if they chose to, or contact me with any last-minute additions.

At this time, I do not plan on submitting this book for publication. I'm a student and I'm compiling this information as a part of my education. This is essentially a term paper. If I change my mind at a later date and do try to get it published, it will only be within the college circuit, as a classroom demonstration and discussion tool for Journalism programs. I explained this carefully to the contributing writers, making sure they all knew that this is not a tell-all gossip book or a screen-play.

(In the interest of eliminating confusion, I should note that Natasha was also known as Natalie.)

Meredith Kendall

May 20, 1998

Time Line

1990

September: Natasha Emily Hillshaw starts college at the University of Arizona at Phoenix.

1991

October: Natasha meets Jacob Charles Grazen, a well-known male model who is in his second year of law school, and they start dating.

1992

May: Natasha and Jacob move in together.

December: Jacob becomes violent.

1993

February: The Phoenix police are called to their residence for a domestic dispute, but Jacob is not at the scene when they arrive, and Natasha expresses that she does not want Jacob charged with any crime. The city files an assault charge but the case is later dismissed due to a lack of evidence.

May: Jacob graduates from law school and begins working at a tax law firm in Phoenix, while continuing his work with a local model agency.

1994

May: Natasha graduates, receiving a BA in human services and counseling. She begins medical school at Arizona State University, in the child psychiatry program.

June: Natasha and Jacob get married.

1995

January: Jacob is arrested for misdemeanor assault, at a local bar, after striking a man he didn't know with a beer bottle. He is released on bail and then plea bargains for a $1,000 fine.

February: Natasha moves out for 3 weeks and stays with a friend, then she and Jacob reconcile and she moves back.

1996

June: Jacob is charged with domestic battery, then found guilty of a reduced charge of misdemeanor assault. He serves 30 days in jail of a 1-year sentence, receiving a suspended sentence for the remaining time, and is assigned to 45 hours of community service.

June: Natasha moves out of their house and stays with her mother in Flagstaff.

<u>August</u>: Natasha moves back to Phoenix and rents her own apartment.

1997

<u>February</u>: Natasha files for divorce.

<u>April</u>: The divorce is finalized.

<u>September 19</u>: Natasha is found dead in Jacob's garage, with a gunshot wound in her head. Alcohol and barbiturates are found in her system. Jake told the police that he had struggled with Natasha for the gun, and that she shot herself in the head after getting the gun from him. He turned over his 22-caliber gun to the police. It had been fired that day and contained the fingerprints of both Jake and Natasha. Jake was taken to the Phoenix police station for extensive questioning and then arrested.

<u>October 7</u>: The pre-trial hearing begins.

<u>October 24</u>: The pre-trial hearing ends, with a verdict of conclusive evidence for a criminal trial.

<u>October 27</u>: Jury selection begins.

<u>October 30</u>: Jury selection is completed.

<u>November 10</u>: The criminal trial begins.

1998

<u>January 19</u>: The state and defense conclude their arguments and the case is given to the jury.

<u>January 29</u>: The jury finishes deliberation, returning a guilty verdict.

<u>February 16</u>: Sentencing begins.

<u>February 25</u>: A sentencing verdict is reached: the death penalty is granted.

Maggie Gellar

Maggie Gellar is a Physician's Assistant in San Antonio, Texas. She was a close friend of Natasha.

September 20, 1997

I've always kind of thought of Natalie as a mirror image of myself. I am a few years older and I watched her go through each stage of the violence, remembering and relating to it. Her life was so similar to mine and we had compared our life-threatened lifestyles so often, that I feel as closely connected to her death as I did to her life. What happened to her, could have very well happened to me. In fact, there was a time in my life when I truly expected that to be the case.

I have learned, from everything that has happened since my dear friend's death, that I need to advocate for everything I believe in, especially now. I was inspired and encouraged by Natalie's strength to stand by her most precious values. If I shut off my emotions, bury my anger, and don't face up to all the ignorant lies people are saying, I won't be doing anything to keep the truth alive.

Natalie would want people to know what her life really was about, what she was really like. Why should Jake have the last word on her private thoughts?

I met Natalie in March of 1991. She had only been with Jake for a few months, but they had gotten serious right away. I was married to Alec Warner (who is now my ex-husband) and he worked for the same modeling agency that Jake did. So, Natalie and I saw each other at all the shows and parties that were basically mandatory for the significant others to the models, especially if you were concerned about your loved one's fidelity. Both Natalie and I had that concern.

We became close friends. We shared the same interests, had the same sense of humor, and were involved with the same type of men, so we hit it off very well. We relied on each other as allies in a secretive war. Although it didn't seem secretive at the time. Or not to me at least, because my life was so completely defined by what Alec did to me, I thought it would be clear to the rest of the world too. I always expected people to know what was going on. At times, I even prayed for it, even though I knew the risks involved, because I thought maybe there could be a way out for me. Maybe someone would catch a glimpse of a bruise, where my make-up had worn off, and somehow be able to help me.

I'd been with Alec for about a year and a half at that point, so I was right into the lifestyle Natalie would have to quickly absorb. In a way, I felt like her supervisor in a difficult job, trying to encourage her and give her advice. I had the knowledge that she was starting to gain on her own. Sometimes I wanted to tell her that everything would be okay, that you got used to it, and that it wasn't as bad as it seemed. Other times, I was too tired. Or I would feel slightly bitter. "You're young, you're just getting into this, so it's not too late to get out," I thought. And since she didn't, she was paving the way for more and more trauma. The bitterness was there because I felt like she was letting me down by not doing what I wished I had done.

One myth about domestic violence victims, which I've heard a lot, is that we carry around a basic belief that things are going to get better. This certainly wasn't the case for me, and from everything Nat told me about her relationship and her basic outlook on it, it wasn't true for her either. Early on in my relationship, I tried having hope that Alec would change, but there just wasn't anything to back it up with. After just one time of getting beat up after a long, drawn-out, seemingly genuine string of apologies and promises of change, my hope vanished. I did create a whole system of denial about how dangerous he really was, but it was always superficial and I knew it. It was more suppression of reality than fading optimism or weak hope for improvement.

As we got to know each other better, we'd exchange coping tactics and engage in long gripe sessions. It was both relieving and depressing. We could confide things to each other that we didn't share with our other friends, which felt good, but it was sad too.

We rarely had light discussions. I don't remember exactly when we figured out that we were both in abusive relationships. We kind of gave off vibes to each other and had intuitive feelings that we were in the same situation, and then one night after we'd both had 4 or 5 vodka tonics, we began discussing it. Natalie was the only person I've ever felt comfortable talking about the violence with, even though I know several other women who have been through it. We were so close and comfortable with each other that there was no hesitation about revealing the most private details of our relationships.

Being in an abusive relationship isn't something you advertise. There's so much shame that your life becomes engulfed in pretense, which causes more shame, unless you're comfortable with lying. I got to the point of feeling that I had no choice but to become comfortable with it. I had to lie to myself about my own safety--"He's really not that bad, he wouldn't ever do anything if it came down to that," and lie to everyone I had contact with about my happiness. That was my biggest reason for finally leaving Alec--I was completely exhausted by the constant acting and lying, both to others and to myself. When I was at the grocery store, I had to act like my biggest concern was picking out the best cut of steak and when I was around my kids, I had to pretend that we were all living in a safe, loving home. It literally gave me a headache, trying to drown out my real feelings with the life I believed I had to live out for everyone else.

The modeling business just intensified the double life, with dose after dose of superficiality. I know it's not a career that many people take seriously, but it brings a whole culture of its own, to the models and their partners. And I agree with some of the skeptical attitudes about the field, so it was one more situation of feeling like a hypocrite. I was sometimes disgusted by all the emphasis I was putting on the most superficial aspects of my life, like what I should wear every day and how often I should change my hairstyle. I felt like I had betrayed my own personality, as weird as that sounds, because my priorities and concerns were very different than the ones I had before the marriage. I had always liked shopping and doing my make-up, but it hadn't been a complete obsession. When I spent hours looking for the perfect dress for a given show, paid ridiculous amounts of money for hairstyles and facials, and killed myself at the gym every day to keep my body firm, it wasn't fun. I was always thinking how Alec would go ballistic if my ass looked fat from any angle, so whenever people would say they wished they had a body like mine, I would cringe.

I was also disgusted by my own sincere belief that I had to do all of it. I could completely understand Natalie's description of realizing she had choices, when she got the divorce, because I went through that same transition from believing I was required to live out the lifestyle my abuser had created, to seeing what a pile of crap that was. But it took a long time to get there. Egos thrive and expand in a context of constant socializing and a microscopic focus on image. When your husband gets paid for looking perfect, he can't have a bleary-eyed, nervous, unhappy wife by his side. And I wanted to hide the secret as much as he did. I didn't want anyone to know my shame. I wanted to look like I could cope with all the pressures and come out on top.

So together, Natalie and I showed off our highly perfected skills of pretense. We would stroll around parties with a martini in one hand and a Sobranie cigarette in the other, and smile non-stop. Our expressions said "Isn't my husband wonderful? Aren't I lucky that he's chosen me? I only wish I could come to these lovely affairs more often!" We comforted each other by the bond we both had with our secrets and with our honest confessions to each other about what was really going on in our lives.

We used to joke about how our friendship was a co-dependent relationship, but it wasn't really a joke. In some ways, I think we fed off each other and wrapped ourselves up in our hopelessness. Self-pity often felt like the only comfort we had. We didn't have to make excuses or explain why we did anything, because we both knew. There was no way out, and our consolation was sharing the misery.

We looked out for each other, but everything was lined with depression, for both of us. We shared stories, but didn't always talk about the real danger. We didn't have to. I couldn't tell her to get out or encourage her to stick with it, because I knew her impossible dilemma firsthand.

I got really worried about Natalie, as time went on, but I felt that I wasn't in the position to do anything. I obviously wasn't strong enough to help her. I would have been a hypocrite if I advised her. She probably looked at me the same way: knowing that something was wrong and feeling helpless to fix it.

I've heard a few people talk about Natalie's depression, but mostly it's been buried. I don't know if her other friends are trying to hide it, or if it's just too painful to discuss. I think that it's an important part of what went on with her and Jake. It's not covering the whole story to simply say "she wasn't happy." I think that's too soft. She was in agony, in every possible way. I'm not going to say Jake was responsible for Natalie becoming depressed because I don't think of it that way. When something terrible happens in somebody's life, they don't just react to one specific problem. The pain spreads out to everything and everyone in your life.

Maybe Jake was the reason she hated herself and her life or maybe it was the effects of loving him. Either way, the depression took on its own personality. It controlled her. She had so much anger, mainly towards herself, and she didn't know how to let it out. She was very self-destructive at times and it was almost as if she was trying counteract Jake's bad behavior by treating herself badly at the same time. She would isolate herself, not seeing her friends or doing anything for herself. It got to the point where it was hard for me to tell which restrictions were hers and which were Jake's. She thought most or all of their problems were her fault, so she felt like she deserved his insults and control tactics.

Natalie and I had some crucial differences. Jake was the first man she loved. He was also the first man she slept with. (I know everyone talks about Ryan as her first love, but it wasn't on the same level as her love for Jake. Ryan was her friend who became her boyfriend, and Jake was always her lover.) I was with quite a few men before Alec. So, I was a little more bitter about men. I went into the relationship with the opinion that men were incapable of committing. Alec was eagerly searching for a committed relationship because he had just been badly hurt by a woman he'd been engaged to. He was very insecure and he threw everything into our relationship, in the beginning. That was a clear-cut example of co-dependency because we were both looking for proof of love, trust, and security. Natalie, on the other hand, got all of her bitterness about men from Jake. She began their relationship with a lot of trust and love, which Jake grabbed with both hands. When he began manipulating her, she didn't see through it for a long time because her trust was so strong.

Another difference was that I have kids. My protective desires came out, when it came to Natalie, because she wanted so badly to be a mother. I just didn't want her to experience the intense fear and guilt that comes along with having kids with a violent man. In my situation, I just couldn't figure out a solution. I have always been very happy that I have kids, but unhappy for what they have gone through. My bad choice in a husband and father for them was their model of behavior. But once I was in the situation, I couldn't dwell on that. I tried weighing my options, but nothing seemed safe. If I left, he would find us. He could get custody, he could hurt them even if he just got visitation. If I stayed, the danger seemed more constant, because he was right there with them, but I could at least be there too and do my best to protect them.

When I first met Alec, I thought that men became models for money only and moved on to a "real career" once they earned a lot. I would never have guessed that guys like Jake, who were lawyers or doctors, would stay in modeling once they finished school and got high-paying jobs in their other field of work. What I soon realized was that models' egos can be much more motivating than money. People make jokes about Jake's strange combination of careers, saying it sounds like a bad soap opera plot, but they don't realize just how serious he was about modeling. Alec stayed in modeling for the same reasons, but he didn't have Jake's challenge of balancing a tax lawyer's lifestyle with the modeling world.

Image was everything to Jake, so he fit right into the business. He set out to gain as much acceptance in Phoenix for his modeling accomplishments as he had gained in the tax law community. There wasn't much doubt among the people who knew him about his ability to do it, Natalie explained to me, and I could definitely see why when I got to know him. Jake is the smoothest person I've ever met. He's consistently friendly, witty, and seems to be a great listener. He is of course extremely conniving, but you'd never really know that because he appears to be so warm and genuine. He seems like he never has a negative thought.

I feel weird when I try to figure out what Natalie was feeling and why she made certain decisions in her relationship. For one thing, those are deeply personal questions and for another, it seems like no one other than Nat herself could ever understand it. And there are a lot of things that she probably never understood either. I feel the same way when I try to figure out my relationship with Alec. Since "hindsight is 20/20," people can sit down with a list of statistics and compare what went on. Now that the relationship is over, all the information is intact. But experiencing abuse isn't something you can get on paper. You just can't.

I didn't know why I did *anything* when I was with Alec. And I don't think it was all about being naïve or totally in love. I honestly don't know what it was about, because I didn't ever sit down at my kitchen table and say, "Gee, why is it that I'm still here after what happened last night?" If I did that, I don't think I would have ever gotten a different answer than "Because I'm a fucking pathetic, stupid idiot." That's what Alec told me and that's what I believed, not simply because he told me it, but because I grew to believe it on my own. I'm not saying Natalie dealt with her confusion and pain like I did. I'm saying I don't think we can sort it all out. We can't come up with ·definitive answers about a woman's most intimate thoughts.

Natalie's letters talk about her shock the first time Jake hit her. That may sound strange. A woman should really know what her husband is like before something extreme happens, but I had similar feelings when the worst times came along. When I first found out he was cheating on me, I felt small. He was physically stronger than me, he twisted everything around to make me feel like I was always to blame, and now he was going elsewhere for sex. I felt like such a loser. He could do anything he wanted and there was nothing I could do.

I don't mean to totally lump together infidelity and violence, because I know you can have one without the other. But in my mind, the two things are very similar. They both cause you to feel shock, betrayal, and fear. With physical abuse you're in fear for your safety and with affairs, you're in fear of not being able to trust again. (Trust *any*one. That's how much it affects your mind.)

I used to think that I would never put up with either. It was so simple for me to picture my actions before the fact. My choices would naturally fall into place, in response to my firm values. I would leave a man at the first sign of trouble. I had a clear idea of what's unacceptable, and if he crossed that line, it'd be over for us. Now I can say that no woman has the right to make that kind of assumption until she's in the position. I would never have predicted the choices I made once I was in deep and it wasn't that I changed my perspective. It just wasn't as easy as knowing what my husband did to me was wrong. He'd be the first to tell you that he thought it was wrong too. That knowledge had nothing to do with stopping it from occurring.

It's really hard for me to clarify my views on domestic violence now. I mean, I know my feelings about my own experience, but when I'm confronted by people who have strong views about it one way or the other, I freeze up. About 6 months after my divorce was final, my sister's boyfriend set me up with a guy he worked with. We had been on a few double dates with my sister and when we had our second date alone, I walked out because we got into a discussion that overwhelmed me. He knew my basic history and I thought I was ready to talk about it, but when he asked me why women stay with violent men, I couldn't speak or respond or breathe. I know that's a simple question that many people have, but I feel like it's an accusation. It doesn't matter how carefully the person sets it up or explains their perspective.

I want to use my experience to help other women and I think I can do that. But I don't think I'll ever be into speaking at education programs or advocacy rallies about the general dynamics of violent relationships or why they happen, because I don't feel like I know. I can't always make the theories about a batterer's insecurity and control issues fit logically in my head. I can relate a lot easier to the typical "symptoms" of a victim because the feelings that the abuse brings out are very fresh in my memory. And it's clearer to me because that's what I went through. I have never felt like I understood why Alec hurt me, despite the numerous explanations by him and many different therapists. I could never identify with his feelings that cause him to be violent, because I can't consider his perspective with any degree of objectivity.

My feelings about blame are simple. I don't think a victim of domestic violence is ever to blame, nor do I think that victims of any other crime are responsible for their own pain and loss. The person committing the crime has complete control over the act and is the only one responsible for it. I've been mugged, my car was stolen, my house has been broken into, and none of those things were my fault. Even if I had done something to entice theft, I wouldn't be to blame because I'm not the one who broke the law.

I'm so upset by all the rationalizing people do who hold the opposite view. What is the purpose of defending a perpetrator and pointing out ways the victim should have acted to avoid the crime? If an act is okay, it shouldn't be classified as a crime. I think rape is the best example of this. I can't hear someone talk about the "she asked for it" theory without feeling sick. It's so unfair to make up this elaborate set of rules for a woman and say that as long as she abides by them, she is not responsible for getting raped. And if she fights back, she will be believed. But if you wear the wrong outfit or give a man the wrong impression, your rights to live a safe life are gone because you're giving consent whether you mean to or not. And knowing this is the way it works, what is stopping a rapist from helping himself?

People outside of this tragedy may wonder why it's such a big deal. I hear complaints that the soaps aren't going to be on when the trial starts. This is a big deal because it's a death that shouldn't have happened. Phoenix is getting all this attention because this tragedy has confused everyone. We're all careful about what we say and when--we have to be. I have tried not to care about what's being said and assumed about me. I still try. I try to just focus on sorting out my own emotions from everything the people around me are saying, but it seems to all blend together. I care what people say because they're combing through my memories and emotions. I feel like my life is an "open book," except it's even more revealing than that. It's like the world is watching a movie about my most private feelings, fears, and values and all I can do is watch along with them.

I would like to be able to talk about domestic violence openly, without people acting like I'm running for office or selling vacuum cleaners. It's one of the chic topics people debate about, trying to find a solution. It's a negotiation. I guess that in some ways it has become my "cause" for the simple reason that it will always be a part of me, but it was an assigned cause that I can't ever detach myself from. I always find myself wishing that people could know just how much I hated that assignment, and how much I would love for domestic violence *not* to be my cause. But the reality is that I just wish the reasons for my connection were different, because I wouldn't walk away from it for anything. I've never really thought of myself as being able to change anyone else's life or as being a decent role model, but I am going to try to help people through their pain, any chance I get. Maybe I wouldn't know how big a problem domestic violence is and how much we need people to give a damn about it if I hadn't been a victim.

Mariah Whitmore

Mariah Whitmore is the Executive Director and a counselor at a treatment center for men who batter, in Phoenix. She has been with the agency for the past 15 years. Additionally, she has a private counseling practice with her husband. She previously worked at a rape crisis center in Minneapolis, and then as a counselor for men's groups, in that same city. She holds a Doctorate in Psychology and a Master's in Social Work.

October 12, 1997

A life is an education. There's a test every moment. What should you do when you see your friend's husband out with another woman? How can you disguise a last-minute zit break-out? Should you move to another state for a higher paying job, when it means pulling your kids out of their third new school? The grading scale is complicated, with several different categories. There's interpretation, prioritizing, short-term and long-term decisions, and values. If the woman is his boss or his sister from out of town, you will look like an idiot for tattling, but if he's cheating, your friend has the right to know. Maybe you want to be seen as someone who's too busy to worry about your complexion. But could the intended message go awry and end up as "I don't take the time to wash my face"? Your kids' well-being is intertwined with financial security, because you have to provide for them. But if you use that as an excuse to pursue your own interests, perhaps you're ignoring their well-being altogether.

Some tests, field trips, and special lab projects are more serious than others and sometimes we spend too much time on the wrong ones. We usually won't see the lesson in something until it's over and some time has gone by. We can always get something out of our experiences--we learn more and more about ourselves as we go along, but just don't realize it at the time it's actually going on. We don't stop and wonder about future consequences. Each choice shows us who we are, what we've learned, and what we want out of life. Yet it can take a while for us to find out exactly what our choices mean.

The tricky part is the grading, since there isn't just one teacher who collects everyone's daily decisions and prints out evaluations. Each of us is in an independent study program, with the occasional group project thrown in. We evaluate our own work. But our paths often merge, so we can't just grade ourselves in isolation from outside opinions. We care about what other people think so we pay attention to their choices. Those choices can inspire us, make us question our own behavior, or validate our own decisions. As a society, we try to fit each method of analysis together, to use as a judging tool for every event we experience or observe. We try to decipher our own beliefs and then determine how each experience impacts us as a group.

This is what's happening in Phoenix now. We have a complicated lesson ahead of us. We all have the same facts: Natasha Hillshaw has been killed, her ex-husband has a criminal record which includes domestic assault against her, he's been charged with her murder, Natasha had a history of depression, and the coroner's office analyses do not rule out suicide. What a list! What are we going to do with these facts? We all have different standards for judging this situation. Our knowledge, experience, and opinions about domestic violence, murder and suicide are working at various levels. If we know the victim or the suspect, that obviously affects our perspective. Or maybe we know someone else who's gone through something similar. Even if it's a fresh situation for us, it's frightening and confusing.

We are sincerely trying to get what's going on. Everyone seems to hold a theory for figuring it out. "Listen to your own convictions." Good advice. "Advocate for your values." Fine if that's clear to you. "Ignore the media." How? "Embrace the media." Why? And so on. The problem is that we are all in different seats in the arena, watching something that's foreign to some of us and common for others. We could be in the front row because we're pushed up the by the crowd, watching out of boredom. We could be standing near the exits, so we can beat the rush to leave, when it's over. Maybe we move every time we see a vacant seat, in hopes of getting in front of a camera. We're there for different reasons and we're not all seeing the same thing.

I want to point out the extreme difference between the people closest to this tragedy and the countless onlookers. I would be disrespecting Natasha's parents and devaluing their pain, if I implied that the discomfort and sadness that people who never knew their daughter feel while watching the news at night, is even comparable to their burden of grief. Every day brings excruciating turmoil for them and my awareness of that fact doesn't get me close to their experience. I'm the first to admit that.

For the rest of us, there are some emotional dips and peaks. It's disturbing to think of the terrible things that happen every day and for most people, violence is scary. My personal plan for dealing with that is to keep on a steady path towards the truth. I tell myself to stop worrying about misquotes and the latest popular opinion, and focus on my own mind. What makes the most sense? We could say that it doesn't matter, that our opinions about what happened on the night Natasha died will be obsolete in a couple of years, but that's not true. It's not about one night of tragedy that ended with the next day's sunrise. It's a permeating loss, so if we let this turn into one more unsolved mystery in a long line, we'll be turning away from the reality of violence. This time of tragedy and confusion is just one puzzle piece of our ongoing education and our perceptions of it will be the markers for how we should react to future crises. We have to watch what's going on--what people say and do, to figure out how to do things differently down the road. This is one of life's pop quizzes.

Did Natasha lose the battle with her depression or did Jake win his struggle to control her? That's where the truth, about what happened on the night of her death, lies. Natasha's depression wasn't a separate event from the abuse and manipulation. It was the result of those factors. She was searching for her identity, when she fought with Jake and when she was dealing with the loneliness after she left him. She was haunted by a poor self-image, which Jake gave her initially, then she came to believe in it too. She and

Jake built up a strong co-dependency and then she experienced guilt when their relationship was over. She was no longer meeting his needs.

For me, it's too early to come up with a definitive answer. There's going to be a trial and the evidence will come out during that. In the meantime, we can think about the dynamics of a violent relationship, in order to be aware of the possible scenarios. That is all I intend to do. I am not going to guess about what happened on the night Natasha died, but I'm going to consider what might have led up to that night.

Those who are unfamiliar with domestic violence see it as a war between a man and a woman, where it would only make sense to support either one side or the other. This will not work. Certainly, a violent relationship has some characteristics of a war. There's physical fighting and constant struggles for control. And there are casualties and emotional scars. However, it's not as simple as eliminating the aggressor in order to end up with a clean solution. You can't separate out a victim's pain and say "This is worth protecting," without looking at how the abuser fits in. It's cause and effect.

Another problem with the war mentality is the delicate, complex inner structure of an abusive relationship. You can't plow in and eliminate the violence without crushing it. This is where the "domestic" part comes in. A man and a woman have chosen to make a home together. They are each other's family. Violence can be become an obstacle for maintaining the relationship, but the connection they have is the obstacle for ending it.

People don't understand why a woman stays with someone who hurts her and there are many reasons, but a big one is love. And no matter how you feel about that and judge it, it's there. That's one of the reasons why a therapist can't think that telling a victim how horrible her abuser is will be the magical solution. The victim may agree with that, but she still loves him. She is attached to him and feels that she needs him.

In some ways the victim does need her abuser, because she's getting certain things from the relationship that she's not getting in any other part of her life. For instance, attention and dependency. Her abuser consistently offers attention, whether it's negative or positive. The attention is intense. And he has convinced her that he is completely dependent on her. He's also isolated her so she can't see the possibility of receiving love from anyone else. She has invested everything into the relationship and the bad things don't push her away because they've simply become things she has to deal with. It feels completely natural to her.

The elements of a violent relationship are building blocks for horrendous endings.

Fear, instability, dominance, control and dependency are constants, but they come in different formulas. Sometimes the batterer is consistently dominant, sometimes it's a co-dependent relationship, and sometimes the victim has alternating periods of submissiveness and rebellion. The dynamics gain strength as the relationship goes on.

The batterer gets used to his power and expects it. In his mind, he deserves it.

Meanwhile, the victim gets more and more confused. She tries to sift through all the chaos and find something solid for support. She looks for consistency and for some kind of reassurance, but the abuse may be the only constant behavior she can find. It's the one

thing she can depend on. She knows it's going to happen no matter what. She tries to please her abuser and control the abuse, but he has all the control and she always falls short.

A woman who is being abused by the man she loves is living a very complicated life. The pain is layered throughout her life and she has to manage it. She wants to appear strong to the people she cares about and she wants to build up strength for herself.

She needs to be seen as worthy of support and love, and she needs to believe that herself- to feel it as her truth.

Another portion of her life is a hard, dirty core that disgusts her. It's in everything she does because there is one plain truth staring her in the face: she is with a man who hurts her. She is ashamed of it and she hates it. He hurts her. It's a small, seemingly simple truth on the surface, but it represents every scary thing she could imagine. He takes her weaknesses and attacks them with full force. He builds upon her insecurities, creating new ones every day. He calls her names that make her body shake, make her nauseous, and make her want to run from him and from herself. "You are worthless, you are nothing." This haunts her and grows into a truth that feeds her mind. This truth justifies the physical pain and makes it logical and necessary. He has to hurt her because she is nothing. She deserves punches and slaps. She deserves rape. She belongs to him.

The bruises and marks are her reminders of what she deserves, as well as her faint hope that she can somehow, someday be good enough for him. Good enough for the pain to stop.

That information directly motivates me to spend my time doing everything I can to prevent women from having to go through that. I know it's going on and I can't ignore it. So, I am really shaken when I get criticized for my work and accused of being a victim-blamer. People can't understand how I can do this work and I can't understand how I can do anything else. Domestic violence haunts me and I can't walk away from it without trying to offer something that helps.

I work with men who batter. That makes me unpopular and puts me at the receiving end of a lot of negative attitudes. I've been doing this for 20 years so I've had a lot of time to think about the reactions. Domestic violence frightens and disgusts people. It doesn't feel right to say "Okay, let's help the batterer." Instead, the assessment is that batterers are the lowest form of scum and we need to turn our backs on them. This may bring a sense of being in a big, bad crime-stopper role, but there is no value beyond that. Even if you believe in a hierarchy of good and bad behavior, you are not supporting the good and hurting the bad with this mind-set. Ignoring violence doesn't punish the batterer or make him feel guilty. If anything, it punishes the victim.

Her pain doesn't matter. He can keep abusing her because she is not worth the time.

A man who abuses his partner needs help. He needs someone to believe that violent men are human beings, that they have rights, and that they are worth caring about and listening to. I believe all of these things. I do not believe that we give up our right as a human being when we do something wrong. As soon as we impose that kind of standard, we will have to push aside a bigger and bigger group of people. And we won't be able to rehabilitate anyone because we won't work at changing behavior.

My job doesn't validate violence or give it a stamp of approval. I am not advocating for my clients' abusive and manipulative actions, or blaming the people they hurt. I have to laugh when I get comments

like "You are giving domestic violence a bad name with your association with batterers." I have no idea how you would give it a good name! Plus, "association" isn't an accurate description of my work. I don't hold poker
games in my house and complain about women with batterers. I don't support their decision to be violent and that's why I want to help them make different choices.

Helping someone get out of violent behavior patterns doesn't mean you just let them talk endlessly about their feelings and call it a day. I have to think the way my clients think. I have to be on the same plane as the hating, blaming, abusive mind-set behind the violent behavior. We're digging up feelings and past experiences that are not only troubling for him, but solidly linked to his violent urges. I have to experience those feelings with him to find out what brought him to the place of craving control. I have to isolate every motivation for violence and find another outlet for it.

He has to trust me so I have to truly understand his emotions in the way he experiences them. Ultimately, he moves from feeling that his insecurities and inadequacies are valid, to taking responsibility for his violence. And that's a tough balance sometimes: yes, your frustrations are real and valid in the sense that they really affect your life. However, you cannot deal with them any way you want to and hurting other people is never an acceptable choice.

I'm in a fairly vulnerable position with my clients. I'm giving them a forum for their emotions and even though it's a very structured forum with clear boundaries, they try to manipulate me. They use the same methods of control and ploys for sympathy that they use with their partners. I solve this problem by constantly explaining my role, as well as my expectations, in clear, non-negotiable terms. Yes, I'm going to help him examine why he got to the point of violence. I'm going to help him deal with his feelings, but that will not amount to hash marks on his score card. We won't have a sparring match between his feelings and his victim's pain.

In an abusive relationship, the batterer is the one who causes the abuse.

Regardless of the victim's actions and all the faults the abuser pins on her, he is the one who decides to use physical violence. So, to stop the violence, you have to go right to the source and deal with him. He is not going to stop on his own, regardless of how many times he promises that.

There are reasons why men become violent. (Sometimes it's the woman who is the abuser in the relationship and sometimes one partner of a same sex relationship is violent towards the other partner. I am referring to men who abuse women because that's the group I generally work with.) Saying that doesn't take any weight away from the severity of the behavior or shift the responsibility away from the batterer. I just mean that we need to address the reasons for the destructive, threatening behavior in order to change that behavior. I guess another way to say this is that they aren't good or acceptable reasons, but they do exist. When I was learning the ropes of parenting with my first child, I quickly learned that starting a question with "Is there a reason why" never really got me anywhere. There's always a *reason*, it just may not be a logical or appropriate one. I'm sure my daughter had a reason, at the age of 2, for painting our bedroom wall with every tube of lipstick she could find, just as I probably had many reasons for all the things I did in high school that landed me in the principal's office. And I am sure that I never articulated one that made my teachers realize they had made a grave error in sending me there.

For a variety of reasons, the batterer comes to a point in his life where hurting his partner is his tool for gaining power. Maybe he was abused as a child. Maybe he had negative role models, somewhere along the line in his upbringing. The specific uses of the tool are variable too. It can be about self-esteem, where dominating and intimidating someone else brings a sense of worth. He's validated. Or it can mean carrying out a deeply entrenched vengeance against women. These issues are very important to him, even if they exist at a subconscious level. When the needs are fulfilled, it's exhilarating for him. He is showing her how things are. He can do anything he wants to her and get anything he wants from her.

For Jacob Grazen's supporters, all of this either becomes diluted when they apply it to his life or they don't accept any of it as being accurate for him. It has to be that way for them to be capable of embracing the delusion that he has never done anything wrong.

I guess it's an attempt to protect him and maybe even reassure him that he won't face the worst possible fate. For me though, the only result so far is a lack of credibility. He has admitted the violence but his supporters (or fans may be a more fitting term) just seem to ignore that.

We see Jake walking into the courthouse, surrounded by his lawyers, with that perplexed, pleading expression that he is making famous. His outfits are the most expensive ones in the courtroom and his hair looks like it's been professionally styled each day. This is not someone who could fit in with all the traits I've mentioned, his backers believe. He just couldn't do such terrible things or have such hatred and disrespect for anyone, let alone Natasha, the woman he loved so much. People don't want to admit how shallow and ludicrous this denial is. Yet it is blatantly so. He looks good, he looks innocent, so he must be.

This kind of denial stings even more when you bring it right next to what happened to Natasha. If you say that Jake did not abuse her, you're saying she was lying.

If you dismiss her death as something he could not have been responsible for, you are capping off the belittling attitude with apathy for her family's loss.

Jake was in denial himself for years and in some ways, he probably still is. He admitted that he abused Natasha when he had to admit it, but even then, there was always something that buffered his behavior. Yes, he hit her, he answered in court when the state had a pile of affidavits from witnesses, but he always had explanations (in treatment we call these excuses, by the way) that he had to get in there. Always something that dismissed him from direct responsibility.

Jake believed that he was the victim. I don't think he would say that today, because the strategy for his defense will probably be to portray a deep sense of regret for the abuse. To do that, he has to say that he admits his mistakes and doesn't blame Natasha for the violence.

I believe that he still thinks, "If only she didn't make me do it." In Jake's eyes, everyone who labels Natasha as the victim is turning the whole thing around. Just like she did when they were together. In the clips I've seen of him in court during the preliminary hearings, I can see this in his eyes. As the prosecution refers to Natasha as the victim, he has this slight look of bewilderment, combined with anger. I imagine the little voice in his head, as he keeps up his perfect pose for cameras: "What are they talking about? How can they get this so backwards?"

The important thing to remember about Jake is that regardless of how upset he acts or how sorry he claims to be, he has a history of charming his way through life. He learned how to lie and pretend when he was with Natasha. He created distorted truths for himself that he probably began to believe. That's what batterers do. Manipulation is a craft and they believe in their art. Now he has to do the same thing but the stakes are higher. He wants the world's respect, he is desperate to be believed, and he is sitting on his guilt. If he did not kill his ex-wife, he only has the guilt of abusing her, which led to her severe depression and suicide. If he did kill her, it is crucial for him to effectively lie about it, so that he doesn't lose his life. So, it all gets tightly woven together: Jake's version of what happened, his feelings, and his friends' view of what he was going through. It's not fair to say that it was all fabrication, but he did manipulate things to build a safety net for himself.

Earlier I wrote about our experiences and what we learn from them. That will happen in Phoenix. We can't just remove all the emotions and analyze this as a remote, fictional situation, so it will be a long road. There will be a lot of arguing, as we sort through the facts and rumors, but I think we will learn a lot about our society and the choices we make. I hope that we can try to understand and respect opposing views. The accusations that have already begun are really hurtful. It's been assumed that I'm trying to step out into the media's eye to defend my field of work. That's nonsense and it would never work any way! Those comments show that people come up with ideas and believe them, regardless of any explanation they hear.

This is just the beginning of this case and the things we're going to hear about are not new events. Physical violence in relationships has been happening for a long time, in every social circle. That's what I hope people can realize, no matter what the verdict turns out to be. Jacob Grazen's wealth and intelligence did not give him an exemption from a violent lifestyle.

Sarah Cronan

Sarah Cronan is a medical secretary in Los Angeles. She was a close childhood friend of Natasha Hillshaw.

November 15, 1997

As everyone probably knows by now, I'm the "hometown girl" character in this whole saga. I went to elementary school and high school with Nat, in Greensboro North Carolina. I'm usually shown as either the country bumpkin type or as a gossip with some big story to dish on Nat's past. I don't think either one of those images is very fair, but it's true that I knew Nat very well. I'm willing to talk about our friendship and her life because there are a lot of lies floating around and people need to hear the truth.

I just moved to the West Coast, but before that I was still living in Greensboro. I was right in the same area where Nat and I lived when we were kids. I was haunted by so many memories. That was part of the reason I moved away from there after she died. It was too much to pass her old house on my way to work, get coffee from our favorite café, etc. Also, I moved out here to be near her family.

It's only been a couple of months since this horrible, horrible thing happened and I'm still a mess. I wanted to write this now though, because I think it's better to capture all my feelings at the hardest time. (I can't imagine things getting easier, but I keep hearing that it will happen eventually.)

I moved from Florida to North Carolina, at the end of the first grade. I thought I was above everyone else, I was cooler. A lot of kids were surprised that Nat and I became such good friends. We were really different, but we just clicked. I was loud-mouthed, I didn't care about school. I have 3 brothers and I was kind of fighting the tomboy image, but it didn't work. I tried to fit in somewhere, but I just had a snobby attitude that rubbed people the wrong way. Nat could fit in anywhere. She was easy-going and comfortable around everyone.

The first thing that jumped out at me about Nat was how nice she was. She wasn't really the goody-goody person that a lot of people have made her out to be. Or at least she didn't ever seem that way to me. She just got along with everyone and was fun to be around. Nat didn't think she was better than anyone else. She never got that typical teen-age attitude of trying to impress people and acting like you don't care about anything. She didn't talk down to anyone or criticize and gossip, she just genuinely cared about people.

It wasn't like she thought she was a missionary, walking around teaching you how to be a good person. But she was someone I looked up to. It's strange that when we were kids I always went to Nat for advice and leaned on her, and then when we got older I had to try to do the same for her-- to give her advice and support her.

Most of my childhood memories include Nat somehow. We had the typical mishaps and adventures of being kids. When I fell off the stage in our 3rd grade production of Oklahoma (Our teacher believed in developing talent at an early age.), Nat got me to stop crying by giving me a big hug and telling me to look at "Curly" from behind-- his pants had split wide open in the butt. I cut Nat's hair in 2nd grade and she stuck to the story of how Billy Grayson, the class bully, had pinned her down and cut it.

I'm sure her mom never bought the story, but I appreciated the effort anyway. I saw it as a big act of loyalty. (I did the job with pinking shears and her bangs were less than 1/8th of inch long.) Nat taught me how to gargle chocolate milk when we were in 5th grade and she pierced my nose in 8th.

Then we suffered through all the trials of junior high and high school together. That was the big stuff, of course. Mainly it was boys, but we stressed our way through things like college entrance exams and state track meets too.

Nat was interested in things that were kind of above the heads of the rest of us. She was more mature. She did a lot of volunteer work, through her church and for other community groups, which was just as important to her as all her school activities, classes, and friends. The rest of us couldn't think beyond dating and sports. Nat was constantly thinking about other people. That's why she enjoyed volunteer work so much. She didn't take anything she had for granted and she was happy when she could help a person who had less than she did.

The way she treated her friends was more proof that she was selfless. When she took a college spring break trip to Cancun, she had been set to cancel it because I was going through a rough time. We talked on the phone the night before and I convinced her to go through with her plans instead of flying to see me. She sent me this postcard which became my security blanket. I'd use it as a bookmark, carry it around in my purse, or put it on my fridge and read it whenever I needed a smile. Instead of writing something like "Having a blast, wish you were here!" she wrote the following: "Sarah, I've been thinking about you. This will sound like a quote from a really bad self-help book, but please just think about it. Don't be afraid of success. We always think it's better to prepare ourselves for failure than to expect the best and sometimes that preparation blocks us. We focus on our limitations and we're afraid of knowing how far we can actually go." She had to write small to squeeze it all in. I could just picture her sprawled out on her beach towel, surrounded by stacks of books, writing out all her postcards with as much thought as she did with mine. Her friends were probably begging her to go swimming and throwing Frisbees at her.

Nat's family shaped who she was. Meeting them made it totally clear where she got her strong values and her likable qualities. They were very close, always supportive of each other, and very involved in the community. Nat and Kristin were the only kids I knew who really seemed to be friends with their parents. And with each other too. It was a family you always felt very comfortable around. They had so many friends, both in town and from all the traveling they did. It seemed like they knew everyone. They were so laid-back and just great people.

Nat's parents' divorce was the most civil one I've ever heard of. Of course, it was tough, but it didn't get nasty. They didn't want to hurt each other or their children. Nat and Kristin seemed more concerned about how their parents would get through it than about how it affected them. I thought that was an unusual way for teenagers to react.

(My parents got divorced when I was 15, they both remarried and then both got divorced again. I didn't handle any of it well.) When I asked Nat why she wasn't objecting at all, she said, "It's not my marriage." She also said, "They would probably stay together if Kristin and I started freaking out, but I can't be that selfish. Plus, they wouldn't be happy and I would feel guilty." She was so logical and calm about it.

Nat's parents have always been really strong people and now they're so vulnerable. I'm not sure whether they feel guilty and responsible for Nat's death. I know a lot of people think they feel that way, but I don't know. I think their main feeling is pure devastation. People are speculating about a reconciliation and saying that both Emily and John want Jake to get the death penalty. There's probably a little bit of truth scattered into that, but I think they're just unsure about most of what's going on right now. They have to deal with the emptiness and anything outside of that is just too much to concentrate on.

Ryan Sheridan was basically the only man Nat ever dated besides Jake. (Well I guess he was a boy at the time.) People are looking to him for some sort of sign about what she was like when she was in a relationship. There are comparisons between him and Jake and he's really upset about that. His marriage didn't work out so there are rumors that he's a batterer, that he can't commit, that he never got over Nat, that he's gay, and the list goes on.

I knew Ryan pretty well in high school and we've stayed close friends over the years. He was a good match for Nat because he was as sweet as she was. And he was really open-minded and mature. (He still has all of those qualities.) They were close friends for a long time and then they slowly started dating. They were serious about each other and wanted a long-term commitment but were worried that they were too young.

They went to separate colleges to let destiny guide them. They didn't think a long-distance relationship would be practical so decided to just lead their own lives and believe that they'd eventually end up together if they were supposed to be together. I'm sure they regretted the decision many times because I don't think that Ryan, Nat, or anyone who knew them, ever believed that destiny had really pointed them the right way.

Ryan and I went to the same college-- the University of South Carolina. We were both Psychology majors and our dorms were on the same section of the campus, so we ran into each other pretty often. We usually tiptoed around the subject of Nat. And when Nat and I spoke on the phone, it was the same situation. Neither of them asked me for information on the other, which I appreciated. We all knew that the situation sucked and talking about it didn't help. They missed each other but were trying to just move forward with their lives.

I visited Nat once at her college, during her first year there. Our schedules were different, so I flew out during one of my breaks and she was still in session, but it wasn't during finals so we got to hang out. I loved it. The night life was really unique in Phoenix and everyone was very friendly. Nat seemed to be happy, which was great to see. Her friends were fun, her professors were motivating and she just fit in. We drank and flirted with a lot of guys, and just talked about how great it was to be young, single, and in college. Now it makes me sad to realize that when we talked about being free, we had no idea what was ahead.

I didn't ever really get to know Jake, which was weird. It was like he was this big mystery in Nat's life. First, I had this idea of him as a great, loving guy, since that's how Nat described him, and I couldn't wait to meet him. Then he became a person I hated and feared because of what he was doing to her, and I didn't even *want* to meet him. I met him at their wedding and that was basically it. He was polite, but he didn't have much use for me because I didn't live in Phoenix. I only had to pretend to like him for a few hours and we never got past small talk. It was like this mutual understanding between us that we didn't need to say out loud: we didn't like each other and Nat was the only reason we were being civil to each other. Couple of clinks of the champagne glasses, then time to move on.

When Jake and Nat visited Greensboro together, he backed out of meeting her friends. It was their Christmas break during Nat's second year of college. They'd been going out for just a couple of months. She and I had planned out the whole week. She was so excited about seeing all her friends and we were all looking forward to meeting Jake. It turned out that Ryan was the whole problem, but we didn't know what was going on at the time.

Jake found out that Ryan and Nat dated in high school and freaked out. Then he decided he didn't want anything to do with any of her friends. Like he was boycotting us to make a point? Childish, I think. They were home for about 5 days and just hung out together the whole time. She and I had lunch one day with a few other friends, but Jake didn't join us and she left early to go meet him. One day they drove 4 or 5 hours to see a couple of his friends who were vacationing here. I thought the whole thing was strange and also really irritating. Jake didn't want to meet us, Nat was blowing us off during this rare chance to see us, and we were all confused and hurt.

Was this guy selfish or anti-social and weird, or what was the story? She hesitated each time someone called and asked them to go out, making up excuses, like they were too tired or had plans with her family. Then finally, she agreed to go to our favorite bar and bring Jake. It was the last night of their visit. A band that one of our friends sang in was playing, we had gotten a big group together, and everyone was psyched. We were supposed to meet at 9 and she called me at 8:30. I was headed out the door. I couldn't understand her at first because she was crying pretty hard. She spoke very softly and sounded nervous. "You're going to kill me, but we can't go out." I asked her what was wrong, telling her that of course I wasn't angry. She said that Jake was really sick. I heard someone yelling in the background and she ended the call.

When I found out later that Jake had forbidden her to see Ryan, my first thought was that he must really be a psycho. If he seriously felt threatened by Nat's engaged ex-boyfriend from high school, something was wrong with him. Not only would Ryan not behave inappropriately, but Nat wouldn't ever flirt with another guy or do anything to hurt Jake. She didn't cheat on people, she had chosen to be with him, so what was the problem? I had never known about that whole jealousy and control thing that happens in relationships like theirs, so I couldn't see beyond my little black and white world.

Before she met Jake, Nat planned on moving back to North Carolina after college. That kind of surprised me because she was always so worldly. I thought she'd be the kind of person who would have 2 or 3 different houses and live in the countryside of Italy or the mountains in Switzerland for part of the year and in a big city the rest of the time.

But she wanted to raise a family where she grew up. When she got serious with Jake, that was no longer an option because he would never move East with her. He said no to her idea of applying to medical schools on the East Coast and told her he wanted to live in L.A. when she finished her education. The divorce made the issue irrelevant, but that had been his plan for them.

Nat would vent to me about Jake at times and avoid the subject altogether at other times-- when she was just tired of being consumed by the relationship. Since I was a childhood friend, lived far away, and didn't know Jake, I was a reminder of a life without him-- an escape. That could either be comforting or depressing for her. If she believed she could get back to that time when she was safe, she felt a sense of hope and she tried to focus on that. However, most of the time she felt so separate from those memories that it was like it never happened. She was sad thinking about what she had lost.

Before I knew about the violence, I just thought Jake was a real downer. He decided where they would go and who they should hang out with. I took this as his egoistical belief that his opinions mattered more than Nat's. Then he made decisions about really personal things. Nat had always cooked but he dictated every meal. He told her exactly how to dress and gave her permission to purchase things. I saw all this as him being picky and whiny. He had to have things his way. Now I can see that my perception was naïve and that I minimized the true implications of his behavior.

I think that sometimes I knew more of the intimate details, about Nat's toughest times with Jake, than her friends in Phoenix knew. I was the outside source she could confide in and not worry about rumors. She also didn't have to worry about me pressuring her to leave him because I was so far away that I couldn't really do anything. Sometimes she wanted advice and sometimes just needed an ear. It was a hard time for me. I missed her terribly and I was helpless to protect her. I didn't really understand exactly what was going on at first, but I knew it was bad and I was scared for her.

I was shocked by what Nat told me. Jake threw her against the wall, dragged her across the floor by her hair, slugged her in the stomach, and kicked her all over her body. She said he usually abused her without any emotion, as if he were bored and it was just something he had to do. Then other times he seemed to enjoy it, which of course disturbed her and I was horrified to hear the descriptions. He had favorite methods and he seemed to deliberately build up to a level of rage that excited him. He didn't lose control when he hurt her. It was actually the opposite. He decided when and how he would hurt her and she just had to go along with it. He told her that he liked to see the fear in eyes and that he deserved to see it. Honestly, I had no idea what that meant but it was definitely creepy.

Threats were a big thing to Jake. It was another huge control thing because he'd promise to hurt her in a certain way and then do it. He had proved to her over and over that he was capable of anything. Nat told me that the mental stuff was an extension of the abuse and that sometimes she hated that more than the physical violence. It exhausted her and of course she couldn't reason with him, but he *wanted* her to argue with him. It was part of his game.

Nat changed a lot. I had expected her to be really panicked all the time and totally desperate. I mean, that's what I would have been like. Instead, she was kind of quiet and sullen. She kept her emotions inside and acted like she didn't really care what happened to her. It was like she had signed a contract that she couldn't get out of and she didn't have the energy to fight it. She got to the point of believing she deserved the abuse and that shocked me. She was always telling me, "You deserve better," when I was with loser boyfriends.

The other day I found a letter that she had written shortly after the first time the police were called to their house. She wrote, "It's not that there are aren't good things about being with Jake. I love him, sometimes he really tries to treat me well, and we can have fun together. But those things don't hold any weight next to the way I feel during and after a violent fight and I don't really think they're the reasons I stay with him. The best answer I have for staying is that I don't know. For some reason, I honestly believe

I have to. Like I've been chosen to do this. Maybe there was a time when I could've walked away, but too much has happened now and it's too late."

That didn't make sense to me, but I knew that it was an honest description of how she felt. She was totally aware that other people didn't understand it. I think that bothered her and made her feel even more isolated and alone. I also think she wanted to protect her friends from knowing the worst details of what was going on and how she felt about it. She blamed herself for having that life and felt guilty for how it was affecting the people who loved her. We were upset and helpless and she felt like that was her fault.

I get really angry when people say things like "If she knew how bad it was from the beginning, she should have known that it would end tragically." We can't pin her own death on her! But the truth is that thoughts like that have crossed my mind. I feel horribly guilty for having them, but they've cropped up. I think we all have become obsessed with questions we can never answer because we want to understand it in order to feel some sort of control.

I of course don't believe that Nat was responsible for getting hurt or that she deserved it. Nor do I believe that she made mistakes that ultimately caused her own death. However, I have often wondered why she stayed in the whole situation if she knew how dangerous it could get. The answer I usually come up with is that she probably did know what could happen but was just unable to stop it. I now know, from learning more about domestic violence, that the most dangerous time for a victim is separation. Therefore, staying is a survival technique. Nat didn't die when she was still in a relationship with Jake, so maybe this point is worth pondering.

I don't know what happened on September 19th. People have called me spineless for not taking a definite position, but I haven't seen all the evidence yet. I don't think it's fair to form an opinion before knowing all the facts. I want to find out the truth. I know that Jake was very, very violent towards Nat and that he had threatened to kill her. I also know that during the last few years of her life, Nat hated herself and the life she had. There were times when she thought about taking her own life.

I've heard people say "Oh, they want to make this into another domestic violence case," and I couldn't believe what I was hearing. How can you *make* it into anything? It *is* about domestic violence because that's what ruined her life, no matter how she died. I think it's insulting to block out that part of her life and say that her turmoil was unimportant. I know people are trying to protect Jake, but they shouldn't do it at her expense.

My life is so different now. A thick blanket of pain has been dropped on top of me and I'm powerless. I don't know what's normal anymore because nothing makes sense to me. I'm supposed to accept something as my reality that is simply impossible to accept. Like swallowing a truck.

Sometimes I'll just sit in a chair for hours at a time, thinking "she's dead, she's dead" over and over again. Then I'll try to will myself into not hurting on that intense, unbearable level.

I have a lot of bitterness towards the media and I know I've made that pretty obvious. I'm seeing people who have done nothing wrong get hurt by all the coverage. John Hillshaw's fiancée left him because she couldn't handle the constant invasion and Kristin has been portrayed as some kind of junkie. How can you grieve and try to defend yourself against monstrous lies at the same time? It's hard enough to find the strength to tackle either one of those tasks. It truly feels like while you're concentrating on getting through one more day, someone is thinking of how to make you look bad or searching for something interesting to expose to the world.

I think of how Nat would feel watching all of this. Her spirit is being punished for her body's death. She wouldn't want all of the speculation and gossip. She wouldn't want the people she loved to go through this. She was hurt and judged for the life she had and she's still being exploited now.

I try to answer the fair, important questions as fully as I can. There are some questions that reporters use to stir up controversy or make an interview more exciting. I won't be bullied into answering those questions and that's sometimes used against me. If you don't cooperate with certain members of the press, they'll get you back by printing something bogus about you down the line. It's a game and some people choose to play it, but I usually don't have the energy to deal with it.

So far, the things that led up to Nat's death have been swept under the rug. No one really wants to talk about the abuse. The focus is instead of Jake's future. He is famous and the death penalty is a possible sentence. Nat doesn't have a future. And if the violence had been stopped, the death penalty wouldn't be something for him to worry about.

Jake Grazen

Jacob Charles Grazen was a model and tax attorney in Phoenix. He is currently awaiting the death sentence. He was convicted of murdering his ex-wife.

November 16, 1997

I decided to write this now instead of waiting until my trial ends. If the worst happens, in terms of a verdict and sentence, I don't know if my head will be clear enough to write anything coherent at that time. And I do want to write this. I know that my words will be misinterpreted or disregarded by those who think I'm a murderer, but I have to get these thoughts out. This is the truth and I've got to at least release it, even if no one will listen or believe me.

When I started therapy for my violence, I was adamant that I didn't fit into any of the profiles for batterers. I didn't grow up seeing violence in my home, I didn't have a traditional view of sex roles, and I wasn't insecure. Well, it was a lie for me to think that, because every single one of those things were true for me. I couldn't see it though. I was different. I was justified to hit my woman because she just didn't understand. I'm sure I was a nightmare to all of my therapists, although my attitude was probably pretty typical. What a pain in the ass it must be, to try to help men who believe they are the true victims.

I wasn't in therapy for the right reason when I first tried it, so I didn't work at it. I wanted to show Nat that I was willing to change because I wanted to make sure she kept coming back after our break-ups. However, I actually wasn't willing to make any changes because I didn't believe I had a problem. It was my way of saying to Natalie, "See, I love you enough to make yet another sacrifice for you." And I truly believed I was the one making sacrifices.

I blocked out most of my childhood. It was like I knew there was a big section of dark memories, but I didn't know the details. And I didn't want to know. When I did start to remember, it really freaked me out. I suddenly had this knowledge of terrible things that had happened to me. So much time had gone by and I was helpless. I couldn't go back and change any of it and I was angry that I had no control over how my life started out. I hadn't chosen for those things to happen to me. It wasn't fair.

I didn't talk about it for a long time because it seemed like I was whining and looking for sympathy. And I really didn't know what to say. I was ashamed and thought I'd done something wrong. When I got to the point of taking therapy seriously, which was after the divorce, I was hit with this feeling that I had deserved it. I saw the tragedy I endured early in life as punishment for all the ways I hurt Nat. Even though those things occurred first, I didn't really experience the full weight of the pain until I was an adult.

I was brought up believing that the best way to deal with pain is to ignore it. That worked for me for a long time, so it was hard to give up. As most people know, my mother was killed in a car crash, along with my older brother and sister, when I was 4.

Dad had a real hard time dealing with it, so we moved in with my aunt and uncle (Mom's sister and her husband) a few months later. We stayed with them for a short while. We moved out because Dad didn't get along with my uncle. He had a nervous breakdown soon afterwards and my aunt and uncle obtained custody of me.

I lived with them until I graduated from high school. It's not a pleasant story. I didn't get to see Dad very often because he had very limited visitation rights and I was not happy living with Mary and George. They fought all the time and I saw a few physical fights, but it didn't seem abnormal to me because there was so much anger in the house. I never thought of them as being my role models, so I didn't worry that I would go on to have a relationship like theirs. I was too young to make connections like that. I just did what I had to do while I was living in their house and then moved on. It was shelter and that was the only positive aspect of it for me. These were people who kept me away from my father and I guess I ended up resenting them for that.

I was pretty quiet as a kid. I had so much going on in my head-- mainly confusion about what had happened to my family. I didn't talk about any of it because I thought people would think I was crazy. I probably got this idea from my uncle, because talking about your feelings was a sign of being "a pussy," according to him. One day I tried talking to my aunt and uncle about the accident and I was so humiliated that I promised myself never to go through that again. I told them about some dreams I was having. Mom talked to me, in these dreams, about what it was like in Heaven and she asked me to take care of Dad. I felt good and like Mom was telling me it was going to be okay, but I was confused by that. Why would I be feeling good when something so sad had happened to me? My uncle told me that if I ever talked about these kinds of things, no one would take me seriously. He said that trying to find something good in something bad was wrong and all I could do was accept that my mom, brother, and sister were dead and that my dad was crazy. My aunt didn't say a word, probably because she was afraid of him, but I took it to mean that she agreed with him.

I decided that I had to take care of myself and shut out everybody else. I knew there were a lot of kind people around me and I wanted to trust them, but I never really did. I was confused and I thought I was weird. I felt like some big plan was going on that I didn't know about. Why else would I be stuck without a real family?

I didn't ever think of myself as sexist. I have nothing against women working, I've had a lot of feminist friends over the years, and I believe in equality. But I have realized that basically these have just been words that sound good, and they don't represent my true feelings. Also, I was defining sexism in a very extreme way. A man who believes women are inferior to men and who demands that his wife stay home and keep house is sexist. Since I don't see things that way, I am Mr. Liberal himself. I didn't see my urge to control Natalie as meaning I hated women. It was just natural. And I loved her. I didn't think my feelings were misogynistic because it was about Natalie specifically, not women generally. I was enraged by her inadequacies, but I didn't see her as representing all women and I didn't think I had this major animosity towards women.

But there was a lot more going on than feeling like Natalie owed me something.

The anger I had went beyond anything she did, didn't do, said or didn't say. I was punishing her for things she couldn't control, because in my mind, she was responsible for everything. When I ranted about how I was the victim and she controlled me, I would accuse her of being a threat to me. That's how I saw it-- she had the control because I was desperate to keep her in my life. The fact that she loved me cursed her. I had to "make her understand" just how much I needed her. It was sick.

It's still very difficult for me to talk about the connection between losing my mother and the way I feared losing Natalie. Just hearing "fear of abandonment" was more than I could handle when my therapist first went into this with me. I couldn't deal with the idea that I was afraid of how someone else could affect me. I didn't need people to treat me a certain way, the only way fear could be a part of my life was if I was causing it for someone else, and who would ever want to leave *me*? This sounds like sarcasm, but sadly it's the actual perception I had.

In my mind, I needed to instill fear in someone else. That was my way of combating against my past and feeling powerful. I was entitled to the position of control, I believed, because of what I had endured. I built every situation into a 2-tiered set-up, where I was on top, dictating Natalie's behavior and her feelings. Even when I broke down and begged for her forgiveness, I was in control because I was manipulating the situation. When I told her I was afraid she would leave me, it was true, but it was also a total mind-game. I didn't have to say "like my mother did," because she knew that was at the root of it. She felt like shit and I had won.

I had a lot of anger toward my aunt, which probably helped shape my twisted view of women. She had let me down by not standing up to my uncle. I thought she and I should be allies because we had both lost family. It was her responsibility to protect her sister's only surviving child. She must have thought about my mother and my siblings every time she looked at me, so why couldn't she fight back-- for my sake and my mother's? Now I have a different perspective. Her sister was dead and she was as confused and hurt as I was. She also wasn't allowed, by her husband, to talk about it.

She was dealing with the same fear that I later caused in Natalie. Now I can see that I really did learn from my uncle's behavior and that I was expecting my aunt to make up for the pain of my mom's death. Of course, no one could ever do that.

Natalie was the first person I opened up to about my past. She was so understanding and compassionate that it overwhelmed me. She never pushed me to talk about my childhood, but she was willing to listen unconditionally whenever I felt like talking. She offered insight when I needed it but didn't judge me. This was new for me.

I've been blessed with a lot of friends and caring people, but I always felt like people expected me to share personal issues with them to prove that I trusted them. I was uncomfortable with that. With Natalie, I felt relieved to have a relationship without that kind of pressure, but since I wasn't used to it, I was intimidated and anxious. I felt like I had burdened her by sharing my tragedy with her.

As my insecurity and paranoia began to flourish, I regretted opening up to her because I felt like I had revealed too much of myself. Privacy had been my shield for most of my life and now I felt vulnerable. This hurt her because it meant I didn't trust her enough to let her in. As with the rest of my issues, my problems of not trusting people had nothing to do with her, but I treated her as if they did.

When I was in my senior year of college, I went through a down period. I'd never had a serious relationship because I hadn't wanted one, I wasn't sure which career was the best choice for me, and I felt nervous when I thought about the future. It seemed like everything I did was trivial and I didn't know how to get out of that holding pattern. I wanted more, but didn't know exactly what that meant for me. I was good at meeting people, but socializing felt really superficial. I got good grades, but being in college felt like an escape. It didn't seem real. I met Natalie and I was stunned that I could instantly feel like my life had direction, that things made sense, and that I could be unbelievably happy-- all at the same time.

I saw Natalie as the key to my complete fulfillment and I didn't realize how much pressure that brought her. I thought it was flattery. She got to be on the receiving end of all my affection. However, her end of the bargain was much more than returning my affection. I held her responsible for keeping my life balanced and ensuring my continued happiness. No one could possibly carry out that kind of role.

We were the super couple of Phoenix and once I took in that image and what it felt like, I became addicted to it. We were popular, rich, beautiful and everyone thought we had the perfect life together and the perfect relationship. I wanted both of those things to be true and I really believed that was what I was fighting for. The term "fighting" certainly sounds inappropriate given the circumstances, but that's actually the way I thought. I saw myself as struggling to keep my life intact and to get what I felt I deserved. And of course, I thought I was doing that for Nat too, so I saw her as ungrateful when she didn't buy into it.

I turned my mistakes into some great romantic phrase. "We are part of each other" was one of my favorites. What that really meant was that I could place all the blame on Nat because she was the evil side of my personality. You hear people say, "we're the same person" or "she's my soul mate." You also hear "we were equally at fault." Well I said those first two things, but I didn't see it as equal at all. She was totally to blame. She was the bad part of our "same person" creation and I was just acting out against that.

I truly believed that the first violent episode was a one-time, isolated event. I had been in fights before, but I never thought I would hurt a woman. I grew up seeing that and identified it as wrong, so when I did it myself, I tried to sweep it under the rug as an embarrassing blunder. I just had one little disgusting urge and I got it out of my system.

My apologies and promises were sincere because I really regretted it and intended to never do it again.

When it became obvious that it wasn't a one-time thing, my mind produced a pile of excuses. This had to be beyond my control. A psychological disorder, something bigger than my own behavior-- anything that took responsibility away from me. I was intelligent and good. There was no way I could be a batterer. Then the excuses easily shifted to Natalie, because believing I was mentally ill or being controlled by some higher force (which of course sounds crazy) was too tough on my ego. It had to be something that she was causing in me. She tried to believe that it was a mental issue because that was less painful for her. However, only one of us could be immune from blame and it was going to be me. So, I came up with every possible reason why her behavior caused me to hurt her and constantly listed those off to her. In our relationship, the verbal abuse became a regular part of our arguments after the physical abuse had already started. It was just one more tool I used in controlling her.

Nat hated herself for staying with me and I fed off of that. I told her how stupid she was and filled her head with contradictions. She had created my anger to begin with and was helping it grow by staying with me. But if she didn't stay, she was weak and she didn't care enough about us to try to make it work. If she wanted to change me badly enough, she'd be able to do it. And if she was worth changing for, I would change. It gives me a headache to think about all this crap now and I said it to her all the time.

The way I truly felt about the situation was much simpler than all of my theories. Since she kept coming back to me after the worst fights, she was giving me the signal that my behavior was okay. She was showing me that I wasn't going to lose her if I didn't stop, so I didn't stop.

I felt guilty, on a pretty regular basis, about all the ways I hurt Natalie, but I suppressed it with my egotistical view of my life. I had taken the attention I got from modeling, from women, and from my success in college and in my firm, and based my self-worth on that. I believed that the positive attention was what I deserved in every circumstance and that it entitled me to do whatever I wanted.

Nat liked my popularity at first because we were both really social, but it got out of hand pretty fast. I couldn't stand it when she went out with her friends, yet I was fine with the double standard of me having a blooming social life. And I threw it in her face. Infidelity slid easily into my rationale that I was above the concept of sin. Just as I wasn't responsible for the violence, I wasn't responsible for cheating. I remember saying, "Plenty of other women don't seem to think I'm so terrible, so why can't you appreciate what you have?" I would tell Nat how lucky she should feel that I had chosen her over so many gorgeous, intelligent women and not realize how stupid that was. I hadn't really chosen to be with her because I was unfaithful, and she certainly wasn't lucky to be the only woman who I beat up. She was simply the only woman who loved me and gave everything she had to our relationship, while I rewarded that with violence.

Usually when I abused Natalie, I didn't see her while I was doing it. I didn't focus in on her face. It was just an intense, hazy moment of attack. I was taking all my anger, frustration, bitterness, and urge for control, and channeling it into the highest level of physical energy I could reach. Usually I began with a complete awareness of what I was doing. I was incensed with something she had done and would scream at her, insult her, demean and humiliate her. I would work myself up until it escalated to violence.

But as I got to the peak of the rage, I separated the person I was abusing from my physical actions. Sometimes it felt like I was beating up a stranger and sometimes it didn't even feel like another person was involved. More like a faceless energy that was threatening me.

Sometimes I felt completely exhausted immediately after a fight, and my memory of it was fuzzy. Almost like I'd blacked out and was slowly coming to. I don't think I was really worn out, I think my mind was trying to protect me from reality. I needed to distance myself from what I'd just done. I had to escape. At other times, however, I relished every moment of the physical exertion-- the rush I felt during it and the release I felt afterwards. Feeling directly involved in the violent act was crucial to my experience. It was the whole point. I had to dominate, I had to put my mark on her-- bruises and abrasions on her body and hideous memories of my cruelty in her brain. She needed to know who she was dealing with, that she could never win, and she had to see and feel exactly how powerful I was. I gave her proof of what I was capable of and she lived in fear that I would become capable of much worse.

The control issues and insecurities have been a hell of a lot easier for me to own than the specific thoughts that went through my head before, during, and after the rages. These thoughts are very ugly and they represent the most base, animalistic side of my personality. It's so humiliating and disturbing to deal with that part of myself. When I uncovered my rage mentality in my counseling group, I flipped out because I didn't recognize the emotions and thoughts as anything I could ever have engaged. They were gruesome and I was horrified to realize, "this is who I am."

It's hard enough to know that Natalie is gone. But my clear memory of the day she died just piles on top of that pain, to make it a million times harder. She took her own life. I was there when she did it and I couldn't stop her. This is what I dream about every night. When people see me crying and say that I'm acting, this is what is going through my head.

Sometimes I feel like I have nothing left. I don't have Natalie. I don't have a lot of the friends I trusted and loved for so many years. I don't have the livelihood that taught me so much and connected me to so many great people. But I still don't want to die. I have worked so hard to own every single one of my terrible acts. I have a long way to go, in healing and repenting. Death would steal away some of the time I desperately need.

Along with every lonely, scary moment that I continue to endure, I am rewarded with a long moment of realizing just how much I still have. The memories of the sweetest, smartest, kindest, most beautiful woman in the world are at the top of this list of treasures that I will carry to my death and beyond. She gave her love to me. How can I have knowledge of that fact without feeling completely satisfied?

I also have my faith. I didn't find it the first night I spent in my cell, but simply embrace what I've had since I was a child. For the short time that I was with my original family, we went to church together every Sunday, said grace at every meal, and prayed together every night at bedtime. I was so young that I hadn't finished learning what all of that meant, but I held onto it as a gift from my mother. I knew it was something special.

Now it has grown into a solid faith that gives me daily strength.

And of course, I have the loyalty of real friends. There are only a few, but their love and trust are worth so much. I can truthfully say that they are standing by me because they know the truth, not because they feel sorry for me. They know I didn't do this.

I know that Nat's family hates me and I don't blame them for that. I deserve a lot of the hatred that people have for me. But if I could choose for anyone to know the truth, it would be them. I would accept being found guilty and taking the worst punishment if I could have that. I know that her parents and her sister are suffering an infinite amount of pain. They never, ever hurt her the way I did. They gave everything they had to her.

Their love, their protection, their respect. They always gave her the right kind of love-- the kind of love she deserved.

I'd like to close with a quote, from a Natalie Merchant song, that reminds me of my Natalie. It sums up how I feel:

"My love is gone and now my suffering begins. My love is gone,would it be wrong if I should just turn my head away from the light? Go with her tonight?"

Josh Van Eiklyn

*Joshua Van Eiklyn is a special needs teacher
at a private high school in Lafayette Colorado.
He was a close friend to Natasha Hillshaw.*

November 21, 1997

I was on the deck of our condo. It was mid-morning and I had on the same boxer shorts and t-shirt that I'd slept in the night before. I don't remember walking out there. It was sunny and windy, but I was oblivious to the weather and the clear view of the Rockies. (We live in Boulder, Colorado.) I was also unaware of my wife's voice, as she ran through the house calling my name. I was crouched down near the deck's edge, staring straight ahead but not focusing on anything, as I clutched the middle rung of the railing with both hands. Every once in a while, I'd say a few sentences out loud. Some made sense and some were very strange. This alternated with blank, white spaces in my mind and a burning sensation in my stomach.

Carolyn found me almost immediately because I always retreated to the deck when I was upset about something. Earlier, I had been screaming and crying without any notice of the volume, but at that point I had exhausted myself into this trance. The kitchen was evidence of my recent break-down, with a broken coffee pot and mug still sitting in a pool of freshly brewed coffee. The living room TV was still on from when I flicked on the news to catch the weather. Instead I caught the most horrifying news of my life.

Carolyn hugged me as I tried to lean back against her. My body felt limp and I couldn't seem to will it to do anything. She had expected to find me in a troubled state, after rushing home in a panic from a meeting. She had heard the same news I had. It was Saturday, September 20, 1997 and Nat Hillshaw had been shot to death the previous night.

It's been 2 months. I don't think I will ever forget the way I felt that day and I've had a lot of days since that are essentially the same. I just can't believe it. At first, I tried to get really philosophical. I was thinking more about what her murder signified than about my memories of her, almost as if I was trying to punish myself by forgetting the good moments of her life. I think I was also trying to bring reason into my mourning, to cover up some of my pain with theories and conjecture. The result was a lot of guilt.

I haven't figured out what Nat's murder "means," in the way of discovering a parallel event or gaining acute knowledge. I don't think that kind of answer is realistic.

She wasn't "supposed" to die in order to balance out some horrible aspect of our society.

However, if we don't put any thought into what happened in her life, we're not taking any accountability. We're treating her pain as irrelevant and showing a continuing apathy for domestic violence. At some point, we have to look at our own actions and make the appropriate changes.

College is the most obvious place for me to start, when I analyze my mistakes and the problems in Nat's life. That's when everything started. Sometimes it feels like I'm looking at an entirely different time period and world. And it's like watching a play. I'll think about the way I acted, the friends I had, the clothes I wore--everything, during a time when I was so much younger. And now that this tragedy has occurred, I can't even relate to those memories in the same way. There's this fog that's suddenly in the way and everything is different.

Everyone who hung out with Nat in college can say that the exposure to a violent relationship forced them to grow up a lot faster. We could list off all the stressful college experiences and say that watching Nat's ordeal just capped them all off. But that makes it sound like an extra credit psychology experiment and a huge act of martyrdom. Nat never asked to be the center of confusion and stress. We didn't ask for it either of course, but I think we should be careful not to give ourselves too much credit.

Especially since we couldn't help her. (Or didn't help her, I should say-- maybe we could have.) True, domestic violence was a heavy thing to throw on top of grades and romance, but Nat paid the highest price. What right do we have, to complain about watching a friend go through a difficult, terrifying time? We were *only* watching.

When I first started dating my wife, I joked with her that my real last name is Cleaver. I grew up in a cozy little neighborhood in Fort Collins. My family had dinner together every night at 6:15, we took family vacations together, and basically did every other stereo-typical perfect family from the 50s thing you could think of. I felt so naïve when I got to college because all my friends seemed to have cultured backgrounds. Now I have many days when I can't remember any of that optimism and naiveté. I'm just bitter. It's not because of college though. It's what Jake Grazen did 2 months ago.

I've read the other chapters in this book and I'll catch a TV interview once in a while. Everyone else who knew Jake and Nat seems to have a grip on their feelings and I'm envious of that. I can't say that I ever knew how to handle the violence or how to be a true friend to either of them. Maybe I should have taken the tough love approach or maybe I shouldn't have judged anything they did. I was confused back then and I still don't have the answers.

I'm not going to really get into my relationship with Nat, mainly because it would upset me too much to detail it. (Also, I wouldn't want a description of all her good qualities to be interpreted as an argument for the fact that it was wrong to kill her. Murder is wrong, regardless of whether or not the victim is a nice person.)

It will suffice to say that she was a very important part of my life, from the time I met her to the end of her life.

I might have been closer to Jake if he hadn't been violent. It sounds kind of noble when his friends talk about their undying loyalty to him, but I didn't have that. I knew him through Nat and thought he was cool at first, but when I found out he was abusive, I no longer felt that way.

I think about Jake and myself, comparing us side by side. We're both men so we must share a lot of the same emotions and interests. According to John Caymen, we all have natural urges to hurt someone. If this is true, I'm able to suppress my urges somehow, while Jake is unable to do so. The reasons could be tied to his childhood traumas. I haven't been exposed to violence or sexual abuse at any point in my life so far. Batterers are searching for control, the psychologists and treatment experts say, so Jake must be driven to overpower women. I do not have any such drive.

I can carefully consider all of these differences and I can try to fit Jake's thoughts into my head, to understand what he's going through. But it all seems kind of pointless unless I can change his behavior. Obviously, I was unable to do that.

I didn't really feel betrayed by Jake or like he'd lied to me, when I found out about the violence. I was basically just panic-stricken. I was in shock and I didn't know what to do. It wasn't a matter of choosing sides because it was something they were going through together. Later on, I had more of a problem with thinking about it that way, because it seemed like I was putting equal blame on Nat. That's how Jake manipulated her into staying-- they were in it together and they both had to fix the problem. I didn't agree. His behavior was the problem, so he needed to fix it.

Jake did not talk about the abuse. He would occasionally make references to it in obscure metaphors and he'd sometimes answer questions if you really pushed. But he never came right out and admitted that he was the reason for Nat's crying spells and her choice to wear long-sleeved shirts all year-round. I don't think it was that he was ashamed. He just knew that not many people were going to listen to any of his excuses or his bragging. (Most of the time he was filled with apologies, but every once in a while, the macho crap came out. Usually during a night of drinking.) One time he told me that he knew he had problems, he wasn't going to make excuses, and he was going to get help. He put some conviction into it, but whenever he made similar statements after that, it was like he was reciting a poem and he was proud of himself for remembering all the words.

Jake annoyed me easily. He was very moody and he'd flip in and out of different personalities. At times he was the suave, laid-back guy you see in the stylish TV interviews. Then he'd be desperate, needy, and antsy. He would get into these moods where logic and rational thought were out the window. He acted like a little kid, asking us to choose between him and Nat, making up ridiculous excuses for his drinking, affairs, and violence. And he would throw little tantrums at the drop of a hat.

Jake was annoyed by me as well, which understandable. I acted ridiculous when I tried to help. I quickly realized that I was simply useless in any kind of crisis. I sounded like I had memorized those little booklets in the bathroom of a doctor's office. I would say things like "Your violence is unacceptable" and "You're not helping anyone until you help yourself." It was pathetic. Jake just rolled his eyes at me or laughed. I intermingled these brilliant tips with pleas and threats, which I genuinely meant, but he wasn't ever moved or scared.

I've forced myself to face all of my memories, in order to tackle my regrets and mistakes. My own denial was one of the things that jumped out at me right away. I didn't want to believe that Jake was beating up his lover any more than I wanted to believe that Nat was accepting it. And victim-blaming or not, the truth is that she was accepting it. She was always saying that Jake's actions were separate from who he was, and I couldn't stand to hear that. "How can that happen?" I'd ask her. "Does a supernatural force take over his body?" I wasn't trying to be a pain in the ass- - I really didn't get it. He was deliberate and manipulative. He had his control down to a science. How could that happen if his mind was separate from his actions? I'm especially skeptical of this theory when it's applied to criminal activity because I think it's even more clear that it's just an excuse. Why don't we ever hear someone say that their friend was totally separate from her mind when she received the Nobel peace prize? We distance ourselves from our ugly behavior and take complete ownership of our successes.

Sometimes I had close to no sympathy for either Nat or Jake because everything they said and did sounded so stupid. I had to force myself to listen to them and suppress my sarcasm. Once Nat told me that maybe the reason she couldn't leave Jake was that she could relate to his control issues. She explained how it was selfish of her to demand control in her life, while denying him control. I blurted, "God, do you actually *buy* that crap?" I was thinking that "having to" control someone else by kicking them in the stomach until they vomit blood, is not comparable to a desire to live a safe life, but I didn't say that. I didn't need to, because she was just consoling herself for my benefit. Or maybe she wanted me to say something negative about Jake. I think she got tired of defending him and listening to the superficial impressions people had of him.

I always had a problem with the word "issue." Nat used it all the time, to imply that Jake's actions were legitimate. Any problem or feeling he had was so crucial that he could do whatever he wanted to deal with it. I hated the way she protected him. She'd tell me how he was so afraid of his actions, how vulnerable he was, and how she was working on being more understanding of his pain. I would tell her that I didn't care why he did it or how it made him feel, and that he needed to be more understanding (or understanding at *all*) of her pain by not inflicting it on her. I told Jake the same thing, but I might as well have been saying it to my plants, in either case.

When I saw the violence firsthand, it knocked me off my high horse of criticism. I suddenly went from imagining it and judging it, to seeing it happen. I didn't get the severity until I saw it. One day I walked into my dorm after lacrosse practice and heard shouting, as I walked up the stairs to our floor. I knew who it was immediately and not just because I recognized the voices, but because I had that sinking feeling of certainty. I knew what I was about to see.

As I opened the stairwell door, I saw them at the other end of the hallway. She was standing with her back against the wall and he was pressing her shoulders into the wall, swearing and yelling. I ran towards them and apparently Jake either didn't see me or was blocking all outside activity from his mind. Nat mumbled something and he grabbed the sides of her face and pushed her head straight into the wall. I broke into a full sprint and shouted his name repeatedly, but the fight just continued. Nat started screaming his name, he grabbed both of her wrists and held on, as she turned away from him. She managed to get one arm free and flailed it around wildly as she tried to lunge away from him. His grip was firm though and he wrenched her arm up behind her back, twisting it. Then he started kicking the back of her knees and shins as she fell to the floor. I had to get in between them and lift him off of her before he stopped.

Jake's reaction to my presence was really disturbing. He wasn't embarrassed, surprised, or upset. His eyes were dull and vacant. He stared at me but didn't say a word, as I yelled at him. I don't remember my exact words, but my guess would be something to the effect of "What the fuck is *wrong* with you?" He just left.

The knot in my stomach had formed as soon as I heard the shouting, and it never went away. If I had ever had any understanding of Jake's feelings, I lost it that day. I couldn't respect him.

When I think about everything that happened and try to figure out how I should feel, two distinct memories stick out in my mind: the fight that day and Nat's laugh. Because I am simultaneously haunted by the horrible truth that my friend was hurt and killed and by the memory of what kind of person she was. She laughed and all you wanted to do was hear that. She was happy and then that was stolen from her. And I allowed it to happen. I can't get away from feeling that way-- I can analyze, make excuses, or blame Jake but we all did something terribly wrong as friends. We couldn't protect her and maybe saying that we didn't know how will be good enough someday, but it isn't right now. Not for me.

Most of the things I've heard about dealing with loss seem to be true for what I've been going through. I still can't believe that I'm in the position where those comments apply to me. That's why I will often look at people like they're crazy when they offer their condolences. The shock has just gone on and on. I'll see Nat's picture on the news night after night and hear my wife talk about the murder on the phone, but it feels like it's all about another woman.

Even though I don't endorse a program of revenge and pure punishment, I can certainly understand the desire for it. All I have to do is think about Nat and I get so angry at Jake. I'm probably going to be messed up for a long, long time and I feel that he is responsible for that. Jake *murdered* my friend. He didn't shoplift or cheat on his taxes. He has to deal with his own guilt and/or denial, and the rest of us have to deal with pain that will never leave us.

Charles Brandt

Charles Brandt is a journalist in Phoenix. He writes for the Phoenix Sun's current event section and is the editor of their business news department.

November 30, 1997

I'm torn between defending my job and agreeing with the seething criticism about it. Some of the controversy about the media is ridiculous. All we do is record events. We don't strive to stir up arguments or provide tantalizing conversation topics for the morning commute. On the other hand, I understand the confusion and discomfort. We're the messengers and our work determines what mood the nation is in. Readers and viewers don't distinguish journalists from stories and they see us as being more responsible for what happens in this world than we actually are. We write stories that become "our stories" in a sense, yet we didn't really *create* the subject matter for them.

Of course, it's only huge, newsworthy stories like this murder that bring out the complaints of any significant magnitude. Otherwise, nobody cares what reporters write. During weeks when my biggest stories are stock market trends and real estate tips, my phone line is open unless my lunch order gets screwed up. Whenever a big story brings out the public's outcry, it takes me a while to get used to the attention.

I can't relate to the position of being at the center of a story. So far, I've always been on the other end of things. It must be hard to suddenly find yourself in the middle of a circus, while trying to deal with difficult or astounding news. When you're hit with the pain and shock of a tragic loss, you're forced to absorb the reality of it and all the immediate and long-term ramifications. It must feel like one more big stab when you're suddenly being followed by cameras. A lot of people deal with this stress by blaming the media for it.

Just as you can't hold the media responsible for the way events unfold, you can't use it to customize your image. If you choose to throw yourself into the public eye, you can't simply highlight your favorite parts of your life and hide the rest. We have to remember this point when we hear complaints of unfair portrayal. People hate to be called a sell-out, but that label will stick when you hunger for money and attention. You pay the price of a nasty reputation for limited notoriety. You're seen as greedy and unconcerned about how your words affect the people in your life. If you deny your true intentions, you're seen as a liar as well. The selfish motives are obvious, so denial makes it worse.

While it's true that people are often unprepared for the consequences of a high-profile position, I don't buy the idea that it shocks people to the point where they don't know how handle themselves. That's a popular excuse for irresponsibility but it's not a valid one. It just takes a little bit of common sense to quickly learn how to deal with a strong media presence. Every move and word could be on the news, therefore think before you act and speak. That's the way to deal with it.

Being a journalist is not a particularly harrowing job. If I tried to draw sympathy for it, I would be mocking the field. It may not be on the highest end of the respect scale, but that's okay. There are pluses and minuses with every career. The criticism about coverage is just a big part of the job that you accept going into it-- we write about controversy. So, it's not a big shock when we become a controversy ourselves. And of course, the bottom line is that nobody forces me to stay with this job and I like what I do, despite the criticism.

Reporters who say they respond to the demands of a democracy, defining and reconstructing the standards of free speech, are telling the truth, but are also fluffing up their self-image a bit too much. All reporters should share the goal of keeping the public informed and accurately capturing people's reactions to events, but we shouldn't really elevate the importance of our jobs more than that.

The most common complaint about us is that we're too aggressive. When you probe this viewpoint, you will find that it doesn't mean that we choose the wrong angle for a story or slant it in a certain way. It's not about semantics, but the extent of coverage. "The media has pounced on this story." "The jury pool was tainted because of the massive media coverage." It's not the specific way we present an event, but just the fact that several stations and papers cover it. If only we didn't cover a story, there wouldn't be so many problems. We wouldn't upset people. Of course, these ideas are not linked to reality.

I don't get the people who say the media is too anxious about breaking stories and then complain when they don't hear enough about a given event. We're a society that's constantly striving to be well-informed and to be heard. That's good. However, people need to own their curiosity. The media caters to it, but doesn't create it. There is essentially a fan base of readers for every type of magazine or newspaper story. The same is true for television viewers and the programs that are broadcast. There is a right to know, but the desire to know can be all that matters. Neither the Enquirer or any of Hollywood gossip shows would exist if no one was interested in them.

The press is not immune to the stress of a tragedy. We don't just stand on the edge and look on, jotting down some notes. We have to report on delicate issues, watch horrible things happen, and do interviews with people who don't want to talk to us about their pain. And we're completely aware of the resentment people have for us. We're invading personal issues and that can be tough to understand and impossible to respect.

People really seem to believe that reporters sit down and plot out the future of someone, destroying their image publicly. I realize this when I hear descriptions of the media as an enemy against our private thoughts. I personally think that's a little dramatic. We're not exactly in an Orwell novel.

A news story is not a personal story. When we cover an event or describe a person's past actions, it's not a biography. We don't seek vengeance against childhood bullies and ex-girlfriends by writing mean things about them. We don't wait around for news stories that touch the lives of just the people we want to hurt or help, suddenly springing into action when something occurs.

Just as lawyers and therapists have to be very cautious in their relationships with clients, journalists have to treat the subjects of their stories with care. If you want accurate stories, you have to treat every source like gold. That can mean anything from anonymous tips to a personal interview. You're protecting the story, as you craft it. As for your interaction with people who contribute to the story, you have to work for the balance between gaining trust and keeping a safe distance.

For me, there are so many polar opposites in my job. It gets to the point where my emotions are my enemy. I'm at battle with how I feel about the story I have to write. Then there are times when my emotions carry me through a project that I start out struggling with. I care about it, so I'm invested in it and I can focus on writing a strong piece.

Objectivity is the biggest thorn in my side. It's not just that it's hard, but it seems so unreal sometimes. Or pointless and irrelevant. Honestly, I don't believe a person can ever be totally objective, no matter what the circumstances are. Everyone has an opinion about a given subject, once they become familiar with it. Objectivity means making up a neutral belief. That forces you into superficiality. You're not being accurate or truthful because you're simply adopting an opinion. You're denying your true feelings. And it's hard to write a realistic story when you get into such a cold frame of mind. If you are pretending that emotions don't exist, you are not able to write a story that involves emotions. (Every story involves someone's emotions.) There's no depth.

I am not implying that I decided not to write objectively, but I guess my definition of that word--or the definition I use as a guideline for my work-- is a little different than the one I just described. I don't empty my head of opinions when I write a story, but I do get rid of value judgments about the non-factual parts of the story. So, if two different journalists write a story, their editing decisions, such as which parts should be highlighted, will be different, but their basic premise should be the same. If an article is written objectively, the reader will not be able to guess what emotions the reporter had while getting the story.

There are times in journalism when non-objective stories are just as critical as factual ones. This case is a great example of that. Domestic violence, depression, and death--these are things that cannot be summed up in a brief, memorandum style article. We have to examine the opinions, questions and emotions that people have about this case because that's where the meat of the story lies. Some journalists become so accustomed to filtering out opinions and emotions, that they ignore some highly relevant views and issues. This is true for myself and the Grazen trial is a chance for me to change some of my stale writing habits.

I've been out of college, writing for city newspapers and the occasional magazine, for 5 years. I've seen a lot but I am often reminded of my age. I am young. I have so much more to learn. I feel like I'm mimicking a cliché as I say this because I've heard a lot of people express similar feelings, but there is just something about this case that has hit me hard. It's got to be the victim's age. Everyone talks about how young she was and I can't ignore the fact that she was my age. It's not an "It could happen to me" feeling or a generational bonding thing. It just takes my breath away when I think about how she and I were in college at the same time and how close her college memories were for her. Mine are too, but my perspective is markedly different from hers.

I have said to my friends, many times, "I feel so old." I truly mean it. I feel like opportunities are flying by me and I am missing out on a lot of things that I can never go back to. Now I'm re-thinking this. I have been forced to re-think it, because of Natasha Hillshaw. Her youth ended in a flash when she had to learn how to protect herself and fit fear into her heart. She must have felt like everyone around her was tempting her, just by doing normal things that she couldn't be a part of. Then in the middle of worrying about getting through the pain and keeping her closest friends, it was all over. I guess that thinking about this is the biggest block for my objectivity in this case. I can be objective about Jacob Grazen by not forming an opinion about his guilt, but I can't drop my empathy for Natasha.

We haven't seen a clear split between people who firmly believe Jake committed murder and those who wagered their house on the suicide theory. There's been a lot of waffling because of the domestic violence controversy. Most people realized quickly that a public proclamation of Jake's innocence would be interpreted as approval of domestic violence. It's come down to a Jake versus Natasha battle, where believing in his guilt counts as support for Natasha's family and believing she took her own life chocks up a vote for Jake. A lot of people have opted to put off this choice by taking a neutral stance.

This case will probably seem like all this nation cares about, for several months. The hype will at least last as long as the verdict delivery and probably a little bit longer. Then it will be replaced with the next big news event. This fact kind of dilutes all the current excitement for me, but I know that some people's lives will never go back to the way they were before this happened. I'm sure I will remember Jake Grazen's name and Kristin Hillshaw's face long after I finish writing about them.

Kristin Hillshaw

Kristin Hillshaw is a physical therapist in the San Diego area. Natasha Hillshaw was her sister.

Interviewed by Meredith Kendall

December 18, 1997

How would you describe your relationship with your sister?

Solid, constant. Precious. She was my closest friend. I looked up to her, I asked her advice on practically everything. People think that's weird, since I'm older, but it's true. I mean, she asked me for guidance too. I think we both viewed the other one as holding all the answers.

From the time we were little, we were so proud of each other and we had this protectiveness thing. We'd always look out for each other and we never grew out of that. We were friends, we liked each other, but we gave each other space too and I think that's why we never went through the heavy-duty fighting stage. We had our own interests and our own friends. My parents said they kept waiting for us to lash out at each other, especially during the teen years, but it never happened.

In addition to the serious bonding, we just liked hanging out together. We had so much fun and sometimes it felt like I was only showing my real self when I was with Nate. We were goofy and obnoxious. I would feel disappointed when I left her and had to go back to my more reserved lifestyle. Because with Nate, there was no pretense. She was honest and direct about everything.

Our relationship was such a sense of security, because I always knew she'd be there for me when I needed her, no matter what the reason. And she always was.

Before I forget to ask, how did the nickname "Nate" come into being?

Oh, my goodness. Believe me, you're going to wish you'd forgotten! Somebody once called me a "pistol." I can't remember why, but I would guess that it wasn't meant as a compliment. Anyway, my sister thought they had said "piston." So, while she was trying to figure out the significance of that, she discovered that piston rhymes with my name. She called me "Kristin the piston" for about a week and I, being the less creative sibling, couldn't come up with any better retaliation than "Nate the Great." Fortunately, my nickname didn't stick, but hers did. And the worst part of the whole thing is that we're not talking childhood incident here. It's much more recent history than I'm comfortable admitting!

Did your relationship with your sister change when she met Jake?

I don't think so. I mean, we changed individually. It was the most intense situation we'd ever had to face. There was no way to come out of something like that unscathed. We didn't treat each other any differently though.

She changed right away because she was a part of a relationship and because she loved someone. Then her life changed more when she acquired a violent lifestyle. I mean, as crass as it sounds, she had to fit that into her life. The lies, the pretense, covering up for Jake, and carrying around her self-hatred-- that was all part of her routine. I changed because I was exposed to something very threatening-- something I didn't understand.

We were both worried that our relationship would change. She thought I would be ashamed of her and I thought she would push me away if I didn't give my approval of Jake. The most important thing was that we needed each other to get through it. So, we just focused on that-- on being there for each other.

Do you agree with the descriptions your sister's friends have given about her?

Well, I certainly haven't read and heard everyone's interviews and comments, but I think most people have been pretty honest and accurate. And I know a lot of her friends, so I think I have a pretty good idea of how they felt about her. Also, it's hard to disagree with someone's memories because you're talking about their own feelings and experiences. I think we should just honor that. It's a special thing.

I appreciate the honesty that her friends have shown about everything they saw. I think it's hard for people to be forthright in a situation like this because it can feel like you're just divulging information about someone who's not around to give you permission to do that. But it's not going to help anything if we try to edit out the unpleasant parts of her life. She suffered and she wasn't able to get people to understand just how much. She couldn't advocate for herself then and she certainly can't do it now, so the very least people can do for her is tell the truth.

It's difficult to hear people vacillate about Jake. You know, there's talk about how it's tough to choose between Jake and our family. It kind of implies that we're making these big demands on people to prove their loyalty. That's not fair. We didn't want this situation. We didn't want Jake to do any of the terrible things he did to her and we didn't have any control over his actions. Also, if someone is suffering through a big dilemma in the choice between supporting us and approving of murder, we really don't need or want that person's support. You know? I mean, it shouldn't be an agonizing decision.

I know that it's really difficult to talk about Nat's life-- the good and the bad, because it means re-living memories, which just magnifies the pain. I of course know that feeling and I know how hard it is to give up your privacy, so I don't want anyone to feel pressured into talking about it. I just ask that those that do speak out tell the truth.

What was your impression of your sister's relationship with Jake?

Complicated. They had alternating patches of rocky and smooth. In the beginning, they seemed really happy and then I could never tell what was going on after that. It was the stereo-typical roller coaster ride.

I think Jake and Nate had a tendency to think more in terms of having their own separate lives and fitting each other into their own plans and goals, than having a life together. That concerned me. I thought it might be a flag that they weren't ready for a commitment. They definitely had the "love will conquer all" mentality. It was like they saw their relationship as a shield to protect them from their own problems.

Somewhere along the line, Nate started believing that the way to help the relationship was to help Jake. They went through a long period of dealing with Jake's jealousy issues, then they fought about Nate's career, then concentrated on Jake's infidelity "vice" for a while. When she described it, that's exactly how she talked. Everything came in the form of a problem that Jake was plagued by, so the solution could only come about by meeting his needs.

Nate said sometimes she felt that he needed power over someone else to feel better about himself, but she said she only got that sense while he was in a rage. The paranoia and jealousy he showed the rest of the time was always backed up with a detailed excuse. He had only thrown a pile of her CDs across the living room, when she came home from having lunch with friends, because he loved her so much that he couldn't stand thinking of her with someone else. The only reason he had hit her when she said she wanted a night out away from him, was because he needed her so much. The guilt-trip attempts were consistent in his excuses, she told me. His good intentions were always behind his outbursts.

How did you react when you found out about the violence?

When she first told me, I was wrapped up in guilt. I kept thinking, "How could I have missed it?" I really hadn't suspected it or picked up on any clues before she told me.

Then I was terrified. I was also devastated and extremely angry with Jake. Those feelings never went away, but I had to suppress them enough to help her. She didn't need lectures and lashing out at Jake wouldn't help her-- those things would only vent my own frustration.

It was hard for Nate to tell me. She knew how worried I'd be. And then she felt like she was letting me down and betraying me. I wish I could say that I was totally calm and knew just what to say and do, but that wasn't the case. It took me awhile to get over the sheer panic and figure out how to support her.

How do you respond to the view that Natasha should have left Jake a lot sooner than she did?

"Should have" just isn't a phrase that works for me. I can't look at things in the past for a sign of hope or for an alternative to the way things are. And I can't place any more judgment on my sister.

I *wanted* her to leave him as soon as he started hurting her and that was never a secret. But that didn't happen and I chose to support her decision. I had to learn why she couldn't, so that I could try to make her feel like she wasn't alone.

Also, the horrible reality is this: if she left sooner, he probably would have killed her sooner.

Did drinking affect their relationship?

I know that they both drank and I don't think that it made their lives any easier. I'm not going to defend it or excuse it. But alcohol wasn't the reason for any of the problems. It didn't make Jake abusive and Nate wasn't subtly encouraging the violence because she drank.

I was concerned about Nate's attitude about drinking and her general patterns of use. She knew of quite a few families that were destroyed by alcoholism and that devastated her. She had a lot of animosity for people who drank a lot, because she couldn't understand how they could hurt the people around them. When she became aware of Jake's drinking habits, she was freaked out. So, when she started drinking on her own and it seemed to increase, I was confused and worried. It seemed to fluctuate. She would be turned off by alcohol for a while because of the way Jake acted when he drank, but then she'd turn to it herself. It was almost like she was punishing herself and trying to show Jake that she had given up.

I think that drinking is one of those convenient excuses people use for problems they have in their lives. It's amazing how it can be both an evil vice and a viable explanation for behavior. And it's something that people are apparently not responsible for. Jake claims alcohol as a big reason why he was violent and had affairs, and he speaks of it as if it were an uncontrollable impulse. He has never admitted to having a drinking problem though and he doesn't see it as a behavior he chooses to engage in. It's just something that happens.

Can you talk about the infidelity issue?

Sure. I think it's pretty cut and dry. Jake cheated on her many, many times and he would give whatever excuse sounded good at a given moment in time. He just wasn't satisfied with one woman. That's a good one to tell his friends, because it makes him seem cool. Apathetic and like it was one more thing in his relationship that was a big joke. Another gem was that he wasn't used to being with one woman, so when he met Natasha, it was hard for him to know what a commitment really meant. And when she started to give him all kinds of pressure, it made it even worse and he couldn't stop the affairs.

I mean, I could go on for a good twenty minutes with that rationalization bullshit, if it didn't give me such a headache, because I know it so well. He was weak, it was wrong, and since he was so noble and brave to admit that he was wrong, it meant he could keep doing it. And of course, the blame falls right onto Nate for this "problem" of his because she put up with it. She didn't force him to stop, she didn't provide him with the appropriate support system to stop, so what was he and his poor penis to do?

To me, it boiled down to just one more hassle Nate had to deal with. Just like with the violence, she knew she couldn't make him stop, but she was constantly trying to amend her behavior so that he would be just a little more bearable. She couldn't win. If she didn't act jealous, he was convinced that she was cheating and if she confronted him about the women, he took that as defiance or that infamous pressure she was always subjecting him to.

Sometimes it seemed like the affairs actually gave her a little bit of relief, because it meant that his sexual demands on her occasionally came down a notch. And I think she became numb at a certain point and expected nothing other than constant pain and turmoil from him-- physically and emotionally.

What's been the most difficult part of dealing with your loss?

Wow. That's hard, there are so many things. Well, I think it's a tie between trying to take in the shock and just trying to "function," as they say. I have to accept that my sister is dead and I also have to get dressed and drive a car and do all those other things that are supposed to be easy.

I guess the process of making her death real and then grounding myself in that reality seems like such an obvious thing. I mean, I *have* to do it, right? So, people assume that I have this basic togetherness and sanity. In truth, I don't have that at all. I don't even see it as a priority. Presenting an image of being strong and stable just doesn't feel too crucial to me right now.

Getting through each day is a challenge. I have to stop and tell myself how and when to do every little thing. I try making lists, I have people call and remind me of everything from dentist appointments to washing my car. It can get ridiculous.

How, specifically, has your life changed since her death?

You know, I honestly can't think of a way it hasn't changed. I'm a completely different person and the world seems different too. Nothing about my life is the same.

I'm no longer a person who makes decisions and behaves a certain way. Everything happens *to* me now. To say I don't have control is a huge understatement. On my worst days, I'm just waiting for the next terrible event to come into my life.

I can get really angry, with myself and other people, whenever there's a flicker of happiness. "How dare you smile because the sun is shining or laugh at a show on TV?" It's like not being sad negates the loss somehow. I try to balance that by remembering how Nate would respond to my feelings. She would understand my anger, but would nudge me towards a laugh or a smile.

I basically have to re-build relationships and start from scratch with people. I don't know how I should be treated or how I should respond to other people. And I judge them as much as they judge me. When someone tells me that I look like I'm doing well, I wonder if they think I've forgotten about her. Then I start to question that myself. If I get through a whole day without crying, it means I have a grip. But does it also mean I'm cold? If I go several hours without thinking about Nate, it means I can get things accomplished, but then I feel guilty, as I worry that it means I'm not mourning enough.

There's a wide gap between my feelings and the way other people see me. Sometimes I want to bridge it and sometimes I use it as some weird, sick kind of self-torture thing. I have kind of resigned myself to the idea that no one's going to know what I'm going through. I mean that's the truth. Sometimes I feel bad about it because I think it comes out as resentment: "They won't get it, so why bother?" I know that's not fair though. People really want to help me. They want to understand and they want to make things better for me. I want that too, but I think I'm somewhat protective of my own experience. I don't want anyone judging it or making any assumptions about it. Also, I'm protective of the people around me. I don't want anyone else to know exactly how horrifying every single aspect of this is. I don't want them to ever have to feel this much agony.

Do people treat you differently now?

Oh, yeah. Yeah, they sure do. The reactions have been everything from swearing at me to offering me money. It's crazy.

A lot of people don't know what to say. I understand that, but I don't really feel like there's much I can do about it. I can't hide my grief and I can't make sure that I'm not offending people or making them uncomfortable. Sometimes I really want to do that, but it's just too much work and it can't be a priority for me right now.

I know that I scare people when I cry or scream in public because they think I'm freaking out. Like I mentioned before, they assume I've accepted that she's dead as a basic reality and so they see my behavior as a lapse in normalcy. To me, it's just what's going on for me. It *is* normalcy. I don't think of it as "breaking down," it's just what I'm feeling.

Other people may laugh a lot or have interesting social encounters, but I'm sad and enraged and I feel completely empty, so I act accordingly. And my outward behavior is nothing compared to what's in my heart.

I know there are a lot of decent people out there and I appreciate the efforts people put into reaching out to me. It really helps. About a week ago, I was walking in one of San Diego's public parks in the early evening, with a friend of mine from work. There were a lot of people out exercising, like there always is, and we walked by a lot of people who recognized me and looked the other way. I was getting a little tired of it. All I wanted to do was enjoy the day, you know? Then a young guy, probably in his early twenties, was biking by us and he glanced at us a couple of times as he rode by. He reversed his direction a few minutes later and rode back to us. He looked nervous, like he thought I wouldn't talk to him. I smiled at him and said "Hi." He said, "I just wanted to tell you that I'm so sorry," and then rode away. I said a loud thank you and felt really good. That's the kind of thing Nate did all the time-- stepping out of your comfort zone to do something that may make someone else feel better.

If you just tell me "I don't know what to say," that's fine because it's honest. I'm not looking for the perfect words, but I don't want to be ignored just because that's the more comfortable choice for someone. You know, I think what stings the most is the fact that I didn't ask for any of this. It's so unfair that I cause people to behave a certain way.

What has surprised you about the public reaction to this trial?

The desperate attempts to support Jake. For the people who have to believe he's innocent, it means they have to trash my sister's name. Maybe part of it is that people get nervous in front of a camera or at the thought that their words are going to be spread across the nation. But it's unbelievable, when someone goes on a tangent about Jake's honor and how unfair it is that his name is being dragged through the mud, and on and on. They'll get all hyped up about it and say things that make no sense. It's ridiculous and I try to laugh it off, but it's annoying and it does actually make me really angry. He doesn't deserve the protection.

I guess I'll never get used to the victim-blaming mentality. People work so hard to come up with excuses for domestic violence. It just boils down to ignorance and I know that, but it still hurts. I don't want to live in a society where people think it's okay to do what Jake did.

How has your grieving process affected your family and friends?

From my perspective, they aren't noticeably affected by my mourning and all my emotional tirades because they are giving me total support. And it's amazing, because they're mourning too, yet they're so solid when it comes to checking up on me and being whatever I need them to be. But I know it was really difficult for them to get through to me in the very beginning because I couldn't accept help.

For the first month, I barely spoke. I didn't know what was going on and I felt like there was nothing to say. Then when I tried to talk about it, I never felt like I could describe anything accurately. I literally couldn't find the words to capture my feelings.

The silence frightened my mother. She felt helpless and couldn't figure out how to help me, since I couldn't tell her what I needed. I felt so guilty for making her deal with that. She was afraid of losing her surviving daughter.

Can you compare your parents' experiences with your own?

Yes and no. I mean, we've shared a lot of course, but we've also had to just ride out our own experiences. We all lean on each other and know that there are some emotions that we all have, we obviously share all the same memories, but we also have differences in how this affects us and how we cope with it.

That widely televised tape of my mother and father literally clinging to each other and sobbing the day after Nate was killed, sums up the raw horror that we carry around with us. Mom is screaming out words so jumbled and loud that you can't understand her, while kneeling down on the ground. My dad is trying to hold her and comfort her, while tears are streaming down his face. I lose it every time I see that tape because I know that feeling so well. And I hate knowing that they have to feel it. The pain is so intense that you want to just shake it out of your body.

You always expect your parents to get you through the toughest times in your life because they have more love and strength than anyone else. It's not a critical, demanding kind of expectation, it's just what you know. They've given you their love and reassurance so often that you assume they have an endless supply of it. At least this is the way I've always thought about my parents. I never separated the way they acted when Nate and I were really little and she slammed my fingers in the car door, from the way they handled all the emotional strife we went through with boyfriends, jobs, et cetera, as we got older. They had this special knowledge, that no one else could access, locked away for all the times we needed their help. When they got divorced, they became even more conscientious about always being there for us.

When my sister died, I wanted to receive that calm, assured strength from them, but I didn't feel it was fair for me to expect it. My parents were feeling that they had failed Nate, that they hadn't given her enough of their love, that they hadn't guided her correctly, and that they were the only ones who were truly responsible for protecting her. On top of that guilt, they felt like they had let me down. They wanted to show me how to get through it and how to be strong, but they didn't know how to do that themselves.

I've tried to think about what it must be like for my parents. Since I'm not a parent myself, I can only imagine, of course. When you give a person life, teach them everything you know and believe in, and give them all the love you have, it must completely change the way you think and feel about everything. Good parents dedicate their lives to bringing up their children in the best way they possibly can. The terrible twos, bickering siblings, and the arguments you have with your children and with the other parents about child-raising techniques, are all part of the struggles of bringing up kids. Once you decide to become a parent, you commit yourself to the ultimate protection of your children. You are fully responsible for not only making sure they have a full, quality life, but for making sure they are safe at all costs.

How can you ever accept even the concept, let alone the actual event, of your child dying? When your child dies before you do, you've failed as a protector. This was what my parents were consumed by, from the time they found out that Jake was abusive, to the rest of Nate's life, because they were confronted by imminent danger. They felt completely helpless about her relationship, like the rest of us who loved her, but they felt it on a higher, more intense level.

I'm so fortunate to have them both in my life right now. They are why I'm making it through this.

What about the rumor that your parents are reuniting?

Well, I usually prefer not to comment on their personal lives because I feel like that's a real invasion However, this is something that has really hurt them-- this particular rumor, so I feel that I should address it: it's not true. My father is engaged and my mother has been in a relationship for several years. They've always been friends and they've probably gotten closer since Nate died, but not in a romantic way.

What is going to the trial every day like for you?

It's very difficult, but it also keeps me focused. I thought carefully about whether or not I should attend and I decided that it would be worse if I didn't. I would feel guilty about not standing up for Nate.

Taking it all in is hard. Some days are worse than others. In addition to the painful memories that all these people are digging up for me, I'm so anxious about what's going to happen with the trial. You know, I want to believe in the justice system and have faith that the right thing is going to happen. But I get nervous and upset every time the defense lawyers make excuses for Jake's violence and downplay the degree of terror my sister went through. I feel like the world is against me, like no one cares.

Listening to every argument, testimony, and presentation in that courtroom is my way of trying to combat the loss of control, which I spoke of earlier. It's so tough for me to walk in there every morning and sit in the same room with Jake all day long, but by doing it, I'm showing him that I'm taking this seriously, that I'm stronger than he is, and that I can get through anything because of Nate.

How would you describe your experience with the media?

Chaotic. Eye-opening. Frustrating. Nerve-wracking. It's inspired me to change careers--I'm just kidding! No, there are some excellent journalists and I've even made some friends with people in the media. But I've certainly been hurt by the publicity too. Like so many things, it's been mixed.

I know it's an important job, but it does cause a lot of stress for the people in the headlines and mourning strips you of any strength to handle that kind of stress. Some stories are exaggerated with untrue details and the tone of coverage sometimes minimizes the pain we're going though. You're so vulnerable to begin with and then you feel like people aren't taking it seriously.

I've been devastated by the heap of stories about me. For one thing, I can never forget the whole reason that it's happening. So even if I were the type of person who liked attention, I'd be wishing for it all to go away. And I'm not that type of person, so I'm even more uncomfortable with it. Then there's the simple fact that it's extremely humiliating to come off looking like a psychopath on nation-wide TV and in every newspaper in print. I'm embarrassed for my family and friends because I worry that they'll get some of the flack for the stories about me.

I have made mistakes and I'm sure I'll make more, as time goes on. I don't know how to handle this. I've admitted that from day one. I'm a mess now, but I was even worse right after she died and that's when the media went wild. I wasn't eating or sleeping properly, I had frequent anxiety attacks, I drank, and I took tranquilizers. Photographers took full advantage of my bad choices. They would follow me into bars on the many nights when I drank and get some great shots of me throwing up on the bathroom floor.

As humiliating as that kind of stuff is, I'd choose it over the negative stories about Nate in a second. It isn't about validity. I'm not worried that people might believe it. I mean, I'm sure some people do believe it, but not anyone who knew her. It's just sick to attack someone who's dead, especially considering the circumstances of Nate's life. I mean, she was battered, manipulated, belittled, and then killed by the same person who did all those things to her. And the benefit of trashing her name is what? Proving that Jake is a victim? That is so backwards.

The positive side is that the publicity has toughened me up. Everyone has this shared knowledge about my life. I know it when I see them, strangers or acquaintances. I feel like I'm walking around topless or something because I'm so exposed. When you feel that way all the time, you stop thinking about it after a while. I have a thicker skin because I'm accustomed to hearing and seeing the worst. Nothing shocks me anymore.

In this trial, Jake's psychologists are testifying about his attempts to change. What do you think about his experiences with therapy?

Too little, too late, and a big performance.

The only reason he ever wanted to change was that he knew he had to prove himself to get what he wanted. The divorce is the perfect example. He loved my sister and wanted her respect. He also wanted her in his life and he wouldn't get those things if he contested the divorce. So, he said he would grant her what she deserved, her freedom, because he realized what she needed. He loved her so much that he was willing to be without her if that was the best thing for her.

I mean, I have a hard time believing a single word out of Jake Grazen's mouth, and I'll admit that. I know him and I know the manipulation. I think he's basically playing everyone around him now, even more than he used to, because he's desperate for support. Now the world has to know how many times he saw a psychologist because it shows that he knew what he was doing was wrong? Who cares? Even if that was true, it's not enough. He knew it was wrong to kill her. Okay, I can sleep better now.

What was your own relationship with Jake like and how do you feel about him now?

The most dominating feeling I have for him is seething anger. I mean, he took my sister from my life. How else can I feel about the person who did that? But as far as the past, there are a lot of layers because so much went on.

Before I knew Jake was a batterer, I really liked him. He is everything his friends say he is. We were friends and I was really happy that he and Nate were together. Then he became abusive and I immediately felt stupid for trusting him. I hated him, I feared him, he disgusted me. I felt betrayed and I was so confused. I didn't understand what was happening in their relationship and in his head and I didn't know how I should treat him. I knew if I got aggressive and accusatory, it would only hurt Nate because he'd blame her for my behavior.

I tried to reach out to him and he got really cold towards me. He wasn't comfortable opening up to Nate's sister and I could understand that. I asked him to talk to someone else about it, I encouraged therapy, but he just dismissed me. Jake has never pushed me to forgive him or to have any kind of relationship with him, at any time after he became abusive. I guess that makes sense because he knows how angry I am. The problem is that my religious beliefs require me to forgive Jake and I know that I'm going to have to try to do that. I also believe in rehabilitation. I'm angry that Jake never got help in time to save my sister's life, but I think he needs to do it now. If I didn't believe that, I'd be giving him the go-ahead to hurt and possibly kill other women.

I feel sorry for Jake. I don't know how long his denial is going to last, but I believe he will be completely and eternally tormented by his own demons, when he finally faces up to what he has done.

When you testified in the trial, you said that you talked to your sister on the last day of her life. Can you tell me what happened?

Gosh. Yes, okay.

I was in Phoenix for a conference that week, so we got together in between my meetings and when she had free time. I'd seen her the night before and we were planning on getting together the day she died. I had wanted to have breakfast with her because I was really worried about her, but she canceled. We were going to have a late dinner instead. I kept trying to call her that day, just to check in, and she'd left me some messages.

I was worried because she and Jake had been seeing a lot of each other and I wasn't sure what was going on. They'd been separated for 2 years and divorced for 5 months and things had been going so well. I mean, I was never hot on the idea of them being friends, but it seemed to have been working. They had separate lives and seemed to really respect each other. Then for some reason they started getting together quite a bit during the last month and it was really turbulent.

She didn't give me all the details and I was trying to be cool about it. She said they definitely weren't getting back together, but she felt like she needed him. I didn't know what that meant.

She seemed to be acting strange and I was scared that she was slipping into a depression again. She was drinking quite a bit and was quieter than usual. Nate left me a message at 3:30, that last day. She sounded drunk and pretty upset. She said she was going to meet Jake, but she was pretty vague about it. I still wonder why she told me that, since she knew I wouldn't have liked the idea. Maybe it was her last call for help.

What is your response to all the questions about her depression?

I'm kind of confused by them actually. I mean, she was living through a crisis when she was with Jake and 3 different psychologists treated her for depression. What's the big mystery? She was depressed, that doesn't mean she killed herself. However, there's no need to conceal the fact that she was in therapy.

I think about all the times Jake threatened to kill her and all the times he hurt her so badly and for so long that she believed she was going to die right then. I also think about the last minutes of her life. I'm sure she tried to reason with him at first. Then she probably got desperate and panicked and … God, I'm sorry. She must have begged him not to kill her. I think about how that level of fear was her constant reality and I think, of course she was depressed. Who wouldn't be?

And I saw how stressed out she was. For instance, I visited her a few weeks before the wedding. She was on the deck, in an oversized flannel shirt and boxer shorts. She had a bottle of Jim Beam in one hand and a cigarette in the other. The way she looked at me gave me a sick feeling. Her eyes were wide, she gave me a very weak smile, and looked away nervously. Her look had a desperate, pleading tone. I embraced her and she stood motionless at first, then hugged me back with an intense grip. Within a minute, she was sobbing uncontrollably. She knew that everything was only going to go downhill. She was drained. She was about to be married and she was scared. She was ashamed of what her life had become and you could see that in her eyes. She looked and felt like crap, all her goals that she'd fought for had slipped away from her, and she was about to legally commit herself to a man who hurt her over and over again.

Can you explain your opinion that suicide could not have been the cause of death, despite your sister's history of depression?

Yes. There are two really plain facts that make that clear to me. The first is that Jake did not have control of his rage. He built up this fantasy of what

Nate had to be, a fantasy that nobody could ever fulfill, and lost it when she couldn't be that for him. I don't know how or when it happened, but something snapped in him and pointed him down the road of obsession. Murdering her was the end of the road. He was out of options. The second reason is that my sister did not want to die. Yes, she had suicidal periods, but she got through them and fought so hard to rebuild her life. She was determined to grab onto life and fight to make it what she wanted.

What have you learned from the ways your life has changed since your sister's death and from the way people have reacted to the case?

I think it's too soon for me to answer that. Right now, I can't step outside my shock and horror to think of this as a learning experience. I know that I'm getting used to things, but it's hard for me to think of this as something I can gain something from. That would mean believing that there's a noble purpose behind the murder.

I know that some people can find a positive angle in tragic situations and I respect that. If it helps them heal, that's great. And maybe that will be me someday, but right now I can't accept the theory that bad things happen to teach us a lesson. I cannot believe that my sister had to die or was supposed to die, in order for the world to see how wrong domestic violence and murder is. She was not a sacrifice.

Do you have any final words?

Assuming you mean for this interview, yes.

I would like to thank everyone who has been showing their constant support. I hope that someday I can be strong enough to repay that by helping other people through their struggles and losses.

I think about what Nate would want, in terms of the way everyone has been acting since her death. She would want us to search out the truth and nothing less. She would want us to talk about domestic violence openly. She would want us to respect each other's own style of grieving. She'd encourage the people who love her to go on with their lives when they're ready, but she would also say that it's okay to be sad. She wouldn't judge us for the pace of our healing.

Tracey Archer

Tracey Archer is a therapist and a coordinator for several domestic abuse programs in the greater Phoenix area. Both Jacob Grazen and Natasha Hillshaw were her clients and the defense called her as a witness in the trial.

December 29, 1997

A lot of confusion surfaced when I was called as a witness in this trial. I wasn't simply giving my professional opinion about a specific disorder or diagnosis, as had been my task in several previous trials, nor was I speaking only about a particular client's situation. I was doing both of these tasks, so I was essentially an expert witness and a character witness simultaneously. It was quite painful for me to talk about the personal details of my clients' lives, especially since Natasha's death was so recent, but I was legally bound to do so. Jake waived his right of privileged information and the judge mandated the information from my sessions with Natasha as admissible in court.

Before I address the details of Jake and Natasha's relationship, I would like to explain a little bit about domestic violence. To those unfamiliar with abusive relationships, the descriptions coming out in this case will appear to be extreme, but they are actually quite typical.

Violence is an attempt at resolution. It is used to express anger and to physically dominate someone else. A person strikes out violently when something upsets them and they want to take a stand on it by exerting revenge. They feel entitled to do so and sometimes they even feel obligated to do so. Violence in a relationship can be complex because the abuser creates layers of excuses for his violence. He is using the relationship to deal with all of his anxieties and needs, which means he expects his partner to provide everything he failed to obtain from past relationships-- both family and romantic relationships.

Plus, she should ease all the stress he feels from his current problems. He puts her through multiple tests. He makes demands on her, requiring her to prove her love for him. He may load the tests, by anticipating failure or placing extremely high expectations on her. Either way, she will be unable to prove her love and loyalty to him because she will never pass the tests.

The specific ways a batterer does these things will vary from relationship to relationship. It depends on what disturbs him the most and what proves most effective. It's a basic supply and demand equation, with the victim supplying and the abuser demanding. Typical methods include financial control, monitoring phone calls, reading letters, and degrading her in front of people who matter to her. Some men will go to the extreme with every method and some will occasionally give concessions. For instance, he may allow her to go to lunch with her girlfriends once a month or so. He then points to these as proof that he loves her and trusts her.

The problem is that it's not actually a positive aspect of the relationship because it's not real. He doesn't want her to leave him and he wants the relationship to appear normal to outsiders. He is maintaining control. This applies to the guilt gifts, apologies, and lavish treatment that sometimes follows big fights. He may feel guilty to a degree, but the real motivation is making her believe that he will change.

Sometimes a batterer will identify causes for his violence as a way to remove himself from being responsible. Some of my new clients will list off their numerous reasons for acting out as if they were reading from a resume, because they believe that pin-pointing an incident in their childhood or naming a Psychological disorder constitutes some kind of magical self-awareness that fast-tracks them to recovery. They don't do it after they've been seeing me for a while, because I don't allow it.

They mix in their excuses with the things their partners do to set them off, to portray the victim as deserving part of the blame. He places her actions on a parallel plane with his problems, which changes the situation from behavior that upsets him to deliberate manipulation on her part. If she burns the toast, that's as significant a reason for his violence as sexual abuse in his past. He expects everyone --his victim, his friends, and his therapist-- to take it all in as justifiable, just as he believes it to be himself.

To complicate all of this, the victim will often see it that way too. She takes the blame because she believes that she deserves what she is getting. She builds up a defensive attitude about the relationship, which consequently means she defends her partner. I do not mean she worships him as a flawless man. However, he is the man she loves and has chosen to be with, so negative characterizations of him reflect directly back to her. The relationship is a heavy investment for her and she has a lot to prove by making it work. She is drawn to the task of changing him, not only because she wants to alleviate the pain, but also because her pride is at stake.

For therapy to truly help a victim of domestic violence, everything has to be the victim's choice. She needs to gain control of her life, which she cannot do with another person telling her what is right for her. If she stays, she is not approving of the violence, she is not coaxing it, and she does not deserve it. And if she leaves, she is not guilty of abandoning an obligation. She has the right to be free of the violence, but there are no legal requirements mandating her to exercise that right. It is not even accurate to say that freedom always comes in the form of leaving the relationship. There is often more abuse and control when a victim leaves because her abuser will stalk her and become more obsessed with her. Leaving is the worst act of betrayal she could commit against him, so he is not going to accept it.

It is not up to the victim to do more to please her abuser or less to avoid upsetting him, but a therapist cannot just present that opinion to her and ask her to accept it. Doing so would imply that if only she was strong enough to be out of the relationship, she would be valuable. Such a presumption only minimizes the emotional investment a woman has in the relationship. It's unfair and detrimental because it sets up the same kinds of rules that a victim is subjected to in the relationship.

A battered woman views her relationship in an entirely different way than all the people in her life who are trying to convince her to get out of it. Even though some of the outside perspectives may have made sense to her before she was in the relationship, she can no longer see the truth in concepts like "no one can change another person" or "everyone deserves to be treated with respect and love." Or she can, but not for her own life. She is living through a crisis, so her field of vision has been altered. Also, her abuser has taught her that the way he treats her is a necessary part of love. He has told her that she has to accept the bad times with the good. That can sound logical, especially when you feel responsible for making the relationship work-- again, it's a serious investment, and to not accept the bad times seems selfish.

Natasha Hillshaw was going through this with Jake. She had plenty of people to tell her that leaving was the only answer, yet she was miles away from that viewpoint. Despite all her pain, she loved him. When she committed herself to staying with him through everything, she resigned herself to a lonely, closed-in, limited world. However, it happened slowly. As she listened to more and more of Jake's minimizing lectures, she began to believe that she alone was responsible for losing so much. She chose him, so every decision from there on out was her fault, not his. She had boxed herself in.

Jake was her voice and she had a lot of shame about that. She arrived in Phoenix as an energetic, assertive, independent woman and within the scope of a year, she lost all of that to one man. That was devastating for her.

As I said during my testimony in this trial, I believe that Natasha's death was a suicide. She was severely depressed, she had been taking anti-depressants sporadically, and she was suicidal. In her sessions with me, she explicitly discussed her thoughts of killing herself.

Natasha first called me in 1993. It was the end of February-- about a week after the police were called to the house she shared with Jake. She was very nervous during that conversation, acting like she expected me to respond with condemning words. I convinced her to come to my office to talk. She had been hesitant, mainly because she did not want Jake to find out. Natasha has been described as strong-willed and self-assured. I could certainly see that as I got to know her, but she was at the opposite end of the scale the first time I met her. She was uncomfortable and self-conscious. She made an early morning appointment, to be sure that Jake would be in class, and she arrived at my building before I did. She was wearing sunglasses and a baseball hat, leaning on her car, smoking a cigarette and crying. She didn't see me and she waited until the exact time of her appointment to come into my office. She had stopped at the restroom and made herself up, taking off the hat and fixing her hair.

Natasha was caught between her emotions and her analytical perspective. She was crying without embarrassment at one moment, then she would try to compose herself and explain her feelings to me. She spoke softly and mumbled a lot. She described the incident with the police and said that she didn't know why she didn't go through with the charges against Jake. She had tried to keep the abuse a secret, but her friends knew about the police going to the house, so she was going through a big dose of shame. She needed to just get all her feelings out, but couldn't think in terms of making any decisions.

I had a feeling that she wouldn't be back to see me, at least for a while, and I was right. I could sense that she felt uneasy about coming to me, like she has had betrayed Jake. (It's common for victims of abuse to feel guilty about revealing details of their relationship to anyone.) Also, she seemed to have the idea that therapy was a sign of her own weakness. She wanted to prove that she could handle all of her problems herself.

The next time I heard from Natasha was in December of 1995, which was a year and a half after she married Jake. She was angry and frantic. She raised her voice as she told me, "Jake believes that I am now legally his property-- that I willingly signed myself over to him when we got married." She went on to tell me that their arguments exhausted her. "He never listens to me, he doesn't respect any opinion I have."

She had gone through a period of not being able to get out of bed in the mornings, which Jake rectified with rages. That was lazy and pathetic, according to him. He couldn't tolerate a wife like that. She was frightened, but tried to cover up her fear with anger. I don't mean that she was acting angry to appear tough. She was clinging to that emotion to avoid a more threatening one. It gave her some feeling of control.

Natasha had been to a psychiatrist the previous August, to get anti-depressants. She said she wasn't taking them consistently because sometimes she felt ashamed about taking them, so she would stop for a week or two. She was also drinking on and off. She told me that her depression seemed to ease up at times. With Natasha's permission, I consulted with her psychiatrist, who said she had diagnosed Natasha as manic depressive. I agree with the diagnosis, but I also believe that Natasha's erratic behavior patterns coincided with changes in her relationship with Jake. If you analyze the entire time frame of the relationship, it becomes clear that Natasha did not exhibit signs of depression during the periods when Jake was not violent.

My contact with Jake began in between Natasha's visits to my office. In January of 1994, he called me, introduced himself, and asked for an appointment together with Natasha. He explained that they were engaged and wanted to talk to someone about their "issues" before getting married. Couples' counseling is not a good idea when you are currently violent and I always discourage it. I feel that it sets up this idea that the violence is something both partners are responsible for. Also, it's virtually impossible for the victim to discuss her feelings openly in front of the batterer. If she does, he will be too defensive to really listen to her.

I'm bothered when a couple with a troubled relationship wants to go to therapy right before getting married, because it usually means they're hoping that their problems will be magically smoothed out at the last minute. Or it can be something they do just for appearance sake, as a way to put worried friends and family members at ease. Sometimes it's almost like a batterer is using his engagement as a weapon in a quest to prove that the relationship is strong. I feel that men like Jake are flashing me some kind of proof of power. And some certainly act like they've got me backed into a wall. They're engaged, that's a big deal, a big decision that they have made as adults, so I would be impolite and intrusive if I said anything against that. But it doesn't work that way with me. Acting polite and complimentary isn't an effective tool for therapy.

I talked Jake into seeing me alone. He came into my office 20 minutes late, apologizing profusely and saying that he had to leave early. He told me that he would call me within the week to set up a few more appointments. I was blunt with him, saying that I didn't think 25 minutes was enough time to adequately deal with any of the "issues" he had alleged to want to sort out. I don't pretend that I'm okay with someone wasting my time.

A client who is out to prove something by going to a few therapy visits does not see the need for taking it seriously. They don't actually believe that they need any help, it's just a show. This was the case with Jake Grazen. He acted like I owed him something and was skeptical of any suggestion or question that challenged him in any way. He wanted to control the situation with me in the same way that he controlled his relationship. He gave contrived, superficial answers. He also used long, confusing metaphors to describe the problems in the relationship. He had a campaign and he wanted to sell me on it.

At one point, I asked him a question that he really didn't appreciate. He had stated how valuable commitment was to him and how marriage was the ultimate and final step in a loving relationship, so I asked him if he thought marriage was the answer to their problems. He stared at me with astonishment. I had offended him. "The only solution is a non-violent home. I *know* that and that's why I'm here." I found that statement to be extremely odd, because he was not taking any responsibility for the violence, but he truly believed that by going through what he believed to be the correct motions, it was going to just go away. So, he was angry with me because I wasn't the puppet he had hoped I would be. He had truly believed that I was going to take his carefully planned speech as either some sort of comfort or as something to be intimidated by. The outcome he wanted was my approval of his behavior and in his mind, he deserved that.

Jake didn't call me again until February of the following year. It was during the time period when Natasha had moved out. I think she moved out for a few weeks and he called me at the end of the first week. He had been arrested for a bar fight, but settled out of court by paying a fine. He saw me twice within the scope of week and his attitude was different than the first time we met. He had lost a good chunk of ego, but I knew he still wasn't ready to get serious about therapy. He was desperate, he swore to me. He had lost her and he had to do whatever it took to get her back. That sounded almost as dramatic when he said it to me as it does now, but he didn't mean it. He wasn't willing to do any work. He thought that feeling guilty about the violence was enough. He couldn't take the time to get help or risk the chance that getting help wouldn't guarantee Natasha's return.

I was very upset when Jake left my office after that appointment. I felt like he was slipping through my fingers. He was crying out for help and even though I knew I couldn't help him, it was impossible for me to say, "He's responsible, I can't help him till he helps himself," and leave it at that. I was worried about Jake because I was afraid that he wasn't going to get help until he had outdone his last rage.

Jake's childhood circumstances had a significant impact on his propensity for violence. When someone endures a string of harsh tragedies at a very young age, it affects their life. There's no way around it. People cannot release pain and unresolved issues from their life unless they address the issues appropriately. The pain will re-surface in some form at some time.

Jake may have had a healthy family before his mother and siblings died, but any positive memories were immediately smothered by chaos. He never comprehended why they had died and he didn't have the support of healthy adults to explain that his mother didn't leave him and to tell him that he didn't do anything wrong. He wasn't nurtured, he was exposed to violence. This point is crucial to studying the root of his own behavior, because it explains his fear of abandonment and resentment towards women.

When Natasha Hillshaw came into Jake's life, she was both a savior and a threat. She gave him love, support, and security, but she couldn't ever give him enough to replenish what he had lost and wipe out his insecurities about the future. He didn't trust women and he didn't know how to accept love. He truly believed that someday she would stop loving him. It was almost as if he was waiting for it.

I heard from Jake again in September of 1996. He called to tell me that he was attending a batterers' group program and seeing a therapist. He said he wanted to thank me for all of my support. He admitted that he had been in denial for years, said that he knew he had a long way to go and that he was really trying to stay positive about his actual chances of changing. He confessed a lot of his feelings about the violence. He apologized for the egotism he had previously shown me. He stated, "I won't blame you if you don't take me seriously, because I know I've never given you a reason to, and I won't waste your time trying to convince you that I'm different now."

I asked Jake to check in with me occasionally and let me know how he was doing. I told him that I would be willing to meet with him any time he wanted, either in my office or together with his men's group coordinator. He expressed an interest in this and he did follow through with it.

I was unsure whether Jake's arrest would motivate him to stay with a treatment program, especially since his sentence was reduced. The actual fight turned out to be the turning point for him, not the consequence of getting arrested. In October Jake came into my office and told me about that night. He had arrived home drunk and Natasha was asleep. The covers were all rumpled up because she always tossed and turned in her sleep. He saw a big lump next to her and thought it was another man. One of her legs was sticking out and he yanked on it, dragging her out of bed. Her head hit the floor hard and the impact knocked her out. He was yelling obscenities at her and kicking her body as she lay unconscious. The neighbors heard him and called the police. They arrived before Natasha came to.

As Jake told me this story, his breathing got faster and faster. Her face was covered in blood from the gash on the top of her head and she was bewildered, as she opened her eyes to the sight of 2 police officers in her bedroom and Jake in handcuffs. "It was so fast," he told me. He said it couldn't have been more than a minute, from when he saw her in bed to when she was lying on the floor. He thought he had killed her and he stared at her body in astonishment, knowing that he had caused that damage to her body and what he believed was the end to her life. He saw dirt marks on her bare legs and on her nightgown, where he had kicked her with his muddy sneakers. He saw his own finger marks on her leg, where he had gripped her tightly and heaved her to the floor.

Usually, an abuser will go through a full treatment program because he wants to preserve his relationship, whether it's reconciliation with his victim or a new relationship.

This wasn't true with Jake. He believed that he didn't deserve Natasha and he didn't want a future with her because he didn't want to hurt her any more.

Rehabilitation is a long process and it requires incredible determination. Jake did commit himself to the process and I believe that he did in fact change. He continued with his group and with individual therapy. He did not see Natasha for several months and when they did begin to talk again, it was at a very cautious pace.

He feels responsible for her suicide because he created the helpless, self-loathing woman she became. He hurt her deeply and his guilt will always haunt him for that. However, he is not responsible for her death.

She took her own life and society cannot hold another person legally responsible for that.

It feels really hollow sometimes, when I tell someone that we can learn from a tragedy, but I believe that. My hope is that this trial will mean something and not be just one more news event. If we can finally take a hard look at domestic violence and make treatment programs a priority and increase available services for victims, we will be able to focus on something constructive.

Laura Morrow

Laura Morrow is an accountant at an architecture firm in Santa Fe, New Mexico. She owns the firm with her husband, David. Both Laura and David attended college with Natasha Hillshaw and were close friends with her.

January 3, 1998

Tasha always told the story of how she and I first met with a little more dramatic flair than my memory's version, but the basics of our recollections are the same. I'll admit, she probably had a better chance at accuracy because she was the objective observer and I was the subject of that pathetic scene.

She walked down to the laundry room of our dorm and found me sitting on the cement floor, crying. I don't remember any audible weeping. But I have the tendency to be in denial about my behavior whenever it's the least bit unflattering. (My husband will be the first to attest that I carry that habit into modern day life. Denial is Laura's friend, as we say.) I'd concede a sniffle or two, but she insisted that I was sobbing in short, heaving grunts, which I alternated with curses. Like I would cry, stop to say "motherfucker," cry again, and so on. And according to her, most of my vulgarities were a lot worse than that one.

I was using the letter I'd just gotten in the mail as a tissue. Its author was the subject of my creative obscenities. In it he announced his new status as my ex. A lit cigarette was on the floor beside me and I was apparently ignoring it, except for an occasional cough through the smoke. She extinguished it in order to avoid a fire. I also had my big tattered backpack next to me, which was tipped upside down with books, papers, make-up, CDs, and various trash leaking out of it. I thought I'd been trying to do some homework before the crying set in, but Tasha's re-caps didn't include any sign of that.

She said I was wearing wrinkled, grimy sweats that looked like I kept digging them up from the bottom of a pile of dirty clothes, to wear over and over. She further described greasy and hair and a bad skin day. My memory's version: baggy, but clean clothes and a baseball hat. The hat probably meant my hair was a little on the nasty side and I'm sure she was right about the bad complexion. I would always break out when chocolate came into the mix and I didn't believe in moderation in those days.

I'm sure I looked like a typical freshman who was trying to maneuver the adjustments of college life, but it was actually my third year. I had a hit a rough patch that definitely surpassed any of my first-year woes. Failed long-distance relationship, freaking out about grades, and a frightening roommate experience topped the list of issues. And I was indulging in a little self-pity, so that added in some exaggeration.

I wanted to get into grad. school, so anything less than an A sent me into a self-loathing slump. Then there was my roommate. I had many nicknames for her, most that I came up with during careful consultations with my friends. (And keep in mind that capitalization was always very important because these were *titles,* not just names.) They ranged from Douche Queen to Schizy (short for schizophrenic). I usually just called her The Crab or something a little more vulgar. She told me she'd been diagnosed as a manic depressive, so I initially felt sorry for her and treated her illness with as much reverence as is possible for a college student to possess. However, that pretty much went out the window when she started doing things like hiding, giving away, or throwing away any of my CDs, books, or clothes that somehow upset her when she was having a bad day, and locking me out of the room when she was having a conference call with her therapist.

Living in a dorm for year number three was definitely not a choice I was overjoyed with. Three of the five people I'd planned to live with, in a gorgeous off-campus apartment, backed out a month before fall semester began. We didn't have time to get anyone else in, so I had to take whatever opening on campus I could find.

My break-up was certainly a dramatic event at the time, but is one of many things I look back at with a queasy feeling. It was pathetic. We'd been going out for a little over a year and it was a security relationship. I would never have admitted that at the time though. He had transferred to Cornell University, I had my first orgasm the night before he left--which I guess symbolized true love to me, we both said we'd be faithful but neither of us really meant it. For me, a long-distance relationship meant not having to work at a relationship and not having to deal with the pain of dating.

However, he was somehow able to deal with that pain. As his detailed letter explained (yes, the one I snotted all over the day Tasha found me in my state of devastation), he had met someone who had stolen his heart away. Why did he deem it necessary to mention that to me? Because honesty was setting him free.

Anyway, it was a perfect time to meet Tasha. Hanging out with her gave my life an instant lift. I've been told I have a hard shell and I blame it on growing up in Manhattan. She was so laid-back and just easy to like and get along with. She made things better. That day in the laundry room is the perfect example. She didn't gush over me, but acted like my behavior was just perfectly normal. She asked me if I was okay as she was folding her towels and made me laugh by saying, "He sounds like a real prick to me" with a straight face and serious tone, after I gave her the rundown on my distress.

She then followed that up with, "Hey, do you know who would be really good for you?" and began describing this absolutely frightening guy who worked at our cafeteria. He had like a mullet/ attempt at Mohawk combination going on, with plenty of peroxide to finish off the look. He always attempted some kind of facial hair action-- either one of those circular 'stache/mini-beard combinations or really sparse scruff. One of my friends called him C.B. and that stood for Chia boy. He wore skin-tight white jeans and sometimes acid-wash, with either one of those netted football half-shirts or the smallest ribbed tank top he could find. He always tried to caress your hand as he checked your meal card.

Tasha got half way through her list of reasons why he would be the perfect man for me, which included a solemnly delivered statement about how great she thought he must be in bed, and we both started laughing uncontrollably. It was one of my favorite moments with her.

Tasha was real and completely comfortable with herself. There was even something comforting about her physical appearance. She was tall and thin, with beautiful dark skin. She had long, smooth dark hair that she either wore straight with the ends curled under, or in big loose curls. She was usually dressed in an outfit that she could have worn to a job interview: in neutral and pastel-colored, layered clothes. She liked to wear short-sleeved light blue or lilac silk sweaters or shells with a loose beige or off-white silk shirt over it and baggy silk pants or skirts, in dark gray or brown. When she wore jeans, she looked just as sophisticated, because she'd wear them with fitted cashmere sweaters or linen dress shirts. We teased her about ironing everything-- bras, cut-off jean-shorts, and bathrobes. She insisted that she wasn't that bad, but I did catch her in the act of ironing her sheets and towels a couple of times.

She always looked like she had just gotten out of the shower, which is a tough look to pull off when you live in Phoenix. Her secret, she told me, was that she was a devoted disciple of moisturizing and crème rinsing. The only time she closed her dorm room door was when the hot rollers were in. Sometimes she'd throw on a facial mask at the same time and only a privileged few of us were allowed admission. I have a photo of her with a face full of Noxzema and a pair of sunglasses that Josh made for her-- that he glued plastic cucumber slices onto.

Tasha was the girl everyone was jealous of, because she appeared ideal. In every respect, she seemed perfect. Beautiful, friendly, athletic, intelligent. But those qualities were just a fraction of who she was. Even reading over those words now, I feel like it misses the mark on her. And she would cringe whenever she heard them. *Those* things aren't important, she would tell you. They're just surface descriptions. Her interests and passions defined who she was and she was insulted when she thought someone liked her just because they thought she was smart or pretty. I can hear her saying "yu-uck" in her drawn out, irritated manner.

I was amazed and amused by her constant energy, her ditziness, and her oddities. She was up for anything. I would occasionally think that she was really weird, but I loved that about her. That was why she was so much fun to be around. She would dance around the cafeteria, whistling the theme song to "Dallas." (Well actually, she couldn't whistle very well, so it was more like this humming/whistling combo.) She would walk into a bar wearing the ugliest outfit available to her from the Salvation Army collection and act like it was Gucci. You would sometimes think "Okay, why?" as a response to these things, but you would also feel completely grateful because she brought joy to the moment. It was funny, it was silly, and it was Tasha. She was confident, comfortable and she felt like it was her duty to bring in the light moments.

We loved going out and we always had a blast. Sometimes it was a spontaneous outing that got us out of studying. We'd drive out of the city to some dive bar, wearing sweatpants and baseball hats. And then there were the rituals of bar-hopping with a huge group of people. Thursday nights were a given. We'd start out with about 15 people and everyone would branch off as the night wore on. Tasha and I joked that these were our weekly therapy sessions, because we'd have long talks about everything: commentaries on the hook-ups, outfit assessments, and endless venting about whatever was going on in our lives.

What's strange is that I now look back at those talks and certain things stand out in my memory. In the moment, it's trivial. You're 19 years old and having drunken discussions about boys and grades. Who cares? it doesn't matter. But when your lives change in ways you never could have imagined, those memories seem to carry more weight, and you feel like somewhere along the line, you missed something really important.

Tasha talked about what she wanted in a relationship. She wanted to be with someone who was secure in his own ambitions, who could respect her goals and interests, without fawning all over them. "I know what I want to do with my life and what I like, so I don't need anyone's approval of that," she told me. She also said that having a secure, solid relationship was her top priority and everything else would fall in place for her. Unfortunately, she ended up living out a scenario that opposed this. A violent relationship meant that everything in her life fell apart.

Tasha liked spontaneity and hated feeling like she was ever predictable. She was bored by consistency. She'd bring out different parts of her life at different times, like buying a brand of make-up she hadn't used in years, or switching to beer that was a former favorite of hers. That kind of stuff made her feel like she was connecting to the specific times in her past. Then she'd want to get away from her past and feel like she was moving forward with her life, so she'd drag me to the hair salon for a "fresh look." As we got older, I realized that the changes may actually be more about trying to find stability than just merely making superficial changes. Connecting to happier times or making a new trend for herself brought her away from associations with life with Jake.

Her changing names was part of this idea of inconsistency too. As everyone close to her knows, she went through alternate stages of wanting to be called Tasha and Natalie. She said that "Tasha" seemed more youthful and "Natalie" was sophisticated.

Her infamous Nadia Comaneci story explained the leap from Natalie to Natasha or Tasha. She told it to drunk guys often. She'd solemnly explain to them that she associated the name Natasha with Nadia because she had worshipped the gymnast as a kid. Her dream of becoming a famous gymnast herself was crushed with a nasty split attempt incident. She always told me I was the only person who ever found the story amusing. Jake called her Natalie, Kristin called her Nate, and I called her Nat or Tasha.

Tasha wanted to experience everything and learn everything. She studied several different foreign languages, played a lot of musical instruments, and read all the time. It could be inspiring to listen to her excitement about all the things she was involved in, but it could also make you feel like a big loser in comparison.

She also mixed in her entertainment activities with the serious pursuits. One night she waltzed into my room with a huge cigar, a can of chewing tobacco, and a copy of Rod and Reel. She plunked down in the middle of the floor and put on her well-rehearsed serious face. "Laura, I really think we're missing out on some of the finer things in life." She decided fly-fishing would be pretty cool, but that was about half-way down her list of dream endeavors.

Tasha could be pretty indecisive because she had to make sure she was always choosing correctly. It didn't matter how trivial the matter seemed. She saw every action as representing, or connecting with, something larger. Despite her finicky attitudes, once she made a choice on the big issues in her life, she was completely committed and unwavering. She tried to balance careful analysis with a from-the-gut style. So, if you were behind her in the cafeteria line, you'd quickly become either frustrated or amused, and if you tried to talk her into a different field than child psychiatry or out of getting serious with Jake, you were wasting your time.

We learned to get through tough situations, in creative ways. Sometimes we'd go for a walk and just swear, shout, and scream. Simple, but effective. Other times we'd sit in silence, listening to Neil Young or Shawn Colvin serenading us, and smoke an entire pack of cigarettes or polish off a carton of ice cream.

One time, she walked into my room and threw down the 3 rejection letters from grad schools that were in her hand. We drank a beer, then walked all over campus, talking about gossipy things. There was no point in discussing the letters because we both knew how they affected her. We just needed to get her mind off those feelings. We walked through all the buildings that were unlocked-- it was about 7:00 in the evening, and went into the first class we found. We took notes (after borrowing paper from someone in the class, as we were not equipped), Tasha asked a couple of questions and answered one. I think it was an Astronomy lecture. We also went to far more intramural games and campus club meetings than we were invited to.

But all of that was before she started going out with Jake. No amount of creative stress relief could get her through what she faced when he abused her. Stress wasn't the issue, she was consumed by fear.

When I write about Jake's personality, I'm going to use past tense, because that's the most accurate way to describe what I know about him. I am no longer friends with him, so I don't know what he's like now. The things I knew about him may still be true today, but I have no way of knowing that for sure.

Jake was manipulative but he also had some admirable qualities. I don't think he maliciously plotted out friendships to use people, or anything like that. I think he was okay with getting what he could out of people, but I also know that he cared about his friends. He had a layer of good in him. Not good intentions, because what he intended to do was equal to what he did, but general decency. And that's what I tried to cling to, when I tried to help him and when I tried to understand why Tasha was so loyal to him.

There is, of course, a separation between my feelings about Jake before he began abusing Tasha and from that point on. Before the violence, I got along with him very well. I considered him a close friend. He was ambitious, intelligent, and very outgoing. He was funny. He had brains and clear goals. He seemed comfortable around people, he didn't talk down to anyone who asked him what the Hell tax law is and why a person would ever be interested in it. Jake was one of those guys you see around and think, he is so cool and gorgeous and smooth, that he just *has* to be an asshole. Then you get to know him and realize you're wrong.

Jake was ecstatic about Tasha, when they met, to the extent of shedding a little bit of the macho, multi-women-craving attitude that college men are apparently required to take on. (There's a contract they're required to sign-- I'm pretty sure about that.) He kept it within arm's length, but in the beginning of their relationship, he was blatantly proud of her and he couldn't seem to see or think beyond her. It was sad and encouraging at the same time, for me to watch them together. I was single and hoped I'd fall in love like that someday-- preferably some time before my biological clock started causing eardrum damage.

When he started hitting her, I avoided him because I just didn't know what to do. I didn't know how to accept it and I didn't know how to help him. I literally could not believe that it was true. To this day, I don't know why I felt that way. It wasn't that I thought only serial killers were capable of violence, or that bad things didn't happen in life, or anything like that. I just couldn't grasp it as something that was actually taking place.

In fact, the way I felt when I found out Jake was violent, was very similar to how I felt when I heard that Tasha was dead. Like every physical thing around me was ripped away in a second's time and I was left alone to figure out why it was all gone. A real "Twilight Zone" kind of feeling-- like a stranger had walked through my door and told me that everything I'd learned in my life was untrue.

I didn't instantly shift from liking, trusting, and respecting Jake to hating him, but my feelings about him did change. I felt like I'd been fooled and like I hadn't really known him. For a very long time, I just felt nauseous when I thought about him or saw him. He was violent and he was hurting my closest friend. It wasn't like I found he was a closet smoker or something. I couldn't just overlook it as a flaw and get over it.

I had empathy for Jake, but it wasn't the same as the empathy I had for Tasha. I wanted him to get help so that she would be safe. I knew that he felt guilty, upset, and out of control, but she was suffering physically (and emotionally) because of his actions. And it was appropriate for him to feel guilty and upset about what he was doing to her.

It wasn't a matter of choosing between them because they were together. Tasha loved this man and was going to be with him-- despite the violence and with or without my support. If I condemned Jake, she would feel like I was judging and abandoning her. And she'd be right.

They started having some major arguments about 3 or 4 months after they started going out, where they would push each other and throw stuff around. I witnessed it a couple of times and Tasha admitted that it had happened before. They both downplayed it and I buried my concerns for a while. All couples fight, I'd tell myself.

Then I noticed that they were withdrawing from their friends, to an extent that went beyond romantic alone time. There was something eerie about it-- like he was scared of being without her and she felt obligated to be around him at all times. They were both anxious about anything that separated them and they acted quieter than I'd ever seen them before. Things became confusing fast because their behavior was inconsistent. The quiet period was replaced by a blissful phase, which seemed really superficial and unnatural. I mean, we all know that love is wonderful, but they were acting ridiculous. I wondered if they were trying to cover something up. As the relationship went on, overcompensation emerged as a habit for them. A day or two after a huge public fight, they would act like nothing had happened and completely gush all over each other.

I think that everyone involved—Jake and Tasha and each person who knew about the violence—was in denial about a lot of things that were going on. Part of it was being young and naïve. When you're not expecting any one you know to ever go through something like that, you don't look for signs. I think we were also trying to protect each other and it seemed easier to avoid certain topics and pretend certain events had never happened. I believed in the privacy rules of relationships because I didn't want to step on toes. I think it's common to say that people's private lives are their own and interfering can offend them, but I also think that's a comfortable out. You want the screaming match in the apartment next door to settle down because you want your neighbors to be okay. But you also want it to settle down so that you won't have to call the police and have your neighbors know it was you who called.

I had these kinds of thoughts. The first time I saw them fight, for instance, I minimized it. They'd been going out for a few months and had gone on their first weekend getaway trip together. I was studying in Tasha's room that weekend and apparently Jake didn't know that, or had forgotten. The doorknob moves, I heard a couple of bumps, then realized someone was kicking the door. I heard a guy muttering obscenities and a key moving in the lock. Then Jake kind of stumbled into the room, as he had been leaning hard against the door while unlocking it. He had been in a rage, but when he saw me, he immediately transitioned into Mr. Smooth/ party-goer mode. Tasha was in the bathroom, he informed me, and they were just back to grab some stuff that she'd forgotten. I found this odd. It was about 11 o'clock on a Saturday morning and they had gone to Sedona, so what could she have possibly forgotten that was crucial enough to drive all the way back? Plus, they were both so anal that they wouldn't have forgotten anything. It just never happened with them. They made lists that they checked and re-checked, and they had this weird methodical packing process, which had started about a week and a half ahead of time.

I also found Jake's attitude strange. He was nervous and he acted like it was really important that I believed what was he was saying. When Tasha came through the door, she went through the same hurried attempt to act happy that Jake had performed for me. She lit a cigarette and her hand was shaking. Her face was red, blotchy, and covered with eye-liner. (She wore the liquid kind that streaks worse than mascara.) They tried to act endearing toward each other, but couldn't keep it up and got into a fight about where they were going next and whose fault it was that they came back early. They seemed to alternate between being conscious of my presence and being so consumed in yelling at each other that they didn't care who else was in the room. They were bitter, sarcastic, and degrading to each other one minute and doting the next. I couldn't figure out what was really going on.

Like I said before, I wasn't in the frame of mind to suspect violence. I thought something was off, but I didn't consider that he was hurting her or that it was heading that way. When I did start to have questions about their arguments, I came up with a quick list of reasons why I shouldn't interfere: I really hadn't known her that long, if I questioned her she might think I was implying that she couldn't handle things herself, and it was none of my business. Besides, I was basically a novice at relationships. How did I know what was normal? Now I believe that the person I was interested in protecting was myself, and that bothers me. It wasn't up to me to determine whether or not the fight was a big deal.

I don't think I ever got to the point of being totally comfortable stepping into the middle of their fights. I usually felt like I was the unwanted invader and I was definitely limited by my physical capabilities. (I was in half-way decent shape, but it wasn't like I was a bouncer or anything.) However, as I grew closer to both Tasha and Jake, and as the fights got worse, it was impossible for me to look the other way. I was less concerned with upsetting them with accusations, and confrontations became typical. Sometimes my anger would block out my inhibitions. For example, one time Jake and I got into a heated argument and he pushed me into a wall. He called me a "fucking twat," one of his favorite expressions, and he kept repeating "Back down, Laura, or it'll get much worse." But I just started yelling at him. It wasn't that I thought I could overpower him or that I was trying to be a bad-ass. I was just so upset with him that I didn't care about his reaction.

Jake became violent about a year after they got together. It was the end of 1992. Tasha didn't talk about it for a while, but when she did, she told me she was shocked at first. She felt an instant surge of betrayal and disbelief. She had professed her love to this man, devoted all her time to him, made plans to build a life with him, and even given her virginity to him. She had believed in him and trusted him. She thought he felt the same way about her. She was always loyal and faithful to him. He discounted all that and began accusing her of horrible things. He was paranoid, he watched her every move and expected her to cheat on him or let him down somehow. Then he topped off the mistrust with violence.

Once violence was a part of the relationship, Tasha was locked into a loyalty to Jake that ran much deeper than the loyalty of being in love with him. It was required, not earned. She had to worry about how he would react to everything she said and did. She was in a panic mode all the time, because she could not make a choice he disapproved of. She had to convince him that she was always happy, even though that was an impossible task. Nothing she did could fend off his paranoia.

Tasha tested her friends. She distanced herself and tried to keep the details of her problems with Jake a secret. Trust was foreign to her because what Jake did to her was betrayal on the highest level. She couldn't trust the person she loved the most, so how could she be expected to trust anyone else? Also, she was ashamed and she couldn't handle the judgment, criticism and pressure to leave him. Maybe she started needing people more when Jake became abusive, but she also gained a harder edge from what she was going through. If you were going to be her friend, fine. If not, fine also. She had more important things to worry about.

Tasha knew Jake wasn't going to change, she knew she had to give up a lot to be with him, and she knew that everyone who cared about her was desperate to help her. But just knowing all of those things wasn't enough. In fact, the knowledge was a burden. I remember her saying, "If I'm in denial, shouldn't I be thinking that my life is great?" She was resigned to the way her life was, but she couldn't take it all in at once. She tried to protect herself from the worst things, by taking one risk in order to avoid a more severe one. Even though she knew that Jake's rages could get worse and worse if the relationship stayed the way it was, she was subjecting herself to a blow-up if she brought up the idea of therapy. (In Jake's mind, therapy meant weakness, which was a quality he simply couldn't handle.) She knew her life was in danger every day she stayed with him, but also knew that he would stalk her and hurt the people in her life if she left him.

Tasha was not passive. She didn't sink into a spineless, weak role in her relationship with Jake. She didn't always yell back or try to push him away from her, but sometimes she did. Sometimes she would scream at him or try to grab his wrists when he was hitting her. When people get into victim-blaming, that's part of the fuel they rely upon—a woman's alleged role in the fights. Tasha never plunged a broken beer bottle into Jake's stomach, smashed his skull into a slate floor or punched him. He did those things to her. I really don't understand why it would have been acceptable behavior, if she had listened to his insults and received all his hits, without objecting or arguing with him. Why would that have been okay, but getting angry and resisting him was wrong?

Jake's threats and rages weren't pushed one way or the other by what Tasha or anyone else said or did. He wasn't looking for approval or permission for his behavior. Perhaps all the young, gorgeous female college students on campuses across this nation, would not be anxiously agreeing to participate in talk show polls, only to flip their hair back, smile directly at the camera, and say that Jacob Grazen was the real *victim* of abuse, like they are now, if Tasha hadn't ever gotten angry with Jake or tried to fight back. But then again, maybe they still would.

I didn't know the first thing about a violent relationship. I was in college, I was experiencing all these new things, and despite my tough New York attitude, I have to admit that I was naïve about a lot of things. All of a sudden, I was in the middle of this horrible situation. I didn't know how to help her. I was confused and it seemed like the more I tried to understand why Tasha stayed and what it was really like for her, the less I could do it. I knew I should validate every feeling she had and support her no matter what, but I felt like I was reading a script when I did it. I wasn't thinking either, "Boy, maybe she's at fault here," or "Any decision she makes is okay," because I was too confused to have a clear opinion like that.

I had no idea what a "controlled relationship" was. I thought it was just another way of trying to get around the ugliness of the violence. The truth is, it's *part* of the ugliness. The things Jake said to her, the way he raised his voice, the way he looked at her, were all part of how he got above her and took over her life. The violence was not separate from that. The degradation and the abuse were all one affliction.

Jake made her decisions for her. He told her how to dress, how often to work out, and what books she had to read. He didn't allow her to hang out with friends unless he felt like chaperoning. He controlled her money, decided when she could use the car (even though it was *her* car), and made her come to him for his approval on everything. Tasha didn't want to discuss these things with anyone. It was humiliating, it made her sick. He treated her like a child.

I didn't know anything about depression either. I mean, everyone says how depressed they are, including me, at one time or another. But that's stress or being in a bad mood. It's not the same thing as going through a terrifying experience and truly losing your idea of who you are. Seeing that happen to Tasha blew me away. She tried putting on the pretense of being totally happy, to protect her friends and to protect herself, but that was the only trace of contentment she showed. She hated herself. She didn't feel like she deserved a better life. All of the things that she had thought were superficial and senseless, suddenly defined her life and she was ashamed of that. She was no longer self-assured and energetic. She was drained.

Jake and Tasha were both infatuated with the concept of a perfect life. They were hard-core about achieving success, in order to prove how valuable their lives were. Happiness meant a successful, fulfilling career; a loving, passionate marriage; and a family. Jake and Tasha were both ambitious, dedicated, and goal-oriented. The conflict was that they disagreed on how to get this life. Tasha had worked with abused kids and was involved in coordinating community programs for kids with emotional problems and violent tendencies. She wanted to go into counseling and had decided on child psychiatry. Jake believe that lawyers and doctors do acceptable work, but psychiatry was unworthy and a waste of time. He saw child psychiatry as being even worse. He told Tasha, "You can't try to figure out what kids are thinking, and that's a parent's job anyway." (I had the privilege of hearing that quote directly.) Jake decided surgery was right for her. She'd be making a lot of money and she'd be doing something he could be proud of. Tasha was also involved in various volunteer projects, which she loved doing. Volunteer work was another waste of time, according to Jake. "Why give your time to someone who doesn't see your work as worthy of payment?" he eloquently philosophized.

Tasha knew I would flip out when she told me she was switching majors, because there would be no question that it was Jake's idea. She told me during the same conversation that she broke the news of her plan to move in with him. I stifled a laugh as she walked into my room, clad in a flannel nightgown and wool socks, with a cigarette behind her ear. The image was so out of character for her, but my amusement quickly faded because I knew something was wrong. It was four in the afternoon and she got up each day at 5:00 a.m. (at the absolute latest), to create the perfect glamour look. Pre-Jake, she didn't even own a mirror—let alone make-up, and she shopped with me at second-hand stores.

She lit her cigarette, helped herself to a swig of my Cuervo bottle, then dove into the news. "I want to go into surgical medicine, instead of psychiatry, and Jacob and I have decided that the dorm environment isn't right for me. Too many distractions. So, I'm moving into his condo." She had spoken very fast and let out a big breath when she was finished. She poured herself a shot of Cuervo and sat down on my couch, nervously awaiting my reaction. (Tasha drank tequila like no one I've ever seen. If we reminded her to do a shot, she would do it like most people, but that was just for show. Otherwise, it was like drinking water after a long work-out. She guzzled it and acted like it was the most refreshing thing she'd ever tasted. It was odd.)

I searched for a cigarette, then took a drag off hers when I got tired of looking. I looked out the window and tried to compose myself, going through my little ritual of self-talk and deep breathing, but this time I did a condensed version of it and it didn't work at all. I suddenly turned around and blurted, "You 'want' to sacrifice the one thing you believe in most? And what exactly is it about living in a dorm that you and 'Jacob' see as being wrong, Tasha? The fact that you have friends? Or is living with the great one right for you because it would give him 24-hour access to a blow job and an outlet for his anger?" There was a sharp silence that would have probably been chilling if not for the heat that had flooded my body as soon as I finished speaking. Tasha's mouth was wide open, she had dropped her cigarette and knocked over her shot glass.

I sat down on the floor and inhaled sharply. Shit, I'm such an asshole, I thought. I said, "Oh my God, Tasha, I am so sorry. I swear. I just get so scared for you, but I didn't mean any of that." I'm sure I stuttered a little, because it was a lie that I couldn't sell to her. I meant every word of my outburst. She just looked at me and we both started crying after a few minutes of silence, but there was no further conversation. What was left to say?

Tasha didn't have a life of her own, once she hooked up with Jake, and I was bitter about that. It made me sad, I didn't get it, and I missed hanging out with her. She had these restrictions on her social life from the person she loved, which embarrassed her and made her miserable. I tried to take her out the few times Jake was in L.A. visiting friends for a weekend, but she felt guilty and anxious the whole time. Once I tried taking her to a party, and when she freaked out about it, I told her she was being ridiculous, that Jake didn't have to check with her before hanging out with his friends, and that I would deal with him if he got mad about it. I now see how patronizing and naïve that was. I implied that the double standard was something she was responsible for and that I could handle the man who physically abused her better than she could. I had no concept of what her fear was really like, yet I was asking her to prove her loyalty to me by risking a rage from him.

Occasionally, Jake and Tasha would make a guest appearance out together, and the rest of us would be pretty much guaranteed to have a horrible time. Tasha was always visibly nervous and stayed within two inches of Jake the whole time, and he drank until he was so obnoxious that people would start avoiding him. We were embarrassed and scared for her. They tried not to argue in public, but when Jake drank, he basically argued with anything and everyone in his path. And he drank all the time. (Josh and I secretly called him the D.A., for designated asshole.) I knew Tasha always faced the chance of a big fight at home. She couldn't relax because he would get angrier as the night wore on and she would totally dread the time when they went home together and no one was around to protect her. She told me that even though she hated his extreme drinking, she always hoped he'd pass out, so she could have a bruise-free night and a chance at getting some sleep.

Having Tasha as a friend meant living with an intense fear every day. Sometimes there'd be a specific source for this fear, like the time Jake showed up drunk at a restaurant where Tasha and I were having dinner with 4 or 5 friends, and pulled her out of her chair by her arm, after calling her a "fucking slut." On nights when incidents like that had occurred, I would lie awake in bed and imagine getting a phone call about her death. Other times, it was a persistent feeling that something was terribly wrong. Something was nagging at me and I felt sick to my stomach.

I can't remember exactly when I realized that Tasha was in serious danger, but the realization brought me a heavy sense of panic. On one hand, it seemed like an irrelevant discovery, as I wondered what the Hell I could actually do about it. However, there was this sense of urgency because I knew things were getting progressively worse.

When I began thinking that Jake had the potential to kill Tasha, I picked up the habit of thinking about emergency procedures during every situation. I would plot out escape routes for Tasha in my head and consider ways to offer protection for her. I viewed Jake as a constant, violent force. I didn't think that his moods or the environment he was in at a given time, either provoked or suppressed his violence. He could break at any moment, I believed. I remember how Jake commented that I looked dazed, one night when we were playing poker at his friend's apartment. Everyone else was into the game and having a great time, but I was fixating on the kitchen window. It looked stuck and we were on the second floor, so I had become particularly perplexed during my routine planning session. I would have to throw a chair through the window and ask one of the guys sitting near the window to hold Jake back, while Tasha jumped onto the dumpster below.

So, it was easy for me to switch into that familiar mode of emergency planning, the night Tasha called me for help. However, everything happened so fast that it was a case of adrenaline controlling my reaction, not rational thoughts. I tried hard to sound calm, reassuring, and like I knew what to do. I also kept the call short so I could call the police and get my ass over three. It wasn't that I thought I was going to save the day by wrestling Jake to the ground or anything. I was going there to be with Tasha and hopefully the police could handle Jake.

On the phone, she was breathing fast and hard. It sounded like an asthma attack. I told her to take slow deep breaths. I didn't even need to hear an explanation of the circumstances. I knew he'd threatened her and hurt her. I didn't need to hear the details to know I had to call the police, but I didn't want to freak her out by hanging up on her. She was crying and could only get out a few words. She said, "Laura, …. shit, … I am so sorry … he's really…. He won't stop." I said, "I know, it's okay. Get out of the house if you can, I love you. We're going to take care of it." She thanked me and hung up.

As I called Dave and Josh and got ready to leave, I kept trying to calm myself down. I wanted to be able to help her and make her feel secure. It would just make things worse if I panicked, so I was trying to think of other things. My mind kept focusing on her face, however. I found myself thinking, "What if I never see her again, what if that was the last time I'll hear her voice?"

The Phoenix police were leaving the house when we got there. Their expressions made it obvious that the call had been a waste of their time. I hurried out of the car, running to the nearest officer. He confirmed my presumption. Tasha had rescinded her complaint and Jake had left the scene. I felt nauseous. Josh and Dave had been running behind me and Josh got to me first. He knew I was going to escalate and he was right. I had started screaming and swearing as soon as I found out what had happened. He grabbed my hand and led me away from the house. He told me that I had to think of Tasha, I had to calm down, get it together and be there for her.

"I know, I know," I mumbled. I knelt on the ground and did a quick self-calming chat. "Don't blame her" was my first mantra. "She needs you, don't judge her," I told myself. Dave and Josh were used to this by now, so they just stood there and acted like everything was perfectly normal. (Josh had once said to me, shortly after I'd started the talking to myself habit: "Ok, you *do* know that's out loud, right sweetie?") I eventually snapped back into my take-action mind-set and walked into the house to find Tasha.

My first thought, as I approached this huddled, sobbing, mess of a person, was "She is going to be apologetic." I felt like shit. I knew she thought she'd betrayed me by staying with him and by dropping the charges, and I felt like I was her worst critic. I hated having that role, but I knew I'd earned it. I made 2 huge whiskey sours and sat down next to her. I gave her my full attention, even though she didn't talk very much. There wasn't much to say, because we both knew all the facts: She was scared, she hated Jake and loved him at the same time, she hated herself for loving him, and she was not going to leave him.

For Tasha, that night was just one real-life nightmare out of many, and one more night that she had managed to get through. It wasn't any more or less dramatic than all the other times he abused her and when it was over, it was over. She didn't think it would be the last fight or that Jake would finally realize how bad things were because the cops had been there. She actually didn't even give much thought to the way she felt during and after a fight. It was a part of her life. In her mind, it wasn't that she *wasn't going* to leave Jake, it was that she couldn't leave him.

No matter how many details Tasha gave me about the fights or the way she felt, I would never, ever get it. (And I don't mean that in the judgmental "I just don't get it" way, I mean that I would always have the 3rd person perspective of panic and fear, while she was the one who lived it.) The episodes would be different, but her fear was always there. Sometimes she would frantically run into my room, to get away from Jake, and other times they would show up at a bar together and she'd calmly tell me about the fight they'd had 2 hours earlier.

One night I paced around my dorm room for hours, after getting home from a night out with Jake and Tasha. He was plastered, and when he decided it was time to leave, Tasha came over to me and whispered, "Looks like it's time to go home and get raped." She wasn't kidding and she wasn't upset. It was simply her reality. I was going to go home and watch a bad TV movie, while eating Cheetos, and she was going home to face whatever assault Jake decided to inflict on her. I had begged her not to leave with him, stammering something like, "Tasha, Oh my God. Please don't leave." She felt like she had to comfort me and told me it'd be okay, but we both knew that was far from true.

The night Jake was arrested for battery, Tasha told me about their sex life. She didn't want to be anywhere near their condo and she didn't feel like making the drive to her mom's house that night, so she and I stayed at Dave's apartment. We went for a walk and then sat on his roof and talked for most of the night. Jake was the only man she had ever had sex with and she couldn't imagine being with anyone else if they ever broke up for good, because she would never feel safe from his rages. She fully believed that Jake would go after any man she ever dated, and I agreed with her. She was sad to think she'd never experience a healthy sex life.

She said that when they first started sleeping together, he was gentle and tender. He was attentive to her needs and she loved being with him. Then he started getting rough, but she thought he was just trying to spice things up. As time wore on, she realized that his strict attitude wasn't just a playful sexual role. His demands weren't a joke and if he told her to do something, she had better do it. He saw sex as the ultimate test. He carried his intense jealousy and paranoia into the bedroom and she had to prove her loyalty to him there, as well as everywhere else. Every time they had sex, she was terrified. He would either hurt her during it or get violent afterwards, if she didn't perform well enough.

Tasha and I argued about Jake and their relationship. *All the time*. I would implicitly and explicitly say that she was pathetic for staying with him, and she would say I didn't know how to be a friend or call me a judgmental, self-righteous bitch. It was like we were desperate to get through to each other and frustrated that we always hit a brick wall. She wanted me to stop worrying about her and just focus on my own life. I couldn't believe she would expect me to just forget about what was going on with her and relax about it.

During one of these arguments, she told me about her dual feelings for Jake. I didn't want to hear it, but she didn't really care about that. She was tired of feeling like I thought she was crazy and tired of dealing with my patronizing attitude. She was alternating between yelling at me and begging me to listen to her and to try to see her side. I remember my guilt oozing in as she finally sat down in a defeated state, grabbed my hand, and looked me in the eye. She said, "Listen. Just fucking listen, okay? You're going to continue to judge me and guilt trip me and criticize me, no matter what I do. The least you can do is listen to how I really feel, or even pretend to listen because no one else in my life does and I can't just exist in isolation."

So, I did listen. She said she truly wanted to leave him sometimes, because she hated what he did to her, his words, and how he made her feel. But she felt this tug to stay—like an obligation that she couldn't get out of. It saddened and depressed her. She also began to hate herself because of it. She'd taunt herself mentally, by thinking about how she had to leave him, and then ridicule herself for being too chicken shit to do it.

In another argument, she told me that all couples go through changes when they get together. I think she wanted to believe that her situation was perfectly normal and if she could get it to make sense to her friends, it would help. When she told me that you become part of a connection as a couple, I inserted a Chuck Woolery joke, but she didn't find it funny. She ignored me and said that it's only natural to consider the opinions of the person you love, because you respect their thoughts. I would get incredibly annoyed with those little speeches, and I pointed out that giving up what's really important to you to make someone else happy, is not love. "How can he really love you, if he asks you to do that?" I'd ask her. That question would usually get an eye roll or two.

Shortly after they announced the engagement, I tried one more time to voice my concerns to Tasha. It felt like a big conference—my last chance to get through to her. I tried to be very gentle and diplomatic, planning out every word carefully. That didn't end up happening though. I called Tasha, the morning after one of my many middle-of-the-night anxiety attacks. I asked her to meet me for lunch, and she agreed, after asking me if everything was okay. I'm sure she guessed that it was going to be an "important" (translation: uncomfortable) talk kind of lunch. We went to one of our favorite delis and ordered Greek salads and Foster oil cans.

I took four long sips of my beer before I dived in: "Tash, have you thought about what you'd do if he really hurt you?" That came out wrong, I thought immediately. "I'm sorry, I know that he has hurt you. What I mean is, do you have some sort of a plan for…" She blew up. "For what?! What I'll do if he tries to kill me?" We used to tease her about her inability to get angry. She was bad at arguments because as soon as she started to raise her voice, she'd feel guilty and back down. This time, I knew that she really was angry, but she was also extremely sad. And I got that because I was as well. Here we were, arguing for the millionth time about her relationship and the underlying emotion for both of us was fear. I was trying to get her to leave the relationship because I was scared for her and she was trying to get me to back off because she knew she couldn't do what I was asking. She followed her angry outburst with sobbing. I felt like shit, as usual.

Tasha stayed silent for a few minutes after that. She had pushed away her salad and began to concentrate on her beer. Then she lit a cigarette and started in on her common defense of Jake. I'd heard it all before. She'd list of all his positive qualities, like she was a car show model trying to make me realize why Jake was the best buy, by polishing him up and putting him on display. She would get flustered to the point of not being able to concentrate on her own thoughts, when she was nervous, and the more she talked, the worse it got. She started out sounding like her argument was completely grounded in logic. She was calm, she enunciated each word carefully, and her posture was relaxed.

This was important to her and she really wanted to deliver an effective sales pitch. But she could not block out the reality that we both knew she was full of shit, for long, so she started speaking faster and louder. Her pitch went up and down like a bad puberty impression (or a good one, I guess). Then she'd shift around in her chair and start doing this fake coughing thing. Like I was going to be distracted by a sudden concern that she was coming down with a cold or something.

Then she started just rambling, spurting out phrases and weird clichés that made no sense at all. "Okay so he's an asshole sometimes. But realistically, Laura, don't we all have our days? He's so intense about being the best tax lawyer and the best model, that he doesn't think about anything or anyone else. Well, he doesn't think about them on the outside, but on the inside, it's all he cares about. It's like he's an undercover cop, because he really does have a purpose and it's a noble one. He's too busy to be Mr. Sensitive Love machine all the time and that's okay because at least he's being real. A diamond in the rough, not a ruby in a display case. He feels safe enough to let down his guard with me. Once he gets his careers balanced, he'll be more relaxed and he'll ..."

I couldn't take it anymore. "Hey! Come back to earth with me for a second. If you are even trying to say that ... well, what the Hell are you trying to say? It's okay for Jake to hit you because he's a good fucking model? Or because, ... Because his violence is …. Is an essential part of the overall plan for your happiness? … or because … he's a … fucking … *diamond*? I mean, … My *God*!" I felt like I was hyperventilating. I would just spew out fragments of sentences like a dry heave.

I closed my eyes, took three deep breaths, two long, disgusting slurps of Foster's (manners are hard enough for me under normal circumstances, so they are out the window when I'm stressed), and lit a cigarette. "All right, sweetie. Just listen for a second. Please. We have got to break through all this 'everything's A-OK' crap and deal with what's going on, but we need to do it without insulting or belittling each other. It's not just that Jake's a really driven egomaniac who's a great guy underneath a hard shell. And if it was just about me thinking he's an asshole, we wouldn't even be talking about it. Tash, every guy I've *dated* is an asshole. You know that." She giggled and wiped at her tears with a napkin. "I don't know what to do, Laura."

And neither did I. I always felt like the right thing to say to her was just out of reach. I thought about it all the time. What was I missing? Why couldn't I be the friend I needed to be? Once I actually got out of bed, during a middle of the night worry-fest, and wrote out a note to her. Its eventual home was the trash can, but the gist is as follows:

> **It's not about me judging Jake. I know it seems that way, but it's really not anymore. It's gone beyond my opinion of your relationship. I love you and I am**

so scared for you. I'm not trying to be melodramatic, I just want to make sure you can think about your life. *Your* life, Tasha. Please just draw a line and when he crosses it, leave. It doesn't mean that you're weak. It doesn't mean that you don't love him enough. And I'm being selfish. I am, because I want you here, God damn it. I am so sorry that I've judged you, Tasha, and I am so sorry that I am such a bitch.

Two incidents in Tasha's life made me rethink my whole attitude about how much Jake controlled her decisions: the fact that she stuck with her original plan to go into child psychiatry instead of going along with Jake's idea about surgical medicine, and the divorce. For the first decision, I thought he must have let up on her a little bit, or maybe something had gotten better in their relationship. Somehow, they had agreed on what was best for her. As for the divorce, it obviously didn't mean that their relationship had improved, but maybe they were accepting that being together was not healthy. Jake wasn't contesting it, so was his obsessive love cooling off? If Tasha was able to stand up to him without getting hurt, maybe he finally got that she deserved to be safe.

When I found out about each of those decisions, I thought that maybe my prediction of a terrible fate for Tasha had been wrong. I prayed it was wrong.

When we talked about the psychiatry decision, Tasha was sullen. "It doesn't mean things are going well. I wish that was the truth," she told me. He had actually gotten more violent than ever and she had reached the point of complete apathy. She knew from experience that nothing she did or didn't do would affect his violence. She didn't care about the relationship anymore because she no longer saw any of his positive qualities. She might as well salvage her one chance for happiness, by pursuing her own dreams for a career.

With the divorce, they had been separated for a while and Jake had given up all hope at reconciliation. He was depressed after his arrest for assault, and believed that he didn't deserve to be with Tasha. (I was one of many who agreed with him.) He didn't see a point in contesting it. Tasha wasn't confident that he would ever leave her alone, but felt like divorce was the only choice left for her.

I think blame is unhealthy, but since Tasha's death, I've learned just how easily it can come about. My blame for Jake has been with me for a long time. Sometimes I try to release it, thinking that will make me feel like a better person, but I've failed so far. I'm pretty comfortable with it because it is so consistent— I do not wake up a single day without it. It's also very logical. There is one cause for the struggles Tasha faced when she was alive, the pain she endured during her murder, the fear and helplessness her friends felt when she was being abused, and the agony of mourning we all deal with now that's she's gone. One cause: Jake.

I also blame him for my brand-new view of the world. My best friend was living a horrifying life at the age of 20 and I began to wonder what would stop me from meeting someone like Jake. I became paranoid and cynical, because I lived in a world where a young, beautiful woman gets punched, thrown, kicked and slashed by the person who claims to love her more than anything. A world where there seems to be no available explanation of why that can happen.

I was probably less cynical of the media and public attitudes before all of this happened. Before, I was an outsider to tragedy. I *heard* about people dying and the pain their loved ones endured. Now it's happening *to* me.

I have days when everything bothers me. Maybe I take every comment the wrong way, or maybe I'm just not strong enough to get into the subject matter. Someone I love is the topic of every discussion and I can't fucking stand it. It feels like we're objectifying Tasha and her life. And everything is past tense, which just sucks. I am not up to it.

Then there are days where a reporter can walk up to me and receive no insults or tears, regardless of what they say. It's not that they've done something to impress me or that I'm in a good mood that day. I'm just numb. When you see, feel, and hear the same pain over and over and over again, you don't have room for anything else. Anger, confusion, happiness—you don't have the energy to feel any emotion.

"Everything's okay." That was probably Tasha's most common line. She said it even when it was so far from the truth and it would have even more power during those times. She would take both of your hands in hers and lean towards you. She'd look into your eyes, take a moment to make sure you were looking back at her, and speak in a soft, low tone. I try so hard to believe those words now. When I'm walking around the house in the middle of the night, when I'm looking at my daughters as they sleep, when I'm staring out our skylight at the stars, as I cry uncontrollably and my husband holds me. I want to believe it—mainly because I know she wants me to, but I always come back to the same conclusion that sits like a rock in my stomach. The only way *any*thing will be okay (let alone everything), is if she will come back to us.

Annia Valdez

Annia Valdez was a co-lead for the prosecution team, in the Jacob Grazen criminal trial. She studied criminal law at Columbia Law School, then worked for New York City's public defender office for 3 years, before becoming a prosecutor. She stayed in New York for another 3 years, working in sex crimes, before moving to Phoenix, where she has been a prosecutor with the Phoenix District Attorney's Office for 8 years.

January 30, 1998

Before Jacob Grazen's murder trial came along, I had been in a niche of working on cases in relative privacy. I have tried a lot of cases that are very similar to the Grazen case, but I haven't seen all the hustle and bustle from the press and crowds of spectators for a few years. I liked it that way because it fit in with my simple work ethic: I like to work hard, but without a lot of distraction or attention.

Maybe the idea of a high-profile, big deal murder case sounds glamorous and fun, to other people. Maybe exciting and a chance to make a name for yourself. Not in my way of thinking. For me, it only means a hassle. Cameras for permanent shadows and the constant tension of knowing everyone is watching your work. No thanks. If I wanted that, I would have become an actress.

I remember how I felt when I first got this case. I had this feeling of discomfort and nervousness, which was really unusual for me. Cases can certainly be complex and preparing for trials on domestic violence cases are challenging, to say the least. But I had never had that foreboding feeling of "this one is going to be bad." Not just emotionally draining or controversial, but something that was going to change me and affect me for a long time. However, I didn't have any thoughts of not taking the case. I knew instinctively that it was a journey I had to take.

I had just gotten back from a weekend of camping, and I was relaxed and refreshed that Monday morning, until I faced the chaos in our office. I had tried to stretch out my break form technology (well, mostly—I have to bring my curling iron along on any overnight…) as long as I could, so I hadn't turned on my television or radio, and I don't read the newspaper until I get to the office. So, I felt like I was the last person to find out.

From the number of people waiting for elevators, and from their anxious attitudes and expressions, I knew something was up. A lot of people were from other firms in the city, as well as some crime lab technicians, scientists, and various consultants from other parts of the country. I don't know everyone who works in my building, but I can tell when people are unfamiliar with our set-up. The directory is confusing and we're always moving offices around, so I'm used to spotting people who are lost and helping them out.

It was earlier than I usually start my workday—about 7:00, and I hadn't expected to see anyone in the building. I had planned on some quiet work time. I went to my office first, instead of stopping by Mark's as I usually do, because I figured he wouldn't be in yet. (Mark Kellar is my assistant.) As I plopped down my huge, bright orange, fake leather hand bag—my favorite that I've had for at least 7 years—on a chair and hung up my suit jacket, I saw a pile of messages on my desk. My message light was flashing on my answering machine. Mark had gotten there first and directed a bunch of calls my way. I listened to a few of the messages, which were pretty vague. A lot of people wanted me to call them right away, but no one left details. John Whitten had dropped by twice already, leaving 2 big notes for me to come find him when I got in. I couldn't seem to find anyone. I called John's office, Mark's office, John's assistant, and no one answered. Then I looked around for some of my interns, which was a futile search as well.

"Am I missing a big lawyers' breakfast or something?" I muttered to myself as I walked down to the elevator bank. (Talking to myself is one of my trademark habits. I don't even get second looks anymore.) I slowly walked by the glass wall of our largest conference room. We use it to meet with clients or for trial preparation if all our other rooms are in use, but otherwise it's empty. When that room is filled with people, you know there's some big deal meeting or conference going on.

Not really wanting to see who was in there, I took a couple of seconds to study the framed watercolor on the opposite side of the hallway. I stretched my arms over my head and thought about getting some hot chocolate. (I only drink coffee if I can't find cocoa.) When I turned around, I saw that the room was packed and everyone was talking in hushed tones and checking each other out, like college kids at a keg party. "Shit," I mumbled, as Heather, one of my interns, walked out of the room and flashed me a nervous smile when she realized she'd been unsuccessful in avoiding my gaze. She looked like she wanted to turn around and walk in the opposite direction. I gave her my "What now?" look and she motioned vigorously towards John, who was close behind her. Whatever had happened, she felt that he should deliver the news. Not a good sign.

John gave me his favorite greeting—the Miss America wave, and quickly came up to talk to me. "Whitten, what the Hell?" He plastered on a grin and waited for more questioning from me. I continued with, "Alright, I find the suspense very dramatic, but I'm ready for you to tell me why I can't leave early today to soak my sore butt in my bathtub." He allowed himself a quick joke and told me the big news. "Oh, how I *love* it when you talk about your ass, but please don't rile me up with details of why it's sore. Natasha Grazen was killed Friday night."

"From hiking and it's Hillshaw," I responded. I couldn't stand to leave a comment unanswered, so we often spoke in fragments. "She didn't take his name,"

I said slowly and softly. As I waited for more from John, I knew it was going to be about Jake's status in the investigation. I knew the basic outline of Jake's history with domestic violence. I thought to myself, "He did it, he killed her." I listened carefully to the details of Jake's arrest and the evidence gathered so far.

Most people are aware of why domestic violence trials are particularly important to me and can affect me on a deeper level than other types of cases. I was in an abusive marriage for five years.

When the stories came out, the theme seemed to be that I had been keeping this big secret. Some articles implied that it was a betrayal because I hadn't been "forthright" about it before. Others surmised that the leak was only supposed to *appear* accidental, while it was really an intentional ploy to get sympathy from the jury. (Apparently some reporters forgot that the jury was sequestered.) It's ironic that I'm a prosecutor and I'm being treated like a defendant.

I was ridiculed and criticized while I was in the relationship, and now I am expected to come out and apologize for keeping this secret. (And it's not a secret because it is public knowledge!) Did we ever hear about every past relationship my colleagues or opposing counsel members have had? It really is outrageous.

The violence was never a secret. Did I call up the New York Times the day I got the Grazen case to make sure they knew that I was once a victim of domestic violence? Of course not, but I never denied it when I was asked. Some of the people who I work with now, as well as past colleagues, know about it, just as some people share personal issues with me from time to time. The subject has also come up with clients before. It is a part of who I am, but victims of domestic violence are not required to put an article in the paper announcing that they have been abused. And since we are so harshly judged for it, why would we want to tell everyone?

I have a job where publicity isn't something you can escape from and I accept that. However, I'm still a person, so it can be difficult to handle at times. I don't understand how anyone could truly believe that my personal history gave the prosecution an unfair advantage in this case. If Grazen had been acquitted, no one would have said this.

The jury did not make its decision because they felt sorry for me. I mean, that could actually be taken as flattery if I believed it, but it would also mean that I believed that they broke the rules of sequestration. I certainly didn't bring it up at trial, as I would be more likely to tell them what color bra I was wearing than I would to tell them about my ex-husband.

There was no political, ethical, or social calculated maneuvering going on during the trial. The D.A.'s office wasn't using this case as a platform for domestic violence education. I did not accept this case to advocate for women's groups. Nor did I hope to engage in a personal battle, get some sort of revenge, or vent about my own issues. I took it because someone was murdered. My job is to hold the person who did it responsible, and there is indisputable evidence showing that Jacob Grazen is that person.

During the trial, I couldn't take the time to address the speculation about my past, so now I'm going to grab this chance to talk openly about the relationship.

I met him when I was in my last year of pre-law studies and he was doing his residency for surgical medicine. We dated for two years and then got married. Eight months into the marriage was when he became violent. He blamed it all on stress. He was on and off the wagon, so he blamed a lot of things on alcohol also. Work drove him to drinking and drinking drove him to hurt me. He was always reminding me how much he worked and how overwhelmed he was. He had to balance his double shifts with raising a family and that was such a huge burden that I could never appreciate. My reaction to that was annoyance, which eventually turned into resentment and hatred. I worked just as hard as he did and I was the one who was raising our kids, while he came home every night to yell at us, before drinking himself to sleep.

I occasionally fought back when he got violent. It didn't do much good and I never stopped being afraid of him. And it was just more fuel for his manipulation. ("I'm not the *only* one who gets physical, Annia," he would tell me. That drove me crazy. He wasn't exactly what Olivia Newton John was referring to ....) The violence wasn't constant. He didn't abuse me during my pregnancies and we had long periods where we didn't talk or interact at all. We would just avoid each other. I tried to focus on law school, work, and the kids. At times, I could successfully deny that I was even married. In my heart, he didn't exist.

We kept the problems in our relationship as quiet as we could. Preserving Howard's starched white reputation among all of his colleagues was imperative to him. Everyone thought he could do no wrong and he wanted to keep it that way. His job was also important to me, because I needed his income to support the kids. For a long time, I didn't have a problem with keeping the abuse a secret because I was really humiliated by it. The fact that I stayed with someone who hurt me was a reflection on my character too. Marriage is a big deal. I didn't want to be someone who couldn't make it work.

When I did leave, the pain didn't stop for me like I had expected it to. Things didn't get easier. I was angry and confused about that. I had gotten away from this man, wasn't that the whole problem? But it was like running from a burning house into the freezing cold, because I had traded one hardship for another one. I was exposed and I felt like I had no support. There were a lot of people who cared about me and wanted to help, but I only noticed the negative reactions because I was in such a vulnerable state.

In the end, Howard's colleagues blamed me for ruining his career. He told everyone that I had made everything up and that I was actually the abusive one in our relationship. And since everyone believed him, his career was *not* ruined. He was convicted of domestic assault, for the damage he did on the night I left, but he got his one-year sentence reduced and only served 30 days. He did not lose his job. He had beaten me in front of the kids, thrown a punch at our neighbor who tried to intervene, and threatened us all with a gun. I had thought a year was way too light, but the judge decided that it was about 11 months too heavy!

I filed for divorce and fought a long, nasty custody battle, which I finally won. Then our oldest daughter, Adriana, was killed in a car crash during Howard's first unsupervised visit with her. He was arrested for driving under the influence of alcohol. He also killed the 70-year-old woman who was driving the other car. He got two manslaughter convictions and is currently serving a 30-year sentence. I felt like the justice system came through, to an extent, but no form of punishment will ever lessen the pain for either myself or my other 2 kids. (Jason is 14 and Sarah is 12. Adriana would have been 15.)

What I went through will always be with me and I will never feel completely healed. I will always grieve for my daughter, wonder what her life would have brought her if it had continued, as well as regret what all my children went through. And I will probably always blame myself for her death.

As I read Natasha's letters, I relived the fear, desperation, and anger that was my world when I was with Howard. But the things we had in common aren't limited to the pain we went through in the duration of our relationships. There's also a residue that you obtain from a violent relationship—a gritty layer that you can never wash off. After Natasha left Jake, she saw people differently. She was more vulnerable. She was afraid at times when it didn't make sense for her to feel fear. She doubted her own abilities and trust was always difficult for her to obtain. All these things happen for me as well.

And there's one more similarity that comes from outside any thought or physical feeling a victim of domestic violence has. It's society's judgment. When Natasha was alive, she met a lot of people who didn't understand how she could have stayed with Jake for as long as she did. "What was she thinking?" "How could she claim to be an intelligent, strong woman if she made those choices?" Regardless of how well Natasha dealt with those questions or what steps she took to end the relationship, people kept asking them and providing their own answers. The same goes for my situation. "Why did you have 3 kids with a violent man?" was the most common disapproval I received.

Even though I've experienced the judgment firsthand, I am still confused about where people's attitudes come from. One afternoon during this trial, I hit burn-out with a stack of witness screening notes, which I'd been sifting through for about 5 hours straight, and I decided to talk to John Whitten about some of my nagging questions. I had been having a lot of sleepless nights and sometimes at work I would find myself stewing over all the comments and arguments that really bothered and offended me.

I walked into his office and opened with, "Why do people look so hard for reasons to blame victims?

Why doesn't that feel wrong?" He motioned for me to sit in my favorite chair (chocolate brown leather, high back—reminded me of my grandfather's living room when I was a kid), slid the files in front of him to the side, and removed his expensive English cigarettes, black onyx lighter, and bottle of Dewar's from his bottom desk drawer. He held out a cigarette and I shook my head. (I smoke about once a month and I have to have a really strong craving to do it.) He poured some Dewar's into a coffee mug and passed it to me.

He inhaled on a cigarette and said, "Admitting the full dynamics of an abusive relationship is what feels wrong. For someone who spends a lot of time in denial and is naturally cynical and judgmental about any situation that makes them feel uncomfortable, there's nothing drastic about it. It doesn't feel like they're looking hard for reasons to blame victims. Also, I don't think most victim-blamers sit down and weigh the worth of the batterer against the worth of the victim, before deciding it's the victim's fault. It's more about putting some distance between themselves and the ugliness of violence. People want to soften the details of a violent relationship, so they come up with thoughts like, 'Maybe it's more mutual' or 'Maybe it's just the ups and downs of a normal relationship that just get a little out of hand once in a while.' Then it's an easy transition into making excuses for the batterer."

Anyone who knows John Whitten will agree that he is a source of comfort. He is the funniest man I know and the most conscientious, so he'll help you get stress of your mind and listen to any problem you have.

I continued on with my questions. "I don't understand. Do they trash Natasha out of loyalty to Jake, because of his reputation in the law community ...?" I saw the smirk form, so gave him the "go ahead" gesture to insert a joke. He suppressed a grin and gave me his best serious expression. "No, it's his reputation in the modeling community, Annia! How could you forget that?!" He knows my favorite Jake jokes involve his illustrious career as a model, so I appreciated the sentiment.

"It seems like the idea of domestic violence as a complex, confusing mystery is widely accepted by everyone else, but it's pretty straightforward to me. I am missing the enigma factor." John knew I wasn't being sarcastic here and that this was something I was really in turmoil about. He said, "There's a fine line between denial and mystery. If you refuse to think about something, it's a mystery. Then you can say it's a complicated issue and leave it at that. It's a mystery that you have no interest in solving. The same thing can happen with child abuse and sexual abuse. No one wants to believe that it goes on. If you just label something horrible as unimaginable and unspeakable, and then disassociate yourself from it, you're free. People have such a hard time accepting that the world they grew up in and are now raising their own kids in, could be tainted by such ills. It reflects directly upon them."

Those talks with John helped prepare me for the public ridicule I'm currently dealing with, plus it helped clear my head for the courtroom. The frenzied, desperate support for Jake brought out an obsessive, panicked, crazed attitude. I am used to receiving venomous attacks from defendants' supporters, but there's not usually such a superficial basis for them. A lot of spectators in this case could probably give a detailed account of Jacob Grazen's wardrobe, but that's about it. They can't believe he's a murderer, simply because of the way he looks, so looking at the evidence that proved his guilt was out of the question.

As far as the courtroom goes, presenting gruesome details of a crime is emotional. I have to balance a calm, professional frame of mind with a passionate voice, because I need to present my ideas clearly and advocate for a just verdict. Sorting out any potential stumbling blocks ahead of time helps me do this.

The defense team put on a very interesting case. They worked very hard and remained loyal to the "I'll do anything for my client" mind-set. I had worked with most of these lawyers previously, so I knew they would take risks and push things to the limit. I think a good defense attorney has to be like that and I respect those qualities, despite the fact that I am frequently annoyed and stressed out by them.

This was just one of those cases where the evidence was piled up so high against the defense that their choices were extremely limited. We had strong physical evidence connecting their client to the crime and they didn't have any solid evidence of their own to dispute the connections. They had to find a way for the jury to minimize our evidence and they tried to distract the jury from the truth with aggressive attacks on our case.

Their technique was swamping the jury with invalid theories, and then asking them to apply the doubt they had to *our* case. Confusion was the key. They gave the jury fragments of ideas and it felt more like a bad lecture than anything else. Labs can make mistakes. The violence has nothing to do with this case. Then they threw in a bunch of contradictions about Jake. On the one hand, he was a poster boy for taking responsibility for the mistakes he made and turning his life around. On the other, he didn't have anything to regret because he was actually the true victim.

They tied all the pieces together by driving home reasonable doubt and the burden of proof. If the jury was confused, they had doubt. So, an acquittal was only fair and logical choice. And "we don't have to prove *any*thing" was their all-purpose excuse for not having a case. Since the prosecution had that burden, all they had to do was ramble on and make sure Jake looked well-groomed each day.

Sam Hadwick kept yelling, "Too many questions!" in his closing. That was why they could not convict Jake, he said. There certainly were a lot of questions, and they were all about the strength of the defense team's arguments.

Despite the defense's claims to the contrary, domestic violence *was* a relevant issue in this trial.

Jake's behavior towards Natasha explains why he killed her. As our expert witnesses explained, his insecurity, obsession, and rage built up to the point of absolute destruction. He literally could not take it anymore. His need to dominate was very real and that's why the defense tried to bury it.

The common view on their decision to put Jake on the stand is that it was a "huge risk." I don't see that. The assumption is that a jury will believe a defendant is guilty if they do not take the stand. The theory being that they have something to hide if they don't. Fortunately, jurors aren't as thick as people think. They think about things like cross-examinations of witnesses and evidence. Also, I have to believe that every once in a while, I get a juror who actually abides by the instructions. They are told not to read anything into the decision of whether or not a defendant testifies, since the defendant is not required to do so.

I wasn't the least bit surprised by the decision to put Jake on the stand. Ultimately, the decision is left to the defendant and self-proclamation is right up Jake's alley. He is a walking ego, so he enjoys talking about himself. I think he did pretty well overall, if you just look at his statements and responses, but I think it seemed staged and over-rehearsed. The direct was well planned. His descriptions of the relationship and his alleged remorse came out in a perfect sequence. It was a gradual build-up, filled with dramatic moments. Jake acted completely surprised by every question. He was really nervous during the cross, but held up quite well. He went for the when in doubt, cry approach. If he didn't seem to know how to handle a question, he would break down, say something like he just couldn't rid his mind of the memories of Natalie, and ask for a moment to collect himself. I was actually grateful for this technique, because I think he gave the jury an inside look at his personality. He is all about theatrics and manipulation. I reacted honestly. I was so disgusted with him and I didn't buy his helpless murderer act.

I expected the defense witnesses, for the character description portion of their case, to be a lot tougher than they were. I was expecting a parade of rich, professional, middle-aged men and women telling us about every law school project Jake did, his community involvement, his impressive tax skills. Perhaps a Sunday school teacher or AA sponsor thrown in. Instead, we were all treated to John Caymen and Sheila Gaelin. They kept everyone awake, but I hold them responsible for turning the trial into a soap opera.

John Caymen's testimony laid the basis for portrayal of Natasha's evil side, apparently. He solemnly told us how aggressive, condescending, and patronizing Natasha was. I guess no one has ever told him that the latter 2 words mean the same thing, but I give him credit for not using "patriarchal" as a synonym for patronizing—as Sheila did. I was offended by his constant insinuation that Tasha deserved the abuse and appalled at his contradictions. He started out denying the violence, but during the cross, he finally admitted that he "guessed" it did happen. He tried to recover by saying, "But Natalie lied about so many things that I wouldn't be surprised if some of the stuff wasn't that bad." Wasn't that bad. Those words made my angry and sick.

By the time Caymen carefully remembered (with his infamous thinking expression, which John Whitten does a perfect impression of) the story of how Natasha "snapped" at him when he visited the condo one night, I had realized that his entire testimony was going to be a joke. We had already heard, from him, how Jake changed from a confident, happy young man to a nervous, depressed, self-hating person—all because of Natasha. Then we were fortunate enough to hear a specific example of the trauma she put him through. The visit Caymen referred to, took place at 3 in the morning, when he showed up at the condo drunk, walked into the bedroom, and began yelling at Jake and Natasha. Natasha's sister Kristin was also staying there that night, and she testified that Natasha had been embarrassed, but had merely asked John to lower his voice. When he continued to shout, she asked him to talk with Jake on the deck. She said that he was very rude and very drunk.

I had a hard time taking John Caymen seriously. He was so obnoxious and self-absorbed. He looked directly into the closest camera, as often as possible. When I was cross-examining him, I finally had to ask him to turn towards me, so I could hear his answers. Also, I just couldn't get this guy to fit with my definition of a close, loyal friend. He didn't seem to care at all about what Jake was going through. He claimed to, but his attitude didn't match up.

Caymen's testimony is an example of the defense's strange tactics. As I listened to him, I kept thinking, "What the Hell are they thinking?" Putting my mom on the stand to talk about knitting skills would have made more sense to me.

Sam Hadwick tried to justify the choice in his closing, but to me, he sent the effects of the testimony from bad to worse than worse. I was offended, as I listened to the following:

> John Caymen's words probably offended a lot of people. This man didn't see Natalie Hillshaw as the squeaky-clean person we've all heard about and nobody wanted to hear a negative word about her. I trust that you will understand that we are not trying to portray Natalie as a bad person. We are not making a judgment on what she should have done or shouldn't have done in the relationship, because that's not our job. Our job is to tell the truth and that means showing you the whole picture, not just the parts that make you the most comfortable.

This was classic strategy of telling the jury you didn't really mean exactly what you told them. It was ridiculous. We are not saying she's a bad person, but she's not squeaky clean. It was in the same tone as

John Caymen's attitude and I lost a little bit of respect for Sam for that.

I actually think that John Caymen's testimony was a set-up, to make Grazen look like a noble, repentant batterer. When Jake got on the stand, he disagreed with his buddy's comments about Natasha being partly to blame for the abuse. Jake had such a strong sense of responsibility, that he was willing to contradict his close friend's words. (And the defense just happened to point this out in their closing.) In a way, Caymen served as a hostile witness.

Hadwick can be long-winded when he doesn't have much to work with. He also offered several contradictions, even though they were subtle and probably intentional. His closing asked the jury to view the character witnesses as canceling each other out, yet he also warned them about giving too much weight to certain testimony (namely that of every prosecution witness), claiming that Natasha's friends were holding a grudge against Jake, while Caymen was bravely giving an unpopular opinion. Again, we're back to the nonsensical.

Perhaps the most puzzling of all defense tactics was, of course, Sheila Gaelin. They never even tried explaining their purpose for using her. My guess is, when they got to the point of preparing their close, they were so overwhelmed by the sheer embarrassment of Sheila's testimony (let alone her overall presence and appearance), that they just prayed the jurors would forget all about her if they didn't touch the subject. That's probably the mind-set

I'd be in if it were me dealing with that nightmare of a witness.

Sheila was Jake's last girlfriend before he became involved with Natasha. I don't know if she was always flamboyant and annoying, or if she just created that identity for the occasion of the trial. (Media attention can bring out weird things in people.) I also don't know if she is actually an extremely stupid woman or if that was all an act.

I seriously thought this woman was a prostitute the first time I saw her. John Whitten and I were taking a break at a deli downtown one evening, after a particularly rigorous day. I believe it was the day of our second or third crime scene tour. It was surprisingly quiet while we were munching on our club sandwiches, but when our coffee and hot chocolate arrived, we saw a big crowd moving down the sidewalk. Reporters had found Sheila Gaelin and she was delighted to be found. She was sitting with two men on a bench—alternating between their laps, laughing in a shrill voice that was unbearable, and occasionally tugging at her miniscule skirt. She turned her attention to the cameras as soon as she saw them, saying she'd be glad to answer questions just as soon as someone ordered her a cappuccino. (In an attempt to make John laugh, I pushed my chair back quickly and pretended to volunteer for that task.)

That day, she had long, straight hair that was bleached to a whitish blonde, with wide streaks of gold and a good inch and a half of dark roots. In court, it was orange and blonde ringlets, with enough hairspray to create a sticky sculpture. The outfit choice for her first day on the stand left a lot of dropped jaws, as she sauntered into the courtroom. She wore a brown wool skirt that was very short, paired with black lace nylons that have a thick seam on the back of the legs and a bright orange ribbed sweater that was way too small. (No bra and she needs one.) Footwear was open-toed brown patent leather shoes with 4-inch heels. She topped off the ensemble with a leopard print fuzzy headband and a gold chain necklace, with a huge cross on it. I literally thanked God that I didn't have to question her first. It was bad enough when it got to my turn, but at least I had time for the shock to set in and to attempt to compose myself.

I'm all for creative wardrobes, don't get me wrong, but dressing like Madonna on a job interview has a time and a place. A murder trial is neither. She was inappropriate, offensive, and treated the occasion like it was a biker bar mixer.

In several post-trial interviews, Jake waffled on the question of the exact nature of his relationship with Sheila. He initially denied that she was ever his girlfriend, but her testimony made it clear that they'd been sexually involved. When a reporter pointed this out to him, he tried the "well, mostly we were just good friends" bit. Yeah.

As I listened to Sheila's testimony, at first, I was just really embarrassed for the defense. Then I became increasingly disgusted by her attitude and angry with the defense for enabling it. She acted like a 15-year-old nymphomaniac, as she detailed sexual aspects of the relationship, which were not asked of her. She tried joking with her lawyers and the judge, flirting with the male attorneys at times, and was constantly scanning the courtroom. When she began to snap her gum and hike up her skirt, I stood up and asked for a side bar. When we reached the bench, I took a long deep breath. "Your honor, I do not want to criticize the defense, but I have to express my extreme discomfort with this witness' behavior. In order to show the proper respect for these proceedings, I think the witness needs to refrain from making irrelevant and inappropriate remarks and attempt to concentrate on the questions presented to her."

John agreed with me and everyone else was silent. The judge said she would instruct Sheila to answer only the questions asked of her and she asked defense counsel to speak to their witness about proper courtroom conduct, in a private setting. Sheila toned down a bit, but her testimony was consistently strange. She transformed from this obnoxious, seductive personality, to a spacey, reflective one. I could see that she was trying to give each answer her fullest concentration, but she just didn't make much sense. Her answers were very drawn out and strayed off the subject to the point where she forgot the original question, and sometimes the rest of us did too. The given lawyer questioning her would quickly pick up the habit of cutting her off.

Sheila Gaelin's habit of making up words has become famous in this trial. While it was amusing, it made it very difficult to decipher her answers. When Adam Riles, for the defense, asked her how Natalie had treated her, Sheila decided to combine the word ostentatious with auspicious, and give it her own meaning of suspicious. Natalie was upset that Jake and Sheila had remained friends after breaking up, so she acted "really auspentatious" whenever Jake and Sheila spent time together. The judge and everyone at the prosecution table immediately turned to watch Adam's expression. No one had a clue of what she was talking about and we were dying to see how he handled it. He pretended that he didn't hear her and repeated the question, apparently praying that she would use a different word in her answer. No such luck. She just said it slower and louder. He had to ask her what she meant and she looked at him like he was a complete idiot. John had to kick me under the table, because I had my head down on the table and tears were pouring down my face.

Sheila didn't seem to have a strong impression of Jake. She said that she knew him for six months and they stopped dating about a month before he began seeing Natalie, but they remained "very close." She said Jake was very nice, he really cared about people, and he loved Natalie. Natalie, on the other hand, was a little snobby. (I was impressed that Sheila remembered that Jake called Natasha "Natalie.")

When John did his cross-exam, he was a little less patient with Sheila than Adam had been, but it was very subtle. He moved her along at a bearable pace. "Please describe exactly what your relationship with

Jake Grazen was like. *Not* how you felt about him, but how you spent time together and how often." From this, we learned that they were never exclusive, were not serious about each other at all, and got together once a week or less. When John asked about Natasha, Sheila admitted that she had only seen her at parties and bars, and that she had never even been introduced to Natasha. "How then, do you feel that you can even speak about what she was like?" he asked her. Sheila leaned forward, narrowed her eyes, and softly said, "It was strong vibes." (Earlier, Sheila had carefully described to Adam how vibes provide her with a large amount of "crypticious" information. Adam didn't even bother to deal with that one.)

Sheila Gaelin was a good witness in the sense that she was brutally honest. (Even though I happen to think her impressions of Jake and Natasha are bullshit, she truly believed them.) There was no danger of a single juror thinking that she staged her testimony. She wasn't bringing any sort of agenda to the table because she was not capable of producing a clear point about either Jake or Natasha. She didn't become defensive during cross-examination because she didn't care enough about the subject matter to extend any emotional energy.

Adam Riles spoke about a jury's "true role" in a trial, during his half of the closing. He told the jury not to think of how anyone would judge their decision, warning them that we would talk about sending a message with their verdict. "If you try to draft some kind of moral agenda for our society, by the decision you make about this man's future, you will only be doing society a grave, grave injustice," he said sullenly. (I hate use of the word "grave," during a murder trial, so I just rolled my eyes at John as we listened to that.) He then went into an emotional speech about how Jake's fate was in their hands.

John stood up and loudly started the rebuttal from our table. "Mr. Riles is asking you to replace a murderer's conscience with your own!" He then stated that the evidence was all they could think about, moving away from the idea that the jurors had to choose between solving all the world's problem's and saving a good-looking man's life.

We need to look at what has gone on for the past 6 months as more than a news event. The trial is all people have talked about and they hungered for the verdict. A conviction is not like a best in show award. I don't feel like I've won a thing, despite being on the "winning side." Someone is dead. Not because of an accident or a fatal illness, but because the man she loved took her life from her, in an extremely brutal way. Regardless of what happens in the sentencing portion of this case, that loss will remain. Whether or not Jacob Grazen should die, is up for discussion. The matter will be carefully pondered before the decision is made. The woman he murdered did not have that luxury, because he took it upon himself to be her executioner.

<u>Samuel Hadwick</u>

*Samuel Hadwick was the lead defense attorney
for Jacob Grazen's murder trial. He has been
practicing with his Phoenix firm for the past
12 years. Prior to that, he was a criminal
defense attorney in Baltimore.*

February 3,1998

Natasha Hillshaw was a beautiful, intelligent, and
kind person. We all know this if we've heard even the
slightest bit of information about her. We've heard the
descriptions about her many endearing qualities and
they're all true. A lot of people loved her and are
reeling from her early death. It's not fair that she was
involved in a violent relationship which led to her
desperate depression, neither is it fair that she died so
young. No one should endure such trauma in their life,
no matter how old they are. However, there's
something else that's every bit unfair and that's what
has happened to Jacob Grazen.

He was chosen as the tool of vengeance, out of a
desperate attempt to balance out a terrible loss. My
client is going to be a sacrifice so that our society can
feel a sense of moral accomplishment. Neighborhood
watch is for pussies, this is the big time. It's a bit more
sophisticated than hanging him in the town square, but
the purpose is exactly the same. We can say that we're
battling domestic violence. We're standing up for
every victim, we're not going to take it anymore. But

it's so wrong and everyone knows it. People can claim that they've seen justice and they're satisfied, but there's a twinge of uneasiness that everyone feels. That twinge is the truth.

The whole story behind this trial is a complicated one and we need to look at all of it. Jake and Natasha did not have a storybook marriage by any stretch of the imagination. And it wasn't just a case of the little disputes here and there that every relationship has at some point. There was violence. This is an ugly, uncomfortable truth, but one that Jake and everyone trying to support him has to face. There was violence and Jake caused it, carried it out, and inflicted it onto the love of his life. However, everyone who holds him accountable-- supporters and despisers, needs to limit the blame also. He is responsible for the damage he did, not for every batterer in the world and all the pain that every battered woman has endured. And certainly not for killing Natasha. It's not fair that we expect someone to change and get help, but then we never give them credit when they do that. We want to hold them to an infinitive amount of blame because that feels better.

Of *course* the ex-husband with a history of violence against his ex-wife is going to be a suspect when she dies. That's logical, that makes sense. There are many, many cases where an abusive man ends his lover's life after she leaves him. But each case has to be tried based on its own evidence. It's sad that I have to even say that, but I do. The evidence that was presented in this trial showed us that Jacob Grazen did not commit this crime. Natasha's gunshot wounds were self-inflicted, she took lethal doses of anti-depressants and mixed them with alcohol, and Jake's blood and prints were on the gun because he tried to get it away from her. These are the facts.

I became very close to my client during his trial. That doesn't always happen. Sometimes there's a superficial bond because the client is terrified and they lean on me as their last chance for freedom. Other clients create as much distance as they can in every relationship they have, because that feels like something they can control. My end of the relationship varies as well. It always starts out as a fairly clinical, non-personal relationship. It has to be that way if I'm going to give them everything I've got. I want to win their case for them, so I can't spend my time worrying about their personal issues. Sometimes I find myself connecting in a personal way and sometimes we never reach that point.

I never really figured out why I developed a connection with Jake. We just clicked. We respected each other. He trusted my advice and I accepted his ideas about certain strategies. I didn't feel the usual pressure of having my client doubt my decisions or trying to get their cooperation on certain things. Jake is extremely intelligent, he's polite, he's likable, and he's very honest. He didn't get into head games with us, constantly ask if we believed him, or hold back certain information from us. He said, "I'll tell you anything you want to know" and he did that. It was a refreshing change.

I didn't try to analyze Jake's feelings when we talked and I'm not going to do that now. I'm not a therapist. Like I stated before, I have to keep my focus on the trial, not my client's emotional roller coaster. However, I am a human being and I can't completely ignore all the emotional situations I see in my job. I don't think I necessarily helped Jake with any of his grief, but I listened to him and I will never forget what I heard. He witnessed a suicide. He was standing right next to the woman he loved when she blew her head off. I will never be able to understand how he is able to put his life together and deal with that. This is part of the reason why I get so angry about all the cruel things people say about this man. I think of what he's been through and I cannot understand all the ignorant attitudes people have about him.

I also listened to Jake talk about his relationship, not in a friend to friend manner, but as his lawyer who needed to prepare a case. Everything he told me, he also told a courtroom of people when he took the stand. I had to take in the information he gave me in the same way the jury was asked to take it in. I didn't judge his actions or Natalie's actions and I didn't sympathize with either of them. All I could do was hope that the jury followed their legal obligation by not judging or sympathizing either.

I learned a lot from him. Most of it was unpleasant, but it was important. I learned what a batterer thinks and feels. I learned how people can live in a sheltered world of abuse while appearing happy to everyone around them. This couple was the envy of all of their friends, yet they were desperately unhappy. At first the story of their relationship sounds like a sweet romance, but the reality is that it was a disaster. Jake became obsessed with Natalie, they both became depressed, and drugs and alcohol became the mainstay of the relationship.

There's a fine line between understanding why someone does something wrong and accepting that reason as a justification for the act. I deal with this issue all the time. I believe in forgiveness, but it has to follow responsibility. When a client who pleads guilty tells me how badly they feel, I put a limit on their speech because I want them to focus on rehabilitation. I didn't have this problem with Jake. First of all, he wasn't guilty of the crime he was charged with, so didn't need to be forgiven. As for the abuse, he had already been through the denial phase. He didn't want people to make excuses for him because he was ready to get help. He did want us to try to understand his past, but he knew that it was difficult for us to do so.

I think Jake is courageous for telling the world about all the disgusting, humiliating and terrible things he has done. He made that choice on his own. He could have sat back and let us run the case without divulging anything. One day near the end of the trial, I asked Jake about his forthright approach. "Not everyone is willing to bring out every cobweb from their life and show it to the world," I told him. He explained that he had to come clean about everything. "Maybe someone else will learn from some of what I went through, but even if that's not the case, I owe it to her" was what he said to me. Natalie was always on Jake's mind. Even though he didn't kill her, he had a lot of guilt for the ways he had hurt her. As he stated during the trial, he feels that he directly caused her depression, so in some ways he feels responsible for her suicide.

People like to talk about Jake's ego and love of publicity. This idea that he loves the attention from the media is ludicrous. He was tried and convicted of murder and being on TV didn't glamorize that or make it fun for him. He hated the fact that his every expression was taped and commented on. He resented being the center of attention for something he didn't do. He also felt that Natalie's death was trivialized by the obsessive interest in the trial.

He chose to give interviews after the trial ended because he wants to take any chance he can at getting the truth out. It's certainly not about bolstering his image. That doesn't make any sense. He's on death row, who would he be trying to impress?

Jake felt controlled by the media and I think that's a pretty accurate way of looking at what has happened to him. When someone gets famous for writing a book or inventing something, they're treated favorably by reporters who want a story about their accomplishment. They can say what they want and it's unlikely that they'll be misquoted or that there will be a lot of speculation about their background. When someone comes into the media's focus for negative reasons, however, that person does not have the basic respect of being believed. Jake hasn't been allowed to grieve for losing the most important person in his life because everyone thinks he is a murderer. If he cries, people say he's acting. If he smiles at something a lawyer whispers to him, that's taken as a sign that he doesn't care about Natalie's death. The world has created a script for Jake and everything he does is automatically edited to fit it.

Our strategy for this trial has been heavily criticized. That happens when you lose a case, so I'm not surprised. I think a lot of our arguments were misunderstood, so I'll briefly explain what we were trying to do. The criminal law procedures which guide a trial like this do not require the defense to prove the defendant's innocence. The state has the burden of proving the defendant's guilt. Therefore, our job is to lead the jury to reasonable doubt in the state's case. We did not have to prove that Natalie took her own life, but that is the clearest way to understand why the prosecution's theory of what happened is impossible to believe. We explained Natalie's history of depression and presented the evidence of her suicide.

We were not trying to use an insanity defense, as some of the trial watchers have speculated. Jake didn't do it, so we didn't have to come up with a justification. We did explain his past, showing his history of depression and instability, because those things are a part of his abusive past. We would have preferred to leave the whole issue of his violence out of the trial because it was not relevant to the crime he was charged with, but it became apparent that we couldn't do that. The prosecution raked through every detail of the relationship so we wanted to make sure the jury got the accurate picture of why the violence occurred.

At this point, I'm probably expected to say that the jury was against my client from the beginning or some equally paranoid statement, but my feelings about it aren't so simple. I have to respect their decision because I believe in the judicial system and the jury system is an integral part of it. I have no idea what goes on in their deliberation sessions, so it wouldn't be fair for me to say how they reached their decision. I don't always assume that a jury followed the law when they acquit and call them tainted when they return with a conviction. But the reality is that they don't always stick to their legal obligations and they aren't always able to look at the case before them in the clinical manner which they need to. I don't believe it's intentional or that they're necessarily conscious of it. Their emotions creep in on some level. I think that might have happened in this case. When they were sitting in that courtroom and when they were lying in their beds at night, they kept seeing those crime scene photographs. They kept hearing Jacob Grazen admit that he abused Natalie. They couldn't forget that a young woman died or that she was in an abusive relationship. Unfortunately, they mixed those 2 facts together.

I don't hold any animosity for the prosecution. They did what they had to do and they did it very well. They know how difficult this case was and still is for me and they have been very supportive. There were some tense times in the trial, but that was due to the stress we were all under and it was about professional differences, not personal conflicts. Most of the squabbling scenes that have been talked about in the press are fictitious.

My only hope now is that people can carefully examine every single aspect of what went on in the trial and realize that a terrible injustice has occurred. Jake Grazen is constantly re-living the details of this mistake that will cost him his life. The rest of us, who do not await the fate of having a toxic gas drilled though our body until we stop breathing, could manage to spend some time thinking about this fatal mistake as well.

Most defense attorneys are used to being strongly disliked and I'm not an exception. People don't respect or understand our job and it seems to be a common sentiment that we are immoral. I wouldn't have lasted in this work for 20 years if I was bothered by that kind of stuff. I know why I do what I do, I know how to do it well, and I care about doing it well. I learned a long time ago that trying to explain my position to people who think I'm completely unethical is absolutely pointless. They will never get it. So, the nasty comments do not bother me. What does is failure. It's not about adding a loss to my record, but about failing a client. Jacob Grazen is going to die for something he didn't do and I was unable to prevent that. If someone thinks that nothing upsets me, I would ask them to ponder that for just a minute.

Thomas Filmore

Thomas Filmore is a homicide detective in Phoenix. He was the lead investigator on the Natasha Hillshaw case and is scheduled to retire in June of 1999.

February 3, 1998

Twenty-two years as a police detective have exposed me to a lot. I've seen tragedies, public controversy, and varied criminal acts. I'm still not immune to the horror I face in my work. I don't think I ever will be.

When I decided to become a police officer, I wanted to find a city that I could work in for the duration of my career. I think it's important, in any job, to know your work environment as thoroughly as you can. In police work, the *community* is your work environment. The only way you can protect it is to know it inside and out. And living here, experiencing the same fears and concerns as the people I work to protect are experiencing, makes my job feel valid. I can truthfully say that I have the same desire to make the streets safe as any other resident, because I intend on staying here.

It wasn't hard for me to know where I belonged, once I came to Phoenix. I had worked in Baltimore for five years and in New York City for four years. I learned some valuable things in both cities and worked with some great departments, but I didn't feel the connection with either of those cities that I do with this one. I felt like I was commuting, even though I lived there. Here I've found the sense of home that I was looking for. This is my city.

The Natasha Hillshaw case is one of many that are hard to read about and even harder to see firsthand. From the very beginning of our investigation, I knew it was going to be a case I couldn't distance myself from. It's not that any murder is easy or comfortable, but some pull you in more than others. Our goal is to eliminate any type of emotional connection to our work, looking at everything as a fact and leaving it at that. Sometimes it is impossible to do that.

At the crime scene, I felt immediately nervous. Not in the sense of doubting my professional abilities or even a pressure to work extra carefully, but I felt close to the actual time of the murder. It was like I was working and experiencing the horror of the murder at the same time. I've worked on many domestic violence cases and surveyed many brutal, disgusting crime scenes like this one. This was different though. It wasn't just feeling overwhelmed by a general sadness that I knew would last for at least the duration of the investigation. I was imagining various memories of Natasha's short life and then feeling those final moments as she must have felt them—the sharp, chilling fear and intense knowledge of imminent danger.

I have a daughter who is a year younger than Natasha was and I think this is the root cause of the anxiety I felt about the murder. I have always been protective of Alicia, but I never had nightmares about her until the day I saw Natasha's body being hauled away on a stretcher. Alicia has been very upset by this case, partially because she knows how it has affected me and why.

When I first interviewed Jake, I felt uncomfortable immediately. As I listened to him talk about his relationship with Natasha, I kept thinking about how he had caused her so much pain. I was angry that anyone could do what he did and I was disturbed that he could be in such a state of denial about it. I listened to his soft, deliberate words and I knew he was a con artist. He successfully conned and charmed his way into many people's lives and he almost succeeded in conning his way out of a murder charge. Fortunately, the jury saw through his scam.

When people talk about police officers slanting an investigation, having malicious intentions, or trying to frame someone, they're really creating a fictitious picture of how police investigations work. A crime occurs, officers are called to the scene, and everyone is assigned a specific duty. There's an extremely rigid, defined protocol for gathering and documenting evidence. Each detective is required to follow official procedures, carrying out the duties efficiently and thoroughly. Every detail of the findings is reported to your immediate supervisor, which will be recorded and passed up the chain to their superiors.

Everything has to happen precisely and consistently or else people would be stumbling all over each other and wasting valuable time. If a detective or officer plants, alters, or hides anything at a crime scene, the change is quickly noticed because we're all there for hours at a time and everything fits together. We all know the contents of a scene backwards and forwards because we have to communicate, analyze, and strategize about every detail. Plus, we're trained to know when something foul is going on. It's our job to do that. So, we know when something is missing or when something has been overlooked. No one can wander into a secured crime scene in the middle of the night to fool around with evidence, because it is guarded like a museum. We cannot allow anything to sabotage an investigation.

The other part of the frame-up theory that doesn't make sense is the intent to single out someone to blame a crime on. The corrupt police system that we hear about is not a well-thought out theory. It seems like an easy source of blame when you don't want to believe that someone accused of a crime is capable of doing it. However, the implications of these theories are too flimsy to be anything more than a fantasy. For one thing, you're assuming that cops have deep grudges against certain people. Maybe we just lust for the power to ruin the lives of people we consider to be evil or maybe we're dealing with some past insecurity. Either we keep a list of "low-lifes" or pick out the higher socio-economic status figures we're jealous of, wait for a crime to happen, and then move in for the evidence-planting portion of our plot. It would be comical, if it weren't so offensive.

There are corrupt cops. There are racist cops and mentally twisted cops, just as there are racist grocery store clerks and mentally twisted doctors. They shouldn't have the jobs that they slipped into and they should lose their jobs as soon as their true motives are discovered. Criminal and immoral behaviors should be taken seriously and punishments should occur as appropriate. However, the cops, grocers, and doctors who are *not* corrupt, should not be painted with the same brush as the bad eggs. We shouldn't have to suffer the cruel, unfair judgments about the careers we have dedicated our lives to. Having people scream obscenities at you and being accused of vile, irresponsible, and manipulative behavior involves more pain than you can ever prepare yourself for or recover from.

My decision to become a cop was a life-changing moment and I will never regret it. It wasn't a result of a career choice test, it wasn't something I did to prove that I could do it, and it wasn't about carrying out some masculine idea of a tough job. I wanted to contribute to the task of making our city safer and breaking down the general patterns of crime in our country. I don't care how corny that sounds. It's the truth. It's something I've always believed in and I've never wanted to do anything else.

I don't love my job because I get a feeling of power and control over people or events. I don't get such a feeling, for one thing. Working a crime scene usually takes me to the opposite end of the spectrum because it's direct proof that brutal crimes are flourishing and people are capable of doing terrible things to each other. There's always a moment of emptiness and a feeling of helplessness when I think about this. I love my job because it shows me that there's a strong effort to stop this frightening, cruel behavior. And I can be a direct part of that effort.

It isn't that I want to be hero. That's not what the job is about. I think some people get that idea when they watch a lot of police dramas on TV, but they miss the point that we work for people in pain. When you solve a crime, you're doing as much as you can to bring families closure from their tragedies, but you can't ever take away their agony.

There's a high price for the satisfaction I get in my job. My work always overlaps with my personal life, which is very difficult for the people in my life. It can't be a matter of ranking the things in my life because every aspect of my life defines me and what I believe in. I have never thought I was obsessed with my job, but I have pushed a lot of people away who have felt that way. I don't think it would be right to give up my career for the sake of eliminating the pressure. Also, that wouldn't achieve the result of healthier relationships or a calmer state of mind for me. I wouldn't be the same person if I wasn't a cop. I would betray my values and sense of duty, by giving up what I believe is my calling.

Despite all the raw examples of criminal behavior that I see constantly in my job, I maintain a basic sense of trust in people. I think that most people know right from wrong and earnestly try to uphold their ethical values. I think that this perspective has shaped my love for the work I do and has strengthened my commitment. I don't think that cops with a generally negative feeling about people can be successful, because they're always at a low point, looking up. I don't mean that we should think of criminals in an endearing way, but we should just focus on protecting the community and solving crimes, instead of having the attitude that the world is filled with scum and that we have to go on a rampage to blast them.

This case has brought out some harsh feelings from a city that I have always respected and felt very close to. That's been difficult for me. Ever since moving here, I've believed that the caring, respectful, protective feelings which I have for this community were reciprocated 100%. So, hearing residents of Phoenix say the police department was out to gain notoriety in this case feels like a brutal betrayal.

Initially, I was oblivious to the popularity of Jake and Natasha. Phoenix is a large city and I do not run with the elite crowd. The names sounded familiar to me, but it wasn't until I learned details of their relationship and Jake's reputation that I realized how big a deal the case was going to be. What's ironic about the rumor that I got involved because of the publicity opportunities (and I won't point out the obvious fact that it was my *job* to be involved, since we have assignments—we don't just pick the cases we think would be the most fun and inform our bosses of our decisions...), is that I resented the popularity angle that everyone kept bringing up. Someone was murdered. That's the tragedy. Not how beautiful she was, how famous her husband was, how well-liked they both were, or how much money they made.

People who haven't been touched by a tragedy like this probably wonder what the big deal is. Emotions come out of nowhere and a community has to learn how to deal with them together. I don't think that we can prepare anyone else for a tragedy they may one day face, but we can hopefully bring some sort of order back to our lives by sorting out everything we've been through. I think that sharing with other people can help with this, which is why I literally forced myself to break my silence, after trying to enclose myself in a shell from the rest of the world. And I feel I've learned more about myself as I've explained my views to other people.

I think that everyone involved in this trial would like to downplay the animosities that have cropped up at various times. There's a lot of bitterness about the media, but we don't want to deal with that directly because it seems like we're just whining and trying to shove the blame for negative appearances onto someone else. I agree with a lot of the points that the other people who wrote for this book have made. I don't think we could have prepared ourselves for the enormity of the coverage. We had no way of knowing exactly what it would mean or how it would impact us.

I think that media-bashing has become an acceptable, sometimes even cool thing to do. Some people have gotten into it to the point of not taking responsibility for their own thoughts and actions. Hopefully we can all remove ourselves from the confusion and examine the choices we made. I think that some criticism of the media is well-founded. Some reporters engage in a pattern of writing fabricated stories that only hurt their subjects. But I also think we need to be realistic in our opinions about the media as a whole, realizing that it's made up of individuals who act independently of each other. They can't be responsible for everyone else's behavior within their field.

I believe that news coverage is very important. I know some fantastic reporters and photographers who consistently show accuracy, respect, and dedication in their work. And then there's the opposite end of the integrity spectrum, but for me, these factors become irrelevant in situations like this tragedy. The media is going to be around every corner—the good, bad, and ugly are suddenly staring you down. It's a given that they're not going anywhere while a story is at your door, so your personal feelings about the coverage are irrelevant. The only important issue at that point is what you decide to do about it. You can open your mouth at every request for an interview, trying to paint a certain picture of yourself and hoping you won't say anything stupid or embarrassing, or you can utter the simple words "no comment" and keep walking. I am not denigrating the people who publicly answer questions and give statements, nor am I implying that it's easy to duck the media. I'm just saying that there are choices. You have control, even though the attention can overwhelm you into thinking you're at its mercy.

I've had so many experiences with the media, positive and negative, that I don't have one solid impression of being in the public eye. There have been times when I felt like the media coverage of a case provided education to the community and times when I felt nothing other than the notion that the reporters and cameras are a pain in my ass. Sometimes it just has to do with the circumstances and my own frame of mind. The stress of a case can definitely affect my reaction to media coverage.

I believe that we should give the media a break, toning down our disdain for them that's become so common, but I also feel that there are times when they should ease up as much as their job will allow. It's a relationship that I've worked on over the years— understanding their viewpoint, trying to get them to understand mine, and bracing for certain inevitable results during a high-profile case. I know that there's bound to be a lies-filled quote with my name attached to it every once in a while, and if I can let it roll off my back, it saves the anger portion of my brain some work. I also know that I will occasionally blurt something out, due to exhaustion or misjudgment, and that I will pay for it.

A lot of it has to do with your own perception of stories, however, so you really can learn to coexist with the media, even during the roughest of times. It would not be reasonable for me to expect that I will ever truly not care what is printed about me, so I don't even try for that. I'm human and I have insecurities. I care about how I'm perceived. I also know that the words on a page can mean absolutely nothing if you read them the right way. (And of course, there's always the option of not reading the articles that bash you and I try to choose that one as much as possible. My newspaper-purchasing friends are my own personal filter for hurtful information.) Everyone's interpretation of a quote is going to be different, so even when you spend days preparing a strong message for a news conference, you may not convince your target audience to see things your way or even understand what you're talking about.

The correct verdict was reached in this case and I have faith that everyone will eventually realize that and accept it. The evidence we collected pointed to the truth and that's the only reason for my support of the verdict. It wasn't about sending a moral message about domestic violence. Regardless of what the verdict was, we still have the problem of domestic violence and we need to work on it together, to prevent more murders like this one.

Regan Maltz

Regan Maltz was the forewoman on the Jacob Grazen criminal trial jury. She is a retired art teacher and avid gardener. She lives with family in Globe, Arizona.

February 7, 1998

A single dove is perched atop the highest, most delicate branch of a tree. The slightest breeze provides a tint of pleasure on the warm spring day, as many creatures in the field below scurry amongst one another, looking for their daily necessities: food, shelter, and companionship. The dove doesn't worry himself with such petty concerns, such mindless details, for perfection is defined on this branch. Nothing else matters.

Suddenly, a gust of wind brings chaos to this exotic existence and the dove has no choice but to reconsider the definition of perfection.

Such is the Grazen trial. (I say "is," not "was," on purpose because Natasha's spirit and her family's love for her are eternal.) Phoenix is the dove and the trial is one of the wind's currents. (The wind is really all of the problems in our world, like violence, drugs, and hatred. This trial was just one of many ways the wind blows its harsh power onto us.) And for the jurors, the dove is our life before the case and the wind is jury duty. We the jury did not ask for the wind and neither did Phoenix. But does that mean we would have been able to preserve our lives as doves without it? The wind was always there, it just didn't touch our branch before now. We must find a way to let it onto our branches, to embrace it as a friend instead of fear it as a foe, and drink in its power, or we will fall off and never be able to find a new branch.

I moved from Scottsbluff, Nebraska to Globe, Arizona about fifteen years ago. I had lived in that comfy Nebraska community all my life and I wasn't sure how I'd survive living anywhere else. That community was my branch and it was sturdy. But I was able to find another sturdy branch in Globe. I learned that you can find a good place when you have a family and a life you love and when you trust in them enough to take some risks. I am seventy-two years young and every day my life is just beginning. I'm a widowed mother of three and grandmother of five. I live here with my middle daughter Mira, who is 44 and teaches art classes at the local community college. I sculpt and paint in my small studio, which my son Koty (short for Dakota) built for me.

I will easily admit that I was happy in my role as an undisturbed dove. I've had a wonderful, simple life and I don't like the idea of anyone or anything interfering with my contentment. I protected my happiness like a glass box, for a long time. I grew up in a conservative, traditional family in a closely-knit community. I don't believe that I was sheltered from the hard truths of crime and other problems. I think I was just lucky to be surrounded by love and safety. I was educated and cultured. I made it my personal goal to be aware of strife and to help people with their problems whenever I could. That's what I was asked to do in the Grazen case and I think I did just that. I don't mean to toot my own horn or anything. I just saw a chance to reach out. I willingly gave up my branch of peace to help someone whose branch had broken. Frankly, I think I have the right to feel good about that.

I know people have strong ideas about me, even though they don't know me. They see things on the news and believe it all. Then they add on their own guesses about what I must be like. That isn't the right way to judge people, but I forgive them for it. I believe that we all make mistakes from time to time and if we try to love each other through it all, we can heal from bad times and grow. That's why I try to simply accept everyone for who they are, even if they hold negative opinions about me. However, I need to love myself too. I have pride in my choices and achievements, so even though I can forgive people who insult me, I don't agree with them. I wish they would take the time to listen to my views like I do with theirs. The only way you can understand someone is to understand their choices.

I was the first juror to come forward to the press after the trial and to sign book and screenplay contracts, but that doesn't mean what everyone thinks it means. It doesn't mean I want money. It also doesn't mean I'm the only one with a story to tell or the only one who wants to speak out. We all have been carrying a heavy basket of secrets and truths around with us for months, while people guessed wrongly about what was in the basket. Now we have the chance to take off the cover.

People can call us selfish. They can say we're looking to get money or attention. But they haven't been where we have been. We worked hard to make a decision that no one else could make and no one else *wanted* to make. Then we were the center of all kinds of arguments and emotional scenes. The little bit of salvation that we have though, is that we know the truth. We know what we did is right and we know what kind of people we really are. Nobody can take that from us. I hope that the other jurors can get a lot of support for these tough times from their families and friends. I also hope they can believe in themselves because that's where the most powerful strength will come from.

I didn't decide to write a book and collaborate on a screenplay to make money. Everyone knows how difficult it is to become rich in the arts, so it wouldn't make sense for me to think I could do it. I don't crave a glamorous life and if I did, I wouldn't go about getting it this way. It wouldn't be right to profit from a tragic situation. I'm going public because it's my moral obligation.

I need to educate people about this case for two reasons. For one, people need to know so they can respect the victim and her family. They can't do that by believing lies. Secondly, I need to do it for my own peace of mind. It is part of my healing process. If I don't speak out, I will be saying that it's okay for people to spread rumors and lies. I have an important experience that I can share with people and I can teach them about domestic violence, so that's what I *have* to do. My book will not try to win anyone over or make the jurors out to be heroes. It will just be an honest, simple explanation of what we went through. It will also give the background on my life and the lives of the other jurors, so that people can see that we're all simple, honest, good-hearted people who searched for the truth until we found it. We didn't have a political agenda or some big scheme to ruin the defendant's life. We did our jobs.

It really hurts me when I hear people say that the verdict was unfair. We were asked to decide whether or not the prosecution proved Mr. Grazen's guilt beyond a reasonable doubt. We listened to everything the lawyers and witnesses said, thought about all the testimony and evidence carefully, and talked about it in great detail. There was a lot of evidence and the prosecution proved it was valid. The time line, blood, DNA, forensics reports, and testimonies pointed right at the verdict we gave. It wasn't about choosing sides and I think most of the people who criticize us actually know that in their hearts. They just don't want to believe that a hero in the community could have killed someone and they're blaming us as a way to deny the facts.

Aside from the physical strain of our work, was the emotional burden it put on each of us. Even though we were able to stay objective and professional, we would get upset at times. We're human, so there's no way to prevent that. Seeing pictures of Natasha's body after she was killed and seeing her family cry and hug each other in court made me feel empty inside. It was helplessness. I couldn't do anything to bring this woman back to these people who loved her. I wanted to erase all the pain. Near the end of the trial, I thought I couldn't handle any more of the stress. I knew it was important though and I got through it.

I didn't ask for any of this to happen. In fact, I'm very sad that it did. But since it did happen and we can't change that, we have to learn from it. I try to take every bad thing that happens in my life and turn it around until I can see the sunny side. And that's what I did with this tragedy-- I have taken a bad situation and squeezed as much good out of it as I could. If there's one thing people can remember about me, I'd like it to be that.

Sharon Kittridge

Sharon Kittridge is an insurance agent in Los Angeles. She is a close friend to Jacob Grazen.

February 27, 1998

They announced Jake's sentence two days ago. I haven't slept and I can't concentrate very well. However, I can't procrastinate on this any longer.

I met Jake when he was 7 years old and I was 9. We grew up in West L.A. together and became inseparable friends. We continued to keep in touch over the years. However, our history and close friendship doesn't mean I'm going to sit here and puff up Jake as being perfect. I'm not going to defend his violent past. But I do want to explain Jake's side of the story as best I can.

I'm not a psychologist and I don't understand how someone's childhood affects their adult life. I'm also not very sympathetic towards people who hurt others, regardless of what happened to them in the past. Therefore, I had a real hard time supporting Jake and understanding where he was coming from. But I knew that the shit he went through as a kid messed him up. There were probably signs that he was headed for trouble and I wish I would have caught them.

Jake wasn't comfortable discussing his past with anyone. He does now because his therapists taught him how to deal with his emotions and he's more open. But he used to avoid talking about the accident and his uncle at all costs. I knew the basics because my parents knew friends of his parents, but Jake didn't tell me much beyond that. He put on a happy-go-lucky face in high school. He just wanted to stay away from the painful memories and go on with his life.

I noticed that when he went to college he became a lot moodier. Maybe his emotions were trying to get out and he had to work harder at stuffing them down. He started drinking heavily and he got into a lot of bar fights. I told him I was worried and he said to stop nagging him.

He had a lot of highs and lows for a while. He'd call me in the middle of the night and tell me how he was in love and he was going to be a rich lawyer, then he'd write me a long, depressed letter about how he didn't deserve Natalie and he wasn't able to measure up in law school. Then the highs pretty much went away. He was always down and he began to show a lot of anger. He'd go on and on about how everyone was against him and the world was so corrupt. He sounded paranoid.

The drinking just made everything worse. It was his favorite excuse for abusing Natalie and for not getting help. I would listen to him, either when he was drunk or when he was giving one of his little alcohol advocacy speeches, and think that he sounded so stupid. I was embarrassed for him and worried, as he gave me lines like "Alcohol is your friend and your enemy at the same time when you're in a desperate place in your life." He told me all about how when you're as desolate as he was, you need alcohol to block out the pain, even though you know it's just causing you more pain. I always expected him to whip out a marker and draw me a fucking diagram of the "wheel of destruction" he seemed to know so much about!

And Jake became an expert on justifying his infidelity. He talked about how much he loved Natalie one minute and came up with a million excuses for cheating on her the next. I was so irritated. I didn't care how common infidelity is or many women did something to trigger it for him, nor did I care how terrible he felt for doing it. He didn't feel terrible enough to stop, just like with the violence, which was the bottom line for me. I felt insulted that he was constantly shoveling all these unbelievable theories and excuses at me. I am an intelligent woman and I've been close to him for a long time, so why was he treating me like I was stupid? Why was I having nightmares and stressing out when he wasn't doing anything to change his behavior?

I was the most concerned by the fact that he was physically abusive. The drinking, lying, denial, and cheating showed that his ethical standards were shot to Hell, but the violence meant that he was dangerous and malicious. It wasn't really that I was afraid he'd hurt me, although that thought certainly crossed my mind. It was more that I was disgusted and ashamed. This was *Jake*. Not a guy I knew at the gym or a co-worker I'd had coffee with. This was a best friend.

Natalie didn't deserve any of the violence. I don't care how many stories someone has about Natalie being mean to Jake or how many faults she supposedly had. That's bullshit. I don't care if she was a complete bitch to him. No one had the right to hurt her.

Having said that, I also have to admit that part of me really wanted her to leave him. It seemed like the best solution because she would have control for once and he wouldn't be able to hurt her any more. I wanted Jake to be with the woman he loved, but it got to the point where he didn't deserve her. Loving her wasn't enough.

It was hard for me to know how to be a friend to him. I didn't agree with what he was doing, I didn't understand it on any level, but I wanted to help him. I don't think I did it the right way. Actually, I *know* I didn't do it the right way. I didn't hold his hand (literally or figuratively) and tell him it was going to be okay, I didn't listen to his "side of the story," and I didn't show any desire to try to understand why he was an abuser. I'm not an actress, so I couldn't have done any of those things. I didn't think that Nat must have done something wrong. The "takes two to tango" shit does not jive with me. I was angry and I was rapidly losing respect for him.

When this whole case started, it was like everything was in slow motion. It didn't seem to matter how many times I heard about Jake on the news or how many times I talked to him about it, I could not believe it was all happening. Natalie killed herself, Jake was in jail awaiting his murder trial, and I was walking around with my mouth hanging open. How could *any* of this happen?

As the trial wore on, it all seemed to speed up. There were more signs every day that this was real. I saw Jake in leg irons, I heard testimony about Natalie's gunshot wounds, and I knew the day that Jake's fate would be decided was getting closer and closer. When that day arrived, every previous moment faded away. I tried to prepare myself for the worst beforehand, but when I heard the word "death," my head just got heavier and heavier. That's all I heard.

I'm jealous of the people who were just spectators in all of this. Reporters or people who thought it would be cool to go to a court case that was getting so much attention in the news. It looks so sophisticated on TV. Everyone gets dressed up and walks up the courthouse steps with a cup of coffee. But when you're one of those people whose world is going to be saved or shattered by the words of 12 strangers, it's not too glamorous. I broke out in a cold sweat every single day. I would chain smoke during the breaks and I cried whenever I looked over at Jake.

I have a lot of anger and I'm in a position of much ridicule right now. My opinion is not respected. It's not okay for me to express my anger at this decision or my sorrow for what's going to happen to Jake, but it's acceptable to wrongly condemn Jake for his ex-wife's death. I've heard talk about how Jake has so much support in this and I don't know where that idea comes from. It is not true. The majority of people in this country are ignoring the hard facts because they don't want to offend Natalie's family. It's more comfortable to believe that he's guilty. That makes me crazy.

I'm also upset with the media's stream of lies. Somehow, they came up with this idea that Jake is proud of his abusive history, that he thought violence was okay, and that all his remorse is a lie. I used to work in the media and I understand their position. They have a job to do like anyone else, but there can be an extreme and this case went there right away. Natalie's family couldn't cross their own lawn without being filmed and nobody seemed to step back and acknowledge how out of hand it was because it was justified as a big news story. It's sad because people outside of this experience cannot see it as a real-life tragedy that is not going to go away. Instead, it's a hot topic for gossip.

I don't believe that only certain people are capable of bad things. I think that anyone could kill if they were in certain circumstances. Therefore, I didn't automatically assume that Jake was innocent before I got the chance to talk to him about it. I asked him straight out if he did this. When he said no, that was it. I accepted the answer and I didn't wonder whether or not it was the truth. If the answer had been yes, I would have supported him and stood by him also. I wouldn't have lied for him, but I wouldn't have stopped loving him.

I have dreams about Jake in his cell on death row. He is crying and begging for God to save his life. I also have dreams about Natalie. She is trying to tell everyone the truth. Despite all the crap Jake put her through over the years, she would not want him to take the blame for this.

Being Jake's friend throughout the years has been trying, and I'm glad that I lasted through it as long as I did. I love him and I'm going to miss him. I will try, as I have so many times in the past, to be strong for him, but he is much stronger than I am. I hope that the truth will come out before Jake's sentence is carried out, but I'm going to do everything I can to make sure it comes out eventually, no matter how long that takes.

Ted Langston

Ted Langston is the executive producer of his own radio talk show in Phoenix. He also writes a bi-monthly editorial for the Phoenix Sun.

March 4, 1998

We are now entering the aftermath of the Grazen trial. All the predicting and the anticipating is over. We know what the verdict is and what the sentence is, so we can finally play the cards on the table. Let's get serious about the issues involved in this case. What really happened on September 19th of last year? Are the verdict and the sentence just? What are we going to do about domestic violence?

I'll start with my own opinions on these matters. The verdict and the sentence are both correct. He did it and since the death penalty is in place in our system, it should apply to all murderers. As for domestic violence, I'm not too optimistic about seeing a change for the better.

Suicide? No way. It doesn't make any sense. They were divorced and she was free of the violence, or so she *thought*, at least. Sure, she was depressed when they were together. I believe that. But she was finally able to put her life back together when she divorced him. Why would she choose to end her life when she had finally gotten the peace and freedom back that Jake had taken from her?

For some reason, people want to protect Jake. And I am certainly the wrong person to ask why that is because it's far beyond my comprehension. Because he's a snappy dresser? Honestly, I'm lost. He abused his wife for years, then killed her. But if we wipe out those two facts, we're left with a detailed description of how great he is and how many tragedies he has overcome.

Maybe he instills fear in people. Even people who believe in his guilt, like Laura Morrow and Kristin Hillshaw, have a habit of smothering that belief with a thick rhetoric about how much Natasha loved him. They apparently feel guilty for condemning the guy she loved and slept with. Then we hear all about Jake's love for Natasha. Everyone goes on and on about it. He was obsessed with her, he couldn't live without her (which is a puzzler for me, given his choice to *murder* her), and all of the mean things he did actually stemmed from a deep love. What? If killing someone is a way to express your love for them, I'd rather get a box of chocolates.

I don't for a minute buy the notion that Tasha wouldn't want anyone to say negative things about Jake. Her letters indicate this, as does common sense. The woman wasn't as much of a sap as her friends make her sound—she wouldn't endorse murderers and want the country to embrace domestic violence as the definition of strong relationships. Please. Let's wake up.

Natasha chose the most unacceptable option, in Jake's eyes, of dealing with his abuse. She left him.

To Jake's ego, what a blow that must have been! What nerve she had, after all he did for her. I can't keep with this train of thought though because I don't get it. I really don't. What the Hell did he do for her? What was the sacrifice?

"Domestic violence." Those two words are always said in a low, serious tone. A black cloud forms and people start squirming. Annia Valdez calls it a mysterious phenomenon that scares people, but I disagree. There are violent sickos out there who beat up their wives. What's mysterious about that? And being scared by the concept is ridiculous. You're afraid of it when it happens to you and other than that you feel sorry for people actually going through it. I don't think it's any more or less confusing or frightening than child abuse, elder abuse or any other type of violence. We're not eager to talk about any of these problems because they're unpleasant to think about and we don't know how to fix them, not because we're confused and scared.

Why do women stay? Common therapists' answer: Battered Women's Syndrome. Common losers' answer: Because she's stupid. My answer: I don't know. It seems logical that women get such a low self-esteem from the way they're treated in an abusive relationship, that they become helpless, but would that dynamic have time to develop if she left the very first time it happened? I certainly don't believe that a batterer is obligated to continue hurting his victim as long as she's with him or that staying is a signal that it's okay—like a secret handshake, but what's the motivation for him to stop? The same urges that drive him to do it once will drive him to do it again and again, especially if there's no obstacle (i.e. victim being gone) in his way.

I want to talk about apathy for a second because it's one of my enemies and I have figured out a way to fight it. Now it's possible that a few residents of Phoenix have heard of this idea, but I wouldn't bet my paycheck on that possibility when I listen to some of the crap being spewed these days. It's called "thinking." That's all it takes to combat the plastic, blank attitudes which haunt this city. The excuses are that this tragedy is too overwhelming and that no one knows what the victim's family is feeling. Absolutely true. Should we leave it at that, walk away, and say we can't reach out to the people going through this pain, because we aren't going through it ourselves? That is so insulting because it implies that people who've lost a loved one have achieved some sort of enviable status. That is obviously not true.

My radio show is about people's opinions and values. It's about how they react to tragedies, scandals, and disasters. That's what I write about in my editorials also because it's what I'm constantly pondering. When our society is upset about something, the result is action and change. When nobody cares, nothing happens. When we can't even take the time to think about something, we cut ourselves off from the chance to learn from it. And when we one day find ourselves or our kids in the middle of a tragedy, we don't have the right to say we weren't prepared for it or we never thought about it before.

On one side of the scale, there's the timid, paranoid crew, who would rather not say a damn word about a controversial topic than risk being misunderstood, misquoted, or insulted. "What if people don't understand what I'm trying to say? What if I offend someone?" That's basically where they're coming from. When they do speak, it's with wishy-washy, ambivalent comments that try to show support for both sides. They don't want to rock the boat and they don't want anyone to yell at them or catch them off guard. High school debate team was not up their alley, in other words.

I actually don't see the Grazen case as a controversial topic. Either you think the man did it or you don't. Why is it so risqué'?

Then there's the more aggressive crowd, who think it's all a game, a fight for fame. Who can say the most outrageous thing to a reporter? Whose face is on the news the most often? That's what's important. Everyone who got their name mentioned on Larry King Live could thank God that they lived in Phoenix. Gee, it's a good thing a woman was killed. Otherwise, you would not be experiencing the rush of having your great Aunt in Michigan seeing you on TV. Nope, I didn't make my promotion, because I skipped work to hang out downtown, but I got to wave to a camera. Write that one in the Christmas card.

The problem with this is that you can't play the media any way you want to. Most people who try to use it as a bridge to success get screwed. The cameras will not necessarily leave you alone on the day that you happen to be walking on the sidewalk in front of the courthouse, so you might not want to pick a wedgie out of your ass at that particular moment. However, if you think up some great speech to say into the microphone of your favorite news anchor, go spend 2 paychecks on a new outfit, and then hang out in front of that same courthouse, that may be the day that half the reporters are sick and the other half are having a beer instead of checking out the trial.

If you try to make a name for yourself by making cute little remarks to the camera or writing a tell-all book, you're going to pay the price of being seen as disrespecting the victim's name and being more interested in scraping up some cash than in the tragedy you're writing about. The perfect example of this is, of course, Sarah Conan. Ah yes, the loyal and grieving childhood friend has come out of the woodwork to tell us all how great Natasha was. Not only that, but we get to hear how noble Sarah is, for standing up to all the negative media coverage about her close friend. The media has negated her dead friend's saintly persona and thank you God, Sarah is here to save the day. She sets the record straight for us. And she doesn't have a bit of self-interest, she explains when she says the following: "Carving out a favorable or memorable public image is not something that interests me." Okay, let's not try passing a lie detector test with that one, honey.

I do feel sorry for Sarah to some degree, because she's going to be really hurting for a long time. I'm sure she feels the stab of guilt every time she thinks about Natasha, Kristin, and their parents because she knows exactly what she's gotten herself into. She knows the term "sell-out" is a perfectly appropriate title for her. I'm sure she didn't intend or want to betray her friend or insult and humiliate her friend's family, but she knows that's exactly what she has done.

Although I understand how everything can be blurred when you're right in the middle of a tragedy and your every move is being watched, she is an adult and she is as accountable for her actions as the rest of the world is for theirs. Her continued choices of making crude comments and pushing her book is not gaining her much sympathy from me and I would guess it's rubbing a lot of other people the wrong way as well.

Sarah Cronan tried to embrace the media in order to establish an image for herself, while simultaneously blaming it for any negative experiences she had. She talks about how the media "assigned roles" to herself and her friends and how it painted them in a negative light. That's bunk. I certainly don't waste any time as a great defender of the media, but they get blamed for a Hell of a lot more than they deserve. They don't pick people out of thin air and create an image for them. Neither do they run around trying to recant stories that upset people.

Kristin Hillshaw's actions with the media represent an opposite course to Sarah's. Kristin has been completely honest about her experiences since her sister's death. She explains her past mind-set of being too upset to care about cameras, without going into a big defense of it. She went through a rough time, made some choices she regrets, and just moved on. She didn't try to make excuses or get people to feel sorry for her.

Jake Grazen has been made into a great tragic hero by this case. It's so pathetic and I really can't understand how so many people are able and willing to lie for this man. I keep waiting for John Caymen to break out of his bullshit blood brother act and say, "Okay, he did it." It must be both exhausting and frustrating to say things you don't believe over and over again. Exhausting because it's tough to come up with a constant string of lies and frustrating because even someone with the slightest fraction of moral fiber can't ignore the nagging guilt of being a fraud.

I have some of the same restricted sympathy for John Caymen that I do for Sarah Cronan. He's going to wake up some night and realize that he's a moron. I understand loyalty. And of course you don't want to believe that your close friend is capable of murder, but this guy is insulting everyone's intelligence and demonstrating the complete lack of his own by insisting that Grazen is innocent. Sheila Gaelin is basically doing the same thing—or trying to at least, but it's a little tougher for her because doesn't do well with things like sentences and thoughts. (The plus side of that is that she makes John Caymen look like a rocket scientist.)

I have yet to purchase a Jacob Grazen criminal trial juror book, but when I hit the book signing circuit, Regan Maltz's autograph is definitely going to be first in my scrapbook of trial memory highlights. Of all the accounts in this book and all the news clips since the verdict was handed down, this woman's words and attitude stick out the clearest in my memory. This is a woman I'd love to have coffee with because I think she's a kick, but I'd have to bring along a bottle of whiskey to periodically dump in my cup if we were going to talk about the trial or her book.

I have read and re-read Regan's section and I cannot come up with any alternative conclusion than that she is just loony. She's crazy and while that can certainly add some interest to a personality, I find it disturbing in a murder trial juror. And the fact that she was the head juror, boggles my mind even more. I have to have a cigarette and a shot of Cuervo each time I ponder this. The *entire* jury was under this woman's leadership. Como se dice "yikes"?

The dove metaphor. I yi yi. What can be said about the dove metaphor? What on *earth* are you talking about, Regan? If you seriously think of the world as a perfect existence, either you have had a life just absolutely filled to the brim with joy, or you haven't turned on the six o'clock news in a few decades. By thinking of the trial as a distraction to an otherwise hunky-dory life, you're implying that denial is the way to go. Given your sanity issues, it probably is a good option in many situations, but domestic violence happens every minute. And I cannot find any amusement or comfort in your solution of not thinking about it.

As for the little juror of the year award-winner speech, describing the merits of being the tool of justice, I'm also a bit bothered. Jury duty is of course important and it obviously brings an incredible amount of power with its responsibilities. You decide another person's fate. This jury sat down and decided whether Jake went to prison and waited for his turn to die, or went home and sipped champagne in bed. The entire nation was watching and maybe that filled their heads with too much power. However, for Regan to feel that her individual opinions on every aspect of the case make up a gospel, unquestionable truth, is not appropriate. And if she doesn't seriously know that, she has a few more problems than psychiatric drugs can address.

I do get the feeling that she really believes each word she utters and as scary as that is, I respect her honesty. It's rare. And I think her energy is admirable too, it just needs to be tamed and focused on reality-grounded issues. Revealing gossipy details about the case to an author doesn't rank right up in my personal definition of working "in the field of art" and the day I look to a woman like this to educate me on justice and domestic violence will be the same as when they check me into her ward. I'm curious as to how her confidence will hold up once people start expressing even harsher judgments than mine, about her campaign for spreading the word of education.

This trial pointed out how stupid our society is. There were many moments when I thought, "We should have learned by now." We should have learned how to behave. The jurors' book deals, the perjured testimony, the changes in testimony, and the ridiculous media battles should have all clued us in on the fact that we have a lot to re-think. We need to re-think our values when we sell naked pictures of the victim to the Enquirer, write books about her sex life, send death threats to prosecuting attorneys, and send condemning letters to the victim's parents. Are we so desperate for any sort of reaction that we betray and hurt people? Is our need to constantly be heard so strong that we have to grab onto every tragedy and rip at the people who are in the most pain?

I'd like to offer my condolences to the Hillshaw family. I'd also like to say something to Jake. Shame on you for continuing to lie about this. I don't believe in God, so I can't get into the whole repentance thing, but I think the least this murderer could do is admit his crime. He doesn't deserve to be forgiven for it, but he is just showing how much of a scumbag he truly is, by not owning up to it.

John Caymen

John Caymen testified for the defense in Jacob Grazen's trial. He has been a close friend to the defendant for several years. He is an architect and a resident of Phoenix.

March 12, 1998

I know I have a sleazy reputation and I probably deserve most of it. I don't think my past is much different than a lot of men my age, but I guess it offers some gossip material. I'm comfortable with myself and I don't lie about anything I've done. If that means I'm egotistical, I'll cop to it. I know the difference between truth and fiction, as do those who know me well. I can handle all the tabloid stories for this reason. It's all good. I just want people to see the truth about my friend and I get upset when that does not happen.

I did a lot of stupid things in college. I came across as this big drinking, smoking, womanizing dumb jock. I liked that image for a while because that's all it was: an image. It was all a game. I was obnoxious, crude, and tactless because I could get away with it. The people who knew me well, knew that it was all harmless. I liked to shock people and take things to the extreme. I wanted to get it all out of my system at an age when it was acceptable.

All that stuff wouldn't have been brought out if it wasn't for this case. And I don't care that it is, as long as it stays about me. People tend to associate Jake with my reputation. That's unfair and inaccurate. He has always been very independent and he doesn't cling to his friends or try to model himself after anyone else. If he did, I sincerely doubt that he would choose me as his role model!

I need to make one thing clear, right off the bat. I would never lie for someone. Especially when I thought they had done something wrong. It wouldn't matter what type of history I had with the person. I believe in loyalty, but I also believe in doing the right thing. If I ever thought there was a slight chance Jake did this, I would have admitted my doubt. There would be no choice involved. But I've never had thoughts like that. With every part of my being, I believe he's innocent.

Jake Grazen is honest, generous, and loyal. The kind of friend he is, I don't even know how to describe it. It goes way beyond being polite and cool to hang with. You're lucky if Jake says, "I have your back." He means it.

I have a lot of friends, but the way I feel about Jake is different. I probably wouldn't be 100% sure in defending the reputation of anyone other than him. It's really hard to trust people and truly know what they're capable of doing, but with Jake, I know. He looks out for people. He would do anything to help out the people he cares about and he has proved that over and over again. He's not a saint and would never claim to be one, but he cares more about other people than about what happens to him.

I've known Jake for 14 years. I moved from Boston to L.A. in the 9th grade. I played high school football and baseball with him. Then we both went to college in Phoenix on scholarships. Mine was for football and his was for baseball. We roomed together in a dorm for the first 2 years and then we rented a house with some friends for a few years.

Jake and I became buddies at a crucial time in our youth. We went through all the major rites of passage together: girls, sports, and partying. We were bonded by our experiences and we got to know each other really well as time went on. He was a positive influence on me during the time when I really needed one. I respected him and liked the way he saw things. I always teased him about being deep. He looked beyond the obvious and came up with the hard truths. My other friends lived for the moment and for telling your friends about the moment. I probably would have been more like that without Jake.

From college on, Jake was the outgoing, friendly guy that he is today. Before that, he was somewhat shy. In high school, he grabbed onto sports, especially football, as his escape. There was a lot of crap going on in his head and he needed a release. He was more comfortable on the field than anywhere else.

He was always likeable and friendly, but he was really apprehensive about asking women out. Once he got to college, he realized that women were really interested in him and his confidence grew. He got into partying for a short time, but he had to put studying first. Law school is vicious and he wanted to be successful.

I met Natalie about 4 months before Jake did because he was away on an internship the semester she started hanging out with Dave Morrow. When Jake first met her, it was like she was a super model. He tried to be cool in front of her, but wasn't too successful with that! He was fascinated by her. I remember how he pulled me aside the night they met, when she was out of the room. He said, "Why didn't you *tell* me about her?!" It was sweet to watch him around her and we teased him relentlessly. He gave us a lot of material: He added an hour to his workouts, started buying new clothes weekly, and got expensive haircuts from the trendiest salons in the city. He wore his shirts one size too small to show off his muscles and read GQ magazine like it was the Bible. For some reason that escaped me, he wore this one beige sweater every time she came over or they went somewhere. It would be like 90 plus degrees and he would slide that thing on. I don't know if she told him she liked it once, he just thought he looked sexy in it, or what the deal was.

I could see why he was attracted to her. Anybody could see why. She was gorgeous, intelligent, and friendly. The first impression that probably most people got when they met her, was just that she was a real sweet girl. And she was an unusual girl. I mean, she seemed different than other women in college. Everything about her was natural, both physically and in her personality. She didn't wear much make-up, she never dyed her hair and she didn't go for that gelled, sticky, big hair look. She dressed in a classic style, not with a lot of flash. As far as her personality, she was really fun, but she wasn't like a lot of the women who tried to get attention and outdo each other. She did whatever she wanted to do and didn't worry about what anyone else thought of her.

The rumors about my involvement with Natalie have gotten way out of control. We went out a few times when we first met, but it never went beyond a friendship. I was attracted to her and I liked her, but we just weren't right for each other and that was clear from the beginning. I was far from being ready for a serious relationship, which is what she was looking for. Not from me, but in general. I was glad she could get what she needed from Jake. I wasn't jealous, there wasn't any kind of rivalry between Jake and I, and I definitely never had an affair with her at any time after they got together. I would never do anything like that to Jake.

It is true that I had concerns about the relationship from the beginning. I was protective of my buddy and I wanted to make sure he was doing the right thing. That's all it was ever about. I get concerned about Jake the way I do about my younger brothers. It was obvious that Natalie really made Jake happy and I thought that was great, but I had reservations about it because it just seemed like it was all too much. They were instantly together when they met. They fell in love fast and hard. They had similar goals and loved being together. But I was uneasy that they were getting so serious so fast and I thought the age difference might turn out to be a problem.

That first year of their relationship, Jake and I were both really busy. I was in graduate school for architecture and he was in law school, so I just kind of heard things on and off. I didn't hang out with them too much, but I got the impression that they were having the normal ups and downs of a relationship. I tried not to judge Natalie, but my lurking doubts were still with me. I wondered whether she was respecting the time demands Jake had with studying, because I noticed that she was insecure about any time he spent away from her. She studied a lot too, but she still seemed to want to see Jake frequently. And it was like he had to account for all of his free time, which I had a hard time with. I think both people in a relationship need to have their freedom and I see jealousy as a bad sign. When one person starts being possessive, it shows that trust is going to be a big issue.

I think they both really tried to make it work, at least in the beginning, because they loved each other so much. They were both good people and they didn't want to hurt each other. (Since I know Jake a lot better than I knew Natalie, I only really feel comfortable talking about his efforts, but I know she tried too.) Jake had a lot of love to give and he was so ready to full commit himself to the woman he loved. I wasn't sure if Natalie could measure up to his intense devotion. I didn't want to watch Jake pour out his heart to someone and not get what he needed in return.

Jake has always been a private person and I think having a relationship was difficult for him. His independent streak kind of took over, even when he didn't want it to. He couldn't communicate certain things because he had a lot of feelings he hadn't sorted out and he wanted to handle everything on his own. It was hard for him to open up and share his problems with someone else. He wasn't used to that. He didn't want to need her. And Natasha had independence of her own, so communication was a battle for them. They built up walls, thinking they were protecting each other from burdens, yet they resented each other for holding back emotionally.

I didn't know much about Jake's past until I'd known him for quite a while. There's so much pain and he doesn't like to talk about it. He wants to move forward with whatever he's doing right now and leave the garbage behind. That makes sense to me. He shouldn't have to re-live bad memories just so people can understand what he went through. But sometimes you do have to let the bad stuff out to get rid of it, and Jake did that. When he told me about his childhood, it explained a lot of the problems he had with Natalie.

I don't believe that if you go through terrible times, you have the right to hurt other people. Jake's past didn't make his abuse of Natalie okay. He didn't think that either. (If he did, I wouldn't have gone along with it—I wouldn't be his friend.) I do think, however, that if you want to know why someone gets into violence, you can learn from certain problems in their past. Jake had to do that in therapy.

I can't say I completely understand either the tragedies Jake suffered or the feelings that led him to hurting Natalie. I know that specific events in his childhood caused him to get to the place of feeling angry with Natalie and wanting to control her and I wish he had gotten help before going there. What I do understand is how he was able to end it all. Despite the years of trauma that he had buried deep inside him, he was a decent, loving person. That part of him was always there and it led him to realize what he was doing wrong and get help.

Maybe it didn't happen earlier because he didn't have the support. No one made the link to predict abuse. I didn't know how to help him and felt some guilt for not reaching out to him in the right way. Part of it was that it took me a while to know exactly what was going on. I would get pieces of information from Jake, like little confessions that he was getting into something deep, but he didn't come out and tell me the real situation. I made excuses for not pushing him to open up. "Maybe he doesn't trust me, maybe I won't be able to handle what's going on." I was in denial because that was easiest for me at the time. I didn't want to hear that he was hurting her. I couldn't believe that.

One time he told me that sometimes he thought about Natalie in strange ways. He was confused, he didn't know what was happening. The paranoia kicked in and he was feeling rage toward her for little things. He seemed clear about the situation, so I didn't think he was in serious trouble. After all, denial is the first sign of a real problem and he seemed aware of his weaknesses.

He said that he felt threatened by things she did, even though he knew it was ridiculous. As time wore on though, he felt more and more threatened. And he didn't seem to recognize his behavior as irrational any more. Whenever she left the house or used the phone, he would think she was plotting to leave him or cheat on him.

It was frustrating to watch them both struggle with their relationship and I often wondered why they bothered to stay together. They just weren't happy. I tried to get where they were coming from and be supportive, but I just saw things differently than they did. I don't believe that love will conquer all and that's why I don't usually stay in a relationship for very long. If I'm not happy, I leave. I know that's one of a million reasons why I'm not someone you'd *ever* go to for relationship advice and I certainly didn't ever try to influence Jake and Natalie with my choices. I think we all accepted that there were just some things we didn't see eye to eye on.

Laura, Mitchell, and Josh have all talked about how they just didn't know what to do when they found out about the violence. I understand the shock and the helpless feeling of wanting to make everything go away, knowing it's not that simple. What loses me is how they make the jump to "I can't be his friend anymore." This was about Jake. It was his struggle. Yes, we were freaked out by it, but he was the one suffering. I didn't ever find myself thinking that if I wasn't able to help him I had to desert him. If you're really friends with someone, you never pull that kind of crap on them. It wasn't about making a big statement to other people about domestic violence. It wasn't a cause that I was protesting for or against, it was my friend's life. I think people are being selfish and lying to themselves, when they twist everything around to seem so complex.

Some people expect me to defend Jake's violence and blame it on Natalie, which is never going to happen. The violence was wrong. There's no two ways about that. But I think there were certain things that went on that no one wants to talk about. Everything has to be sugar-coated so you don't sound like a jerk. We need to get over that, it just blocks us from the truth.

No one wants to say that there can be some problems in a relationship that both partners are responsible for. It's true though. People don't get upset unless something is going on in their lives and that usually means a conflict with another person. That's what happens when we get into arguments with people: We're cruising along with our own plans for how to get what we want and someone else throws a curve in, whether it's a comment or an attitude.

Men and women are different. I don't think too many people would dispute that. That's why relationships are such a challenge. The feelings and hormones are just flying all over the place. These two people who love each other get so crazy because they can't take in what's happening. They can't express themselves in a way that the other one will understand. Men want to get their frustrations out in the most aggressive way they can, which can mean violence. Women want men to listen to their needs and pay a lot of attention to them and they can't understand where all the aggression comes from. Society doesn't stop to see this basic conflict though. Instead we just get labels of "abuser" and "victim," to simplify the problem. It's easier to lay blame.

Before we judge Jake as some sick bastard who hates women, we should be honest about the basic make-up of men. What I'm going to say about this will not be popular. It doesn't fit in with the sensitive man fantasy that women have, but it's my honest opinion. Not all men hit, but probably the majority of us have experienced violent urges at one time or another. It's a natural feeling, even though not all men act on it. Anger goes farther than flaring tempers. It's a forceful emotion that gives you a sense of release. When you let out stress and anger in a physical way, it's a concrete feeling and it's like you got something done. You've dealt with a problem directly. It can be harder to talk something out, for men, because that doesn't express just how intense the anger is, and hitting or screaming does express it.

It's hard to admit, but I understand all those feelings, somewhat, and I understand the feelings that lead to infidelity too. I don't think it is right, but I understand the weakness. Again, I think a lot of other men can understand it too, if they're being totally honest. For a lot of us, being with just one woman is very, very difficult. Sex is a strong part of a man's daily choices. It's a crude truth, but it's the truth all the same. Men want diversity, we have egos, and that's why it's a real struggle to stay committed to one woman.

With Jake, I was kind of confused because he really wanted only Natalie. He loved her and wanted to be with her forever. All that hopeless romantic shit was totally him. When he turned to other women, it was more about insecurity than just pure lust or not being satisfied with Natalie. He thought that she wasn't being loyal to him and he wanted to get back at her. Also, the attention from women made him feel better about himself. He liked feeling wanted and he didn't always get that from Natalie because there was so much tension between them.

I have never believed that an outside person killed Natalie. It was clearly a suicide. Everything points to that. She hit the bottom of the barrel. She and Jake were not together and that's not what she wanted. (That point has been covered up because so many people want to believe that Natalie was strong enough to lose Jake and move on.) It was a situation where the phrase "can't live with 'em, can't live without 'em" fits perfectly. That's exactly what it was.

Suicide is such a painful event. Of course it's something friends and relatives don't want to accept. Taking your own life hurts other people. It makes them think, "What did I do wrong?" There's guilt that just takes over people's minds, which I think is too bad because it takes away from the pain the victim went through. I don't think it's fair to say that people who do it are weak. Depression totally smothers a person and can lead them straight to suicide. They feel suffocated by all the pressures in their life and see that as the only route out. I think depression is a natural thing that happens to all kinds of people. When you're hit with more problems than you can handle, you sink into it.

I feel this way because I saw it firsthand, with both Natalie and Jake. Jake didn't get to the extreme Natalie did because he got help in time, but he certainly had desperate times. He hated himself for all the pain he caused. I think he could relate to Natalie's suicidal feelings. He had times when he contemplated taking his own life.

When I was a witness in this trial, I was amazed that I made it through my testimony. I was so overwhelmed every day I sat in that courtroom. I couldn't believe why I was there. The only way I could get through it was by forcing myself to believe that justice would prevail. When that didn't happen, I went crazy. How could a jury make such a terribly wrong decision? I'll never understand that.

To write this, I've had to sort of separate myself from the worst of it. I didn't want to write it at first because I thought it would be too painful to re-live everything. I wanted to just lock myself in a room somewhere and wait for it to be over. I have to fight the denial, which is not an easy task. Sometimes it seems easier to trick myself into thinking it's one long nightmare.

I know that I have to face to Jake's upcoming death. And he doesn't have much time left, so I have to find a way to deal with it. Truthfully, I don't know how.

Alyson Shyers

Alyson Shyers is a legal analyst, a lawyer, and a journalist. She covered the Grazen trial on location. She currently resides in New York City.

March 26, 1998

My husband loves telling people that I make my living by taking notes on tragedies, following lawyers around, and watching a lot of "Court TV." He's essentially right, although I could certainly come up with a more eloquent and professional-sounding description. His is more amusing though.

I couldn't decide between journalism and criminal law, so I got my BA in journalism, then went to law school. I have been fortunate to incorporate both into my career, as a lawyer who writes about legal strategies and decisions.

During the Grazen trial, I concentrated on the journalism side and limited my trial work to part-time advising for another attorney in my practice. I worked for one all-news network, as their daily correspondent from the courthouse and I guest-hosted a current events discussion program for the same network. I also wrote a few guest column articles for a Phoenix newspaper.

The judge for this case, Margaret Lange, addressed the publicity issue by saying that she would "accept nothing less than a trial focused on proper legal conduct." She promised that she would not tolerate a trial that was catered to the public. However, she did not issue a gag order and she denied the defense's application for a closed trial, reasoning that the speculation caused by closed proceedings would be more distracting than the normal attention of keeping them public. She insisted that there would be strict guidelines for her decision and said that she would make amendments or even change her mind altogether if problems arose.

Her choice didn't hold water with me because she was claiming to be intolerant of the press, yet she was giving us free reign. (She did sequester the jury, but that doesn't affect the media's activities in a trial.) Judges who allow cameras in their courtroom and claim a distaste for the press are hard to take seriously. They open themselves up to criticism and frankly, I think it's well-deserved. I was told that Judge Lange has a reputation for being tough, but I certainly don't think her behavior in the trial supported that characterization.

Working on this trial has been unique for me. It was the first time that I got a real feeling for a community's view of a tragedy like this. I never spent as much time in direct contact with the various people involved in a case as I did in Phoenix. Usually, I stay in a hotel room for a few days and just hope that I happen to be there for an interesting part of the trial. I'm typically doing so many different jobs at once that I don't have the time to devote to an entire trial. Or sometimes I'll work for a network that divides up a crew of reporters for coverage. I was fortunate for the opportunity to focus on this trial exclusively. I moved to Phoenix for the duration of the trial and I really feel that I became a part of the lifestyle there. I learned what people thought about every step of the trial, as well as their opinions of what led up to the trial.

If you don't live in Phoenix, it's hard to get just why Jake Grazen has become such a figure of fascination. When a famous athlete or movie star is accused of a crime, people are shocked that it could happen to someone they feel they know. Jake Grazen was famous in a different way. A lot of people in Phoenix actually knew him personally. Even though Phoenix is a city, there was kind of a small-town quality about the way this man was revered. He had started getting nationwide recognition in modeling and a lot of residents were proud of him. They were also very protective. It was almost like a sense of ownership—like the city was responsible for taking care of him.

Once I realized all this, I could understand the intense loyalty of this defendant's supporters. If I hadn't gotten to listen to so many people explain their connection to Jake, I would have passed it off as ignorance. People saw his integrity as sacred and fought for it with a serious sense of obligation. I saw it as a clear-cut for better or for worse type of relationship: His success and popularity had been the better and being charged with murder was the worse.

Some of his supporters were not familiar with the statutory laws and seemed to have no interest in learning about the justice system. They're just fans and they want to make noise. Others may have tried to follow the procedures of the trial, but they could not accept any decision that didn't favor their hero. They saw it as unjust because in their minds, he was falsely accused and shouldn't receive any negative consequences or forms of punishment.

When Jake was not granted bail, for instance, his supporters were outraged, declaring that the phrase "innocent until proven guilty" had been ignored. This shows a real lack of knowledge. Bail is rarely issued to a defendant charged with such a serious crime. When it is set, it's usually too high for the defendant to afford because the concern is safety for the community.

Jake's lawyers asked for bail instead of a no bail hold, as a standard strategy for the case. They also asked for dismissal before presenting their case. Defense attorneys on murder cases don't necessarily expect favorable rulings for these issues, but they want to give their client a chance at every possible break and cover themselves for the possibility of an appeal. They also need to make sure their requests to the court are reasonable, so a request for release on personal recognizance would not be something an experienced attorney would argue for on a murder case.

Another misconception people have is that a judge's ruling on bail is an indication of his or her personal opinion on the defendant's guilt or innocence. Judge Lange did not deny bail because she "had her mind made up from the beginning" that Jake was guilty, as I've heard people say. The decision on bail is not a judge's comment on the defendant's guilt or innocence. It's an assessment of safety factors, which includes legal precedents set in previous cases, the defendant's criminal history, and the specifics of the crime. This issue is separate from the evidence that is presented at trial. In the Grazen case, case law showed bail denial under similar circumstances, Jake had violent crimes on his record, and first-degree murder is the most serious crime a person can be charged with.

This case drew people in for 2 reasons. The first is the admiration for Jake that I just described. The second is the subject of domestic violence. Again, it would have been hard for me to understand what people were feeling if I hadn't been right in Phoenix learning about it firsthand. People saw this case as a chance to address a problem they really cared about. It was a case that got the entire public's attention and advocates for victims' rights groups wanted to take advantage of that attention. It quickly became a very personal debate that was fueled by incredible vigor on both sides. It wasn't just a public dialogue about the need for new programs, but an all-out argument about the character of an idolized man.

Those in favor of Jake complained that the focus on advocacy assumed Grazen's guilt for the murder, accusing their opponents of wanting to use Jacob Grazen as their poster child for batterers. The response to this was the sentiment that Jake shouldn't be treated any differently than other killers. A counselor at a Phoenix women's center made the following comment early on in the case: "He doesn't represent every violent relationship in the world, but we shouldn't pretend that he is exempt from the truth. He does not deserve to quietly slip away from the public's knowledge of his brutal crime."

Samuel Hadwick, who came into the case with the reputation of a ruthless, controversial defense attorney who liked to stir things up, actually made rare statements to the press concerning this case. His refusal to comment about his client surprised many people, but I understand it. From what I've seen of him, he can be obnoxious in the courtroom, but it's really all for his client. He breaks rules when it will help him win cases, but it's not about his ego or trying to get attention for himself, despite the rap he often gets and sometimes goes along with.

His rebuttal to the above comment was one of his exceptions in refusing to speak out. He made a spontaneous call in to a televised talk show, while the comment was being discussed. He spoke slowly and deliberately, and I thought he sounded upset. He said, "I have absolutely no disagreement with the opinion that a person who kills someone should not be granted special privileges. They have to answer to society to what they've done. That's the least they owe. Jacob Grazen, however, is not in this category. He needs to own up to his violent past, but he can't own up to this murder. He's not responsible for it."

Hadwick was criticized for this choice. It's never a good idea to comment on a pending case, but he didn't take any questions about the case and kept his statement very brief. He took a risk but I think he decided that not saying anything would be worse than taking a stand on it. (I don't think I would have done it, but I do understand why he did.)

Along with the advocacy for domestic violence treatment, came a melancholy atmosphere. Of course, not everyone favored Jake. Natasha's death left a significant gap, as she had been quite popular also. The first surge of publicity suggested that she was only well-known for her connection to Jake, but that was not the case. She touched a lot of lives, even before she met him. Some people simply believed that Jake killed her, whether they knew her or not, while others were unsure about his guilt, but disgusted by his violent history. It seemed that knowing her made the whole grieving process much more painful.

The trial proceeded relatively quickly. There is usually a period of at least a year between an arrest and a criminal jury trial, but Natasha Hillshaw's family did not want such a delay. They asked the Phoenix District Attorney to push the case through right away and he successfully did so. (I had heard that story as it happened, but it wasn't confirmed by either the family or the D. A's office until after the trial ended.) The judge, the court's docketing clerk, and some of the attorneys with cases pending were willing to swap things around so that the Grazen trial could get started earlier.

In a criminal trial the state is responsible for the entire process of charging and prosecuting a defendant, so the victim's family doesn't necessarily have an active role in the process. While their interests are often a focal point for the prosecuting lawyers, they don't have the same type of control that they would have in a civil case. In a wrongful death suit, the victim's family is essentially running the case because they have chosen to bring forth an accusation against a specific party and have hired their own lawyer.

Some prosecuting attorneys will consult with the victim's family and consider their needs at each step of the case. Others will run their own case and limit the contact they have with any interested party. For the Hillshaws, the former situation occurred.

The defense attorneys wanted a speedy trial also, so they did as much as they could on their end to move the case along. They combined the arraignment with the initial appearance and waived the preliminary hearing. This decision caused rumors that Jake was "giving up" from the beginning, but it was merely a practical procedural decision that made things more efficient. It was clear that probable cause existed, so disputing that would only delay things for their client.

Lawyers on opposing sides can either work towards each other or against each other and in this trial, they chose to cooperate for the most part. They shared information even when they weren't required to and were generally cordial to each other. The nastiness came out after the trial concluded and maybe that happened because emotions had been kept in check for so long. I also think that the courtroom atmosphere was very formal and professional, despite the emotional nature of this case. For the most part, everyone managed to keep a flat, calm demeanor while court was in session and that's not necessarily a common occurrence in murder trials.

Even though the case moved along efficiently, it was not a situation where anyone was cutting corners. (Some people seemed to think the defense was doing that, but they were simply choosing legal options that aren't commonly used.) In fact, I felt that there was almost a zealous regard for procedural details. The District Attorney's office was probably the most careful. For instance, they pushed the Phoenix Police Department to ask for an ex parte hearing to gain an arrest warrant, even though there was clearly probable cause.

They also had a tendency to go through a lot of formalities in court that the judge assured them were unnecessary. Some analysts complained that the prosecution was too picky, but I think the goal was not to draw any accusations of trial procedure mistakes, sloppy work, or mishandled evidence. A capital case with a lot of public attention can make the attorneys working on it especially meticulous. The world is watching and their work is being monitored by the entire nation. Any mistakes will be remembered and may affect the public's view of future trials.

Jacob Grazen was arrested on September 23rd, 1997. His initial appearance and arraignment were held on September 25th, and he entered a plea of not guilty. The grand jury met from October 7th to October 11th and returned with an indictment. The trial began on November 10th. The prosecution and defense took roughly the same amount of time presenting their arguments-- about 4 weeks each, and the case was given to the jury on January 19th, 1998. They deliberated until late into the evening on January 29th and delivered their verdict of guilty the next day. Sentencing (the court hearings and deliberation process) took place from February 16th to the 25th. The death penalty was announced on the 25th.

With high publicity cases, it seems to be a trend now to have a big team of lawyers. Sometimes that works well. If you're using lawyers who can focus on specific aspects of the case, you can save time and seek out quality witnesses and accurate analyses of the evidence from experts. For example, some lawyers specialize in DNA evidence, so they are familiar with the process and have close contacts with experts in the field. It can be a situation where attorneys want to be involved to gain notoriety, but some personalities tend to dominate the arguments, so the overall presentation of the team appears to be disjointed when that happens.

I've heard of cases where 10 different people write the closing argument. With high publicity cases, everyone wants to get their name on it, but the result is a choppy statement. When you write and deliver your own argument, you have creative control, and you can improvise effectively. You're adding or subtracting to your own argument and you know the case well, if you have been the primary attorney throughout the entire trial.

It can be easier for a small team of attorneys to build a rapport with the jury. It's a personal relationship and it's difficult to present a consistent, persuasive argument with multiple voices.

The number of lawyers used in this case was moderate and both sides divided up their arguments and witnesses. For the prosecution, Annia Valdez and John Whitten shared the courtroom presentation. Annia is the Assistant District Attorney and John is a Deputy District Attorney. For the defense, Samuel Hadwick, Adam Cole, and Mary Solnik were the attorneys who presented arguments at trial. On both sides, there were several other lawyers consulting and researching.

In the beginning of the trial, each lawyer showed their individual characteristics. They personalized their styles of arguing and used the contrast between their methods and other attorneys' methods to highlight their unique strengths. For example, Mary Solnik carefully led the defense's medical expert witnesses through complicated testimony, quietly prompting them to explain their opinions to the jury. Samuel Hadwick was a sharp contrast to that, with his loud, brash side comments during cross-examinations. I don't know whether this was intentional. I'm more inclined to think that everyone was trying to come across as extremely confident, embracing their quirky characteristics. As the trial moved along, however, the individual traits became blurred. Attorneys were slowly taking on each other's mannerisms and seemed to be getting sucked into their opponents' arguments, sometimes to the point of losing their train of thought.

John Whitten started raising his voice almost as often as Samuel Hadwick did and Mary Solnik seemed to be abandoning her original points and focusing on an attack against Annia Valdez's assertion that suicide was impossible. It was a strange thing to watch. Each side seemed almost intimidated by the strength of the opposing team's arguments, so everyone seemed to be getting defensive. After a while, everyone started sounding alike.

Each lawyer was extremely experienced and that was obvious throughout the trial. They also showed a real passion for their work. However, it just wasn't a very even case, in terms of presentation. There were some brilliant arguments from both sides, and also some mistakes. The biggest issue seemed to be inconsistency. There wasn't always a good flow between each part of the case. So, the points brought up in opening argument weren't necessarily addressed during testimonies. The result was that the attorneys appeared disorganized and I think the jurors were left with the impression that the issues that seemed important early on and then disappeared, were either mistakes or points that the attorneys could not prove.

I'm not sure whether it was the prosecution or defense that originally came up with the domestic abuse relevancy issue, but it ended up being a blessing for the prosecution and a nightmare for the defense.

Initially, the defense brought up the past abuse as a way to appear that they had nothing to hide. They didn't want to downplay either the fact that Jake had made mistakes or the seriousness of domestic violence. So, in a sense, they were saying that his past was relevant in the overall big picture of who he is. Unfortunately, they didn't hammer home the point that his past was irrelevant to the charge he was on trial for.

The prosecution connected the domestic abuse and Natasha's death so solidly that they acted as if the two were one in the same. The implication to the jury was, "Look, if you believe the defendant hurt her, you have to believe he killed her." This argument was dangerous for the defense because if the jury accepted it, there was no way to convince them to view the two issues as separate. It was clear that Jake hurt Natasha. He was convicted of domestic assault and admitted his guilt. Ultimately, the jury followed what the prosecution was asking them to do and made that leap from assault equating to murder.

Judge Lange's instructions to the jury included the standard definition of evidence: The opening and closing statements are not evidence, nor is any comment an attorney makes about testimonies. Some judges will go further and tell the jury that they can accept an attorney's argument if they find that the evidence supports it. Judge Lange did include this point and I think the jury was influenced by that specific instruction. In general, they would hang on every word the judge said and a couple of the jurors who have discussed the case since the trial have mentioned that instruction specifically. I think the jury believed that they needed to choose one sides' argument exclusively and accept it verbatim.

Every juror showed favoritism for the prosecution's case at some point in the trial, because they felt sympathy for the victim's family. The defense team couldn't do anything about that. The circumstances of the case brought a strong feeling of sorrow that was present throughout the entire trial.

The strongest part of the prosecution's case was the testimony from their expert witnesses. They brought in therapists to talk about patterns of power and control in violent relationships, and about suicide. They also had blood and DNA experts who described the presence of the defendant's blood and fingerprints at the crime scene. If Whitten and Valdez had highlighted the blood and DNA testimony more in their arguments, the case would have been tighter. They didn't present the evidence as a central part of the case. Instead, they just referred to it occasionally and spent more time trying to dispel the defense arguments about the relationship.

John Whitten gave the opening statement for the prosecution. He's been labeled in the media as "the lecturer" because he can be pretty wordy. He had some strong arguments, but it could take him a long time to get to them. He seemed to be teaching the jury and sometimes he sounded like he was giving them a pep talk.

Good morning. I'd like to thank each member of the jury for the time and careful attention you are willing to devote to this case. You are all in an unenviable position. This is a tough situation. The tragic, untimely death that has brought us all here together will undoubtedly haunt each person in this court room, regardless of our individual opinions, for a long time after this case concludes. This will be a complicated, emotionally-charged, and exhausting trial. You will see and hear a lot of disturbing, confusing, and upsetting things, and there will be many points of disagreement between the people who are speaking to you. We are all starting at the same point of not knowing exactly what will go on each day that we gather together or how we are going to feel about what we see and hear in this trial, both in and out of the courtroom.

Among the many repetitive themes that will develop in this trial, is the idea of relevancy. Who should you listen to and which evidence is accurate? I apologize ahead of time for all the confusing, contradicting statements that you will hear. The reality is, of course, that the two groups of lawyers seated on opposite sides of this room do not agree on many aspects of this case. It may be frustrating for you to hear conflicting theories and viewpoints.

However, you have the control here. Your reasoning and listening skills override everyone else's opinions. *As jurors, you have the power to decide which points are relevant and which ones are not.*

I think that common sense is the key to making the right decisions. It will guide you through the evidence and testimonies and help you to distinguish truth from diversions. Perhaps the most controversial and important arguments you will hear are those about Natasha Hillshaw's relationship with the defendant, the role of violence in that relationship, and whether or not Mr. Grazen's violent history is important to the question of how his ex-wife died.

Anyone who uses common sense will not have any trouble with these issues.

Witnesses who knew this young couple very well will tell you countless stories about the abuse Jacob Grazen inflicted upon his wife on a consistent basis, therapists and domestic violence experts will tell you that Mr. Grazen didn't ever reach a significant level of rehabilitation while Natasha was still alive, and you will see evidence connecting him to the crime scene. There is no separation point between Jake's violence and the murder. The same rage that caused him to hurt Natasha when they were involved, caused him to murder her after they got divorced. His rage increased even more after they broke up because he felt betrayed by her. He needed to follow up the control he had created so carefully, for so many years. That was too big of an investment for him to suddenly stop caring about it.

The defense is probably going to tell you that our intent is to make this case into a social conscience-

raising effort. That is not true. Our goal is very, very simple:

We want to tell the truth. A young woman was killed and the man who killed her needs to be punished for it. We are not using her death as a rally for a social issue or to wave a red flag at the oppression that marked her life. Would it be nice if some of the people who follow this case can think about domestic violence and be motivated to make some positive changes? Sure. However, that's not an agenda for us. We are concerned with this man, not society. Despite any way that the community or the foster care system may have failed him, he committed a crime. He's the only defendant in this case, so he's the only person we're focusing on.

Despite the lengthy testimonies, the technical language, and the conflicting arguments that you will hear in this trial, the facts are going to be straightforward. Jacob Grazen is a violent, controlling man. He has a record of domestic assault against Natasha Hillshaw. His blood was found at the crime scene—on the victim's body and on the gun. The gun was registered to Mr. Grazen and had his fresh fingerprints on it.

These facts speak for themselves. The defense will bring witnesses in here who will speculate about an alternate course of events, but the truth is just too strong. All the postulating in the world won't make the facts go away.

You are probably going to hear more about the defendant than about the victim in this case. And unfortunately, you're going to hear some victim-blaming. It may be subtle, but it will surface nonetheless. Some witnesses will talk about Natasha's behavior in the relationship—her faults, what she did to upset Jake, and her failed attempts to make the marriage work. Some therapists will imply that the defendant was actually a victim himself in many ways.

Why did the violence occur? Why did a tumultuous relationship end up in tragedy? The defense will provide you with many reasons. Jake was emotionally unstable. He was mentally unstable. He grew up without a mother. He was insecure, he didn't know how to control his anger, and the list continues into the horizon if we choose to follow it.

Again, I'm going to bring you around to the concepts of relevancy and common sense. If you keep those 2 concepts in mind throughout this case, you will ensure that justice is served. Thank you.

I think John's opening would have been stronger if he tightened it up a bit, but he delivered it with passion once he got going. He's the type of lawyer who wants to use every minute before the jury, to make sure he gets it all in there. It can present as overkill or extremely conscientious.

I'd seen John in a few other cases and knew that juries respond well to him.

He has the right balance of confidence and humility. He carefully regulates his speech and variation in his tone, putting emphasis on the most important points. Too much drama will not reach a jury because they will become distracted by it. When every argument is brash, loud, and aggressive, the impact can become dull. (Samuel Hadwick and Adam Cole both made this mistake.) The same is true for the opposite end of the spectrum: A soft-spoken, calm lawyer can appear passive or timid if they never raise their volume or vary their tone.

The defense divided their opening between Mary Solnik and Samuel Hadwick. She spoke about the relationship and described the basis of their suicide evidence. He explained their theories about the crime scene evidence and talked about Jake's past. Their arguments fit together well because they both touched on the prosecution's basic arguments. There was an implied patronization towards the prosecution, as if their arguments were ridiculous.

Mary's opening was straightforward. And while I wouldn't go as far as describing it as hard-hitting or dramatic, it was definitely a strong argument. She brought emotion to her description of the relationship and she was very good at building up to her key points. Her presentation was plain, which went well with her simple style. She didn't pace or point at her client, just stood at the podium and maintained eye contact with the jury, carefully laying out her argument. That actually made her argument stand out, because no other attorneys did that. (The following is the beginning part of her statement.)

Good morning ladies and gentleman. I share Mr. Whitten's gratitude and appreciation of your time.

When I first met with my client, he didn't have much to say. He was distraught. He listened carefully to our advice, which we gave him plenty of, because we are never at a loss for words. When he finally spoke, he said "I just have one request. Let me tell the truth at my trial." We are of course going to honor his request, so you will hear everything that we have heard from him. I mention this because it gives a snapshot of what our case is about. We're going to tell you about our client, his relationship with Ms. Hillshaw, and how she died.

You won't get an edited version or an exaggerated version. You will get all of it.

Jacob and Natasha were involved for 6 years and it was never a healthy relationship. Obsession, neediness, jealousy, paranoia, violence were there for just about every step of the way and not on both sides, but on Jake's. He was the one who was cruel, degrading, and abusive. He was the one who received fines and served jail time for bar fights and domestic assaults. Today he admits that he alone is responsible for all those things, but for most of that 6-year period, he did not admit that. He blamed Natasha for most of it and everyone else for the rest.

Natasha loved Jake immensely and she tried really hard to make the relationship work. She lost friends and jobs, she endured years of insults and physical pain, and she became depressed. The man she loved made her believe she was worthless, after she had sacrificed everything for him.

This case is not about fault and blame in the relationship. Your job is not to decide whether Jake was a violent man or Natasha was suicidal. Both are true. We are not judging her as weak or unstable, but we have to tell the truth. Jake has to admit his faults and we have to draw the line at a murder charge.

She went on to describe the therapists who would testify that Natasha was suicidal. She kept it brief and Hadwick's statement was slightly longer. The jury seemed to react favorably to her argument. If she had followed up these ideas throughout the trial, they would have felt more valid, but she didn't do that. I expected her to question Jake and treat him as a hostile witness, because that would have been consistent with her opening, but her attitude about his responsibility for the violence slowly faded out in the course of the trial.

Samuel Hadwick's part of the opening was toned down compared to his usual style. He threw in a little bit of sarcasm, but saved most of his aggressive attitude for his cross-examinations and his part of the closing. He hinted at the tragedies Jake endured as a child, without spelling them out. I think he wanted to create some suspense, plus he didn't want to appear to be going for sympathy. He stuck with the same theme that Mary had introduced, as he explained that they weren't trying to make up excuses for Jake, but were obligated to tell the truth about him.

I'm including the latter part of his opening, because it brings all of his points together. Also, it's the only time in the trial when he spoke in a sensitive manner. He usually glosses over any emotional issues and rarely refers to a victim's family. In this case it was appropriate for him to make the change and to do it early on in the trial. He was directly acknowledging the pain involved right away, not tacking on a few comments as an afterthought.

I know this is a lot of information and I've gone off in several different directions, so I'm going to briefly re-cap for you. My client has a lot of stuff in his past and you will hear about it, in order to understand who he is. You need to know that he was a violent man because that is what he learned. After years of hurting the woman he loved, he made the choice to break away from what he had been taught. He got help and learned a new way of life—a healthy, safe way that he had never known about. That part of his life is very, very important. Understanding how he changed is the key to understanding why he did not commit murder.

We are not telling you that Jake is a nice guy and that's why he couldn't have done something bad. We are not suggesting that a few therapy sessions will cure a person from violent tendencies. It's not that simple and we know that.

You will need to look at each part of Jake's life and examine everything that was going on for him. Listen to every witness and consider every piece of evidence.

This is a difficult case. I'm not going to stand up here and pretend that it's a clinical, objective situation for anyone involved. That would insult your intelligence. Despite all the resentment and skepticism that many people have for me, I truly feel for everyone involved. My client and Natasha's family are going through turmoil that none of the rest of us can begin to understand.

There's a lot of stress and tension in this room that will only increase as time goes on and just saying that we all have a job to do is not going to make it go away.

I think that Samuel's opening was his most effective argument in the trial. He was direct, clear, and he didn't overdo it.

Samuel Hadwick's general court presence is closer to Annia Valdez's than it is to John Whitten's. Where Whitten opts for muted tones, reflective moments, and drawn-out arguments, Hadwick chooses a loud voice, exaggerated body language, and fast-paced speeches. He uses rhetorical questions quite often, but they're much more accusatory than John Whitten's.

Both attorneys have been noted for their emanating egotism and patronizing attitudes in court. I think Hadwick's behavior is more genuine than Whitten's. John often acts bored and I think it is an act, to keep up with Sam and show a little bit of a rough edge. When Sam seems bored, I think he really is. He behaves as if every argument and presentation besides his own is a waste of time and I think he often feels that way. He suppresses this feeling during his colleagues' presentations, then brings it out again when he takes the floor, suggesting in any way he can that the audience needs to save up their attention span for him—he carries the defense team, as his colleagues offer valuable information and he brings it all together.

Sam shared Annia Valdez's tendency to move things along, which the jurors seemed to favor over Whitten's habit of lingering on each topic. He chose quality over quantity, as he simply made each point, with a raised voice and juicy, sometimes off-color language, then moved on. This came across as an impatient, agitated lawyer. He played it up, like one of Jack Nicholson's spookier characters. The message was "I'm stressed-out, I'm losing my energy, so you better listen now." I've seen him in interviews and casual conversations—it's real.

Both sides used a lot of expert witnesses and it got confusing because a lot of them were so similar. It was hard to keep track of which side they were testifying for. The jury became restless after a few days of listening to these witnesses. They were shifting in their seats, gazing all around the courtroom. One was even caught dozing off. (The judge gave them a little lecture about attention spans and made sure they had coffee during their breaks from that point on.) All the expert witnesses seemed credible and knowledgeable, so the result was a "cancelling out" effect in the eyes of the jury. From comments jurors made to the media at trial's end, it was apparent that they figured that neither side's witnesses stood out to give more weight to arguments.

The character witnesses made up the most chaotic part of the trial. For virtually every witness, I kept waiting for a significant fact to surface and that never happened. When people say the trial turned into a joke, this is the part of the trial they're most likely thinking of. There didn't seem to be any reasonable purpose for most or the witnesses and the questions seemed to get more and more obscure.

Once the cross-examination began, it was like a battle of wills between lawyers. The tension kept rising and there were times when Whitten and Hadwick were just zeroing in on each other. Despite the lack of direction, they both made an impact because they got everyone's attention. Ordinarily that doesn't mean much in a trial, but in this case, it broke up the monotony of the confusing evidence analysis. The jurors woke up and probably took that section of the trial more seriously. The subject matters seemed more important because the lawyers were making a big deal about them. It's likely that they concentrated more on the character witnesses, in their deliberation, than on the expert witnesses.

John Whitten gets what he wants from a witness by creating a character for them and interacting with it. He will subtly direct the questions towards the information he wants to bring out. Usually, you can see where a lawyer is going with their questions. With John, the witness can't tell what he's looking for, so they can't brace themselves for a difficult question or uncomfortable topic. He frequently uses long pauses in between questions, as a strong part of his presentation. He will hint at sarcasm, in reference to the answer a defense witness has just given, by squinting slightly, stroking his chin, and nodding his head. He is showing an exaggerated level of interest in their testimony, pretending to be intrigued. He gives himself away with the occasional eye roll though.

Samuel, on the other hand, took more of a blind-siding approach. He bulldozed his way through questions, regardless of who was on the stand. At first, I wondered if his ego had carried him beyond any sense of tact. Now that I'm in the position to reflect on his choices and fit them together with the way he acted in the rest of the trial, I think he was trying to show that he didn't have any favoritism towards defense witnesses. By treating every witness with the same hostile attitude, he took personality out of the picture and focused on getting his final product from them.

He preferred short testimonies and at times he would rush witnesses through the questions. Some were caught off guard by the way he treated them and became flustered. Others tried desperately to combat his attitude with a confident, defiant air. He wasn't shaken by any negative treatment, whether it was a witness' complaint, an objection from the prosecution, or words of admonishment from the judge. I interpreted his careless approach as another subtle message to the jury—a signal of extreme confidence in the evidence. He didn't need to worry about offending anyone or even about the specific answers because the evidence was the strong part of their case. Everything else was extra.

From a spectator's standpoint, it appeared that each side picked out a witness to attack. I felt like we were all supposed to know what the significance was, but I didn't get it. I don't know what connections they wanted the jurors to make and they never explained it.

Whitten took on John Caymen, showing disgust and annoyance during the cross-examination and then referring to his testimony as a joke in his closing. He told the jury that this defense witness represented the views of the defendant and all of the other defense witnesses. He didn't prove that, but he asked the jury to go along with that presumption.

I've included Mary Solnik's direct examination of John Caymen, to show what preceded Whitten's cross. She didn't lead her witness too much, but some of his answers sounded rehearsed.

Question: *When did you first meet the defendant?*

Answer: *It was in our first year of high school.*

Question: *How would you describe his personality at the time?*

Answer: *He was shy, but friendly when you got to know him. He was extremely smart and a great athlete.*

Question: *What changes did you see in Jake as you grew up together?*

Answer: *Um, he was a lot, he became a lot more social. He had been shy around girls, but that changed in college. He was more confident when he saw how much people liked him.*

Question: *Mr. Caymen, please describe your relationship with the defendant, and specifically, your knowledge of his relationships with women.*

Answer*: Okay. Well, before Nat, or ...?*

Question: *Before and including, please.*

Answer*: He was, well, we were really close friends all along. Um, we hung out in high school and then we roomed together in college. Jake was someone who ... he was unique. I mean, you have a lot of people in college who you hang out with, but not that many you can trust the way I have always trusted Jake. He took things more seriously than people that age, even though he liked to have fun too, so I felt more comfortable telling him personal stuff than most of my other friends.*

And the women. Well, Jake's social life was pretty typical for college. He dated a lot of women, but not seriously until he met Natalie. Oh, Natasha, but he called her Natalie. I definitely thought that he would be ready for a serious relationship sooner than the rest of us, but I also knew he would be really particular about it. He respected women. You could tell that right away, when he was dating someone.

Question: *Did he change when he began dating Natasha?*

Answer: *Yes.*

Question: *How so?*

Answer: *Let's see. He became nervous, withdrawn. Um, he seemed to defend her a lot. He was pretty protective of her and I wasn't really sure if he was jealous or if he, like, got insecure again. If he thought he would mess up and lose her, or what.*

Question: *Was he crazy?*

Answer: *No, he wasn't crazy. He just had a lot of past issues that he had to work through, like low self-esteem, fear of abandonment, protectiveness, and he was overwhelmed when he fell in love with someone as great as Natalie.*

Question: *Do you think that Jacob Grazen killed Natasha Hillshaw?*

Answer: *No, I do not.*

Question: *Why do you have this opinion?*

Answer: *He loved her in such a delicate and protective way. If he was "obsessive," it was just because he wanted to be with her. To have her out of his life, was just unthinkable.*

Question: *Often times, when a person commits a crime, close friends of that person will try to protect them. Is that the case here?*

Answer: *No. My loyalty for a friend doesn't extend to covering up a crime.*

Question: *Thank you, I have no further questions for this witness, at this time.*

I think she made some crucial errors with this witness, but to give her some credit, I have to say that I'm not sure how I would have proceeded with him either. I just don't think he had very much to offer to the defense's case and he certainly invited criticism from the prosecution. Solnik's direct was so basic and skimpy that it seemed like she wanted to get him off the stand fast. She never established why he was there in the first place. Her questions didn't really make sense and she didn't go anywhere with them. I was astonished when she asked the question about Jake being crazy. It was one of the times in the trial where it seemed that the defense was implying that they thought Jake was mentally unstable, but they never pursued that in any direct way. At first, I assumed that

Solnik was trying to draw attention to something, with that odd question, but she never followed it up.

When Adam Cole talked about John Caymen in his part of the closing, he might as well have been referring to another trial. He spoke very favorably about Ms. Solnik, acting as if she had delivered an airtight proof of Jake's innocence with that testimony. He was giving her too much credit.

John Whitten had a golden opportunity to blow Caymen's testimony wide open and he went for it. He kept his questions simple and let the witness do damage to himself.

Question: *How are you, Mr. Caymen?*

Answer: *Fine.*

Question: *Good. I'm glad to hear that. How well did you know Natasha Hillshaw?*

Answer: *I would say that I knew her very well in the beginning of her relationship with Jake, but as we all got busier, I spent less time with her.*

Question: *Did you spend less time with Jake as well, or just less time with Natasha?*

Answer: *Both, but I made more of an effort to see Jake when I could.*

Question: *In your opinion, what were Natasha Hillshaw's negative characteristics, as they related to her involvement with your friend?*

Answer: *Oh, that's a hard question. Well, I mean, Jake adored her so much that I tried to keep a positive opinion of her, but I saw some changes in Jake, since they met, that worried me.*

Question: *Could you please list her negative characteristics?*

Answer: *Yes, I'm sorry. Okay, she was demanding of his time. I felt she was aggressive towards Jake, in the sense of trying to control him and shape his image into what she was comfortable with. Um, she had a superior attitude at times, and she would embarrass him in front of his friends.*

Question: *Did you think Natasha was a jealous person?*

Answer: *Yes, I think she was.*

Question: *Did Jake and Natasha have a committed relationship from the beginning of their involvement?*

Answer: *Yes. They got serious right away.*

Question: *Was Jake faithful?*

Answer: *No.*

Question: *Approximately how many affairs would you say Jake had, throughout the time he was involved with Natasha—both before and during their marriage?*

Answer: *I honestly can't give an accurate number. I would say that it was more than 5 and less than, um, 30.*

Question: *Was Jake a jealous person?*

Answer: *Somewhat ...*

Question: *How did Jake feel about Natasha's male friends?*

Answer: *Oh. He liked their mutual friends and then there were some people he didn't like for her to hang around with.*

Question: *Can you explain to me, Mr. Caymen, exactly what that means—that he "didn't like for her to hang around" with her male friends?*

Answer: *He got upset, sometimes, if she wanted to go out with them. He thought that was strange. If she was with him, she shouldn't be going out with anyone except him.*

Question: *By "going out with," you don't mean sleeping with, do you?*

Answer: *No, but Jake was worried about that. That having some drinks would lead to something more. I think it was more that he didn't trust other men, not that he didn't trust her.*

Question: *Oh, really? That's interesting. Okay, so your friend sometimes got upset if his woman wanted to go out and have drinks with male friends. Did he forbid her to do so?*

Answer: *Not that I'm aware of, but I didn't know about their private conversations.*

Question: *Right, right. Like what went on behind closed doors?*

Answer: *Well, yeah.*

Question: *Did Jake drink heavily after college?*

Answer: *Yes.*

Question: *Do you recall any occasions when Jake fought with Natasha publicly, or humiliated her in any way, while he was intoxicated?*

Answer: *Yes, that happened a few times.*

Question: *A few times? More than 5 and less than 30?*

Answer: *Um, something like that, probably, yeah. Yes.*

Question: *All right, thank you. Now, you explained to Ms. Solnik, just moments ago, how Jake loved Natasha, or Natalie as you both called her—in a delicate way. You told us that he wanted to protect her, right?*

Answer: *That's right.*

Question: *I'm having trouble with that, Mr. Caymen, to be completely honest with you, because your friend Jake violently abused the woman in his life, the woman who is no longer alive, on many, many occasions, correct?*

Answer: *I don't know how many times, but he did have a problem with violence.*

Question: *We're in agreement on that one, Mr. Caymen. What was he trying to protect her from?*

Answer: *Oh, I don't know if there was anything specific he thought would happen to her, but he was always very concerned about her. He wanted to make sure she was safe.*

Question: *Did you ever hear him threaten her life?*

Answer: *When he was angry ...*

Question: *Yes or no is fine, sir.*

Answer: *Yes.*

Question: *More than once?*

Answer: *Yes.*

Question: *All right. Now I'd like to ask you about something else that you discussed with Ms. Solnik. You told her that you know Jake did not kill Natasha and that you wouldn't lie about that out of loyalty. Do you remember that question?*

Answer: *Yes.*

Question: *Well, this is very confusing to me also, Mr. Caymen. Did the threats and the violence and the paranoia about other men, ever lead you to worry that your friend was capable of murder?*

Answer: *No.*

Question: *Did that concern ever cross your mind?*

Answer: *Not really sir, no.*

Question: *Can you explain to me why this jury should believe that A) you are absolutely certain of your close friend's innocence, despite your knowledge of his violent behavior, and B) you wouldn't lie for him?*

Answer: *I really don't know how to explain it any better than saying that I know Jake very well and I know that his feelings for Natasha would never let him take her life. He needed her.*

I could tell that John wanted to comment on that answer, but he restrained himself and went on to ask about specific violent episodes that John Caymen had either witnessed or heard about from the defendant, pushing him to reveal the ugliest details of the violence. There was a change in Whitten's tone, when he got to this part of the questioning. Earlier, he had acted bored, as if he was just going through the motions. He glanced at his watch frequently and would lean against the table behind him and tap his fingers on it, during the longer answers. He reacted to each question with doubt, but also with a touch of apathy. He didn't believe Caymen was being truthful, but he wouldn't lose much sleep over it.

As the questions began to turn to the subject of violent fights, John became angry. He paused between questions, as if he needed to compose himself and calm down. He would loosen his tie, squint at the witness, and shake his head. He no longer doubted what the witness was saying and he was really disturbed by the subject matter. Whitten explained his feelings about John Caymen in his closing arguments, admitting that his reaction caught him off guard. He said the following:

I have tried to distance myself from the most emotionally-draining parts of this case and that has been difficult. On the afternoon that I questioned John Caymen, I became lost in anger and disbelief. It wasn't an act, it wasn't a plan. As I stood here listening to a man defend his abusive, misogynistic friend, I realized that he didn't see anything wrong with any of it. He didn't think it was wrong to abuse your wife, to kill her, and to lie about it. Jake Grazen is a liar, John Caymen is a liar, but you know what is sick about it? They have done it for so long that it's okay in their minds. It's okay because they're protecting themselves and they're surviving, and they're getting revenge against every woman who has ever done something to piss off her man.

They deserve it, Natasha certainly deserved it and all these two men have to do is take this one dirty little secret to their graves.

The defense chose Kristin Hillshaw, Natasha's older sister, as the witness to get aggressive with. Her time on the stand was extremely emotional. By that time, I knew how much Hadwick was willing to push, so I expected his cross-examination to be bad. I was astounded, nevertheless, by his complete lack of empathy.

Question: *Do you hate my client, Ms. Hillshaw?*

Answer: *No.*

Question: *You do not hate the person who you believe to have killed your younger sister, is what you are sitting before us saying.*

Objection by Annia Valdez, for the State: *Asked and answered, Your Honor.*

Judge Lange's response: *Sustained.*

Question: *Well you certainly haven't shown much affection for him with your testimony so far in this trial, which makes me wonder why you would perjure yourself now ...*

Objection by Annia Valdez, for the State: *He is badgering my witness, Your Honor.*

Judge Lange's response: *Sustained. Let's try something new, Mr. Hadwick.*

Question: *Okay, I'll assume you're telling the truth for a minute and ask you this. You do not hate my client. Why?*

Answer: *Because I have an excellent therapist and I've learned how to understand my anger about everything that has happened. I used to hate him.*

Question: *Okay, your anger "about everything that has happened." What, specifically, has happened that has made you angry?*

Answer: *Specifically, he violently and repeatedly hurt my sister, and it is my opinion that he killed her.*

Question: *You think he killed her, you loved her— I'm assuming, yet you do not hate him?*

Interjection by Judge Lange: *Mr. Hadwick, five minutes ago I ruled that this question was asked and answered. It wasn't open for interpretation. Why are you still asking it?*

Response from Samuel Hadwick, for the Defense: *I'm sorry, Your Honor. Can she just explain her answer?*

Response from Judge Lange: *Only if it ends here. If not, you are done with your cross.*

Question: *Thank you, Your Honor. Ms. Hillshaw, can you answer please?*

Answer: *I sure can. Your assumption that I loved my sister is correct and that is exactly why I have worked so hard to let go of my rage towards Jake. She loved him for years and she would want me to let go of any destructive feelings for another person.*

Question: *Rage? Wow. Okay, thank you for clearing that up for me. Do you have a problem with alcohol, Ms. Hillshaw?*

Objection by Annia Valdez for the State: *Relevancy?*

Response from Judge Lange: *Excellent question, Mr. Hadwick. I'm all ears.*

Response from Samuel Hadwick, for the Defense: *Witness' capacity for judgment, Your Honor.*

Response from Judge Lange: *I'll allow it.*

Question: *Do you need me to repeat my question, Ms. Hillshaw?*

Answer: *No thank you, I remember the question. I drank for about a month and a half after my sister's murder, but I do not drink now.*

Question: *Ever?*

Answer: *Never.*

Question: *Have you ever abused drugs?*

Answer: *Yes, I was addicted to sleeping pills, during the same time period I was drinking.*

Question: *Have you ever tried to commit suicide?*

Objection by John Whitten, for the State: *Objection, relevancy.*

Response from Judge Lange: *Mr. Hadwick?*

Response from Samuel Hadwick, for the defense: *Establishing family traits, Your Honor.*

Response from Judge Lange: *Sustained.*

Question: *Was your sister suicidal?*

Answer: *I think she struggled with it, but I think that ultimately, she didn't want to die.*

Question: *And what proof do you have of that?*

Answer: *As much as anyone could know, I would say. She confided in me, and told me what she was feeling.*

Question: *So, you have her descriptions of what she was feeling.*

Answer: *Correct.*

Question: *This morning you went into great detail, with Ms. Valdez, about my client's mistakes. He hurt your sister. He drank a lot. You didn't like* *him. Is it fair for you to blame Jacob Grazen for every problem your sister had in her life?*

Answer: *I don't think that would be fair, no. I have never said I blame him for ...*

Question: *You believe he was the cause for her misery, do you not?*

Answer: *He was the cause of the violence, which made her miserable, so ...*

Question: *So, why wouldn't that be a "yes," am I missing something here?*

Objection by Annia Valdez, for the State: *Your Honor, is this sarcasm necessary? I think we're flirting with badgering here.*

Response from Judge Lange: *I agree, Mr. Hadwick. You are dangerously close.*

Question: *Your Honor, I apologize. Withdrawn. Was Jake's drinking the main cause of their fights?*

Answer: *I personally don't believe so, but I'm not a psychologist or expert on alcoholism.*

Question: *That's a very good point. Did his drinking bother your sister?*

Answer: *Yes.*

Question: *Did your sister drink?*

Answer: *Sometimes.*

Question: *Is that a yes?*

Answer: *Yes, sometimes she drank.*

Question: *Did my client's drinking bother you?*

Answer: *Yes.*

Question: *And you drank, as we've already discussed. I wonder, do you truthfully think it's fair of you to make any type of judgments about someone who did things that you yourself have done?*

Answer: *I don't think my judgments of ...*

Question: *Yes or no?*

Answer: *Yes.*

Question: *You think that's fair? Hypocrisy is fair, in other words?*

Answer: *I have never been violent towards ...*

Question: *That's not a yes or no answer, Ms. Hillshaw. But let's not waste any more time. I have no further questions.*

Sam Hadwick didn't have a legitimate point, so the questions were just attempts to make the witness look bad. He skated from one obscure point to the next, inserting sarcasm and biting comments along the way. A comparison between Kristin's drinking and Jake's didn't make a bit of sense and I have no idea what he was getting at with the obsession of whether or not she hated Jake. I think he was trying to distract the jury with multiple topics, so they wouldn't notice that the cross-examination had no relevancy to his case.

Annia Valdez's work in this trial gained a lot of attention. She was very effective in her arguments about domestic violence and in her descriptions of Natasha Hillshaw's situation, because she was straightforward, specific, and graphic. She uses simpler syntax than John Whitten, and gives unique examples to keep the jury's attention. She was harsh in her descriptions of the defendant and never backed down from that, but she didn't go for overkill either. This was also true for her cross-exams. She was blunter than Whitten was, opting for confrontational, aggressive tactics over subtlety. Her low, throaty voice and no-nonsense attitude fit her style of argument.

Annia's closing argument was strong because it was direct. She was easy to follow, as she explained her points without pushing them. I've included the beginning part of her statement.

(With a reflective, pondering demeanor, she slowly walks parallel to the jury box, pivots, and looks at Jake. She holds her eyes on him for a few seconds—despite the fact that he does not look up at her, then turns to the jury and begins.)

You know how much work you have in front of you, so I'm not going to belabor that point. I don't think any lawyer in this courtroom should stand here and tell you how to process everything you've heard. We don't have that right because we don't have any kind of authority over your choices. You have a job to do, just like the rest of us.

If I were granted one request, I would choose the following one: Please, please try as hard as you can, not to think about the way people will feel about each possible verdict. You will not bring back a fair decision if you decide the case based on pity for either the defendant or the victim's family.

And that's all we're asking from you: a fair decision.

Did Jacob Grazen murder Natasha Hillshaw? You can easily find the answer to that question, by answering several smaller questions. Was he at the murder scene the day she was killed? What was his state of mind that day? Did he threaten the victim that day?

The answers to these questions are very clear and so is the necessary verdict. Yes, volatile, yes, and guilty.

The defense, during their closing argument, will surely reiterate the point they've made repeatedly during their presentations: the relationship between Jacob Grazen and Natasha Hillshaw is irrelevant to the question you're here to decide. In other words, years of violence and manipulation are not important factors in this case. We shouldn't consider these things at all. Why? Why would the defense make such a point? Because they want to bury the seriousness of the violence and its ultimate repercussions. They have been very careful in the way they've dug the hole, but they did dig it and now they're ready for you to pile on the dirt. Mr. Hadwick told you that all his client wants to do now is tell the truth. The defendant himself told you the same thing. "I have nothing to hide," Mr. Grazen said to us all. But I assure you, ladies and gentleman, there is very little that he would not like to hide from you.

The defense doesn't want you to remember the evidence about his violence and "leave the past in the past" has been one of their favorite quotes. You need to decide whether or not the violence is important. Is it an important part of who Grazen was, at the time his ex-wife was killed? Did the years of violence create a life-threatening situation that followed the victim after the divorce? Did Mr. Grazen's limited amount of therapy allow him to release the rage he had during the entire course of their relationship, in time to stop short of killing her when she left him?

You've heard domestic violence experts explain the statistics of murder victims who were in violent relationships. They have told you why men like Jake cannot let go of the women they dominated and controlled for years. You have heard witnesses to his violence and manipulation. They have described the immense anger he had towards the woman he had a life with, the woman who is no longer alive. Mr. Grazen himself described that anger. This is all the information you need, folks. You do not need persuasions. You do not need emotional blackmail. You have the truth before you. Thank you.

Annia had an interesting approach. She asked questions instead of stating her opinion. She led the jury to each of her points that way. She took herself out of the equation, which is a principle most attorneys should apply. The case is not about them, it's about the evidence. The arguments can be egocentric when attorneys lose sight of that.

I attended the sentencing hearing also. The atmosphere was completely different. The verdict had been delivered, and the focus was only on what the punishment should be. I think a lot of people were still in shock over the conviction, and they had to transition into listening to arguments for and against the death penalty. It was tense and emotional.

It can be difficult for defense attorneys to smoothly switch from arguing their client's innocence to arguing for leniency in sentencing. Once the verdict is reached, it's the official decision and attorneys can't dispute it. However, they don't want to admit their client's guilt, contradicting what they said during the trial, as that would hurt their credibility with the jury. So, the defense team couldn't say, "Well, as we've said all along, Mr. Grazen didn't commit murder, so he shouldn't receive any punishment, let alone the death penalty." Nor could they appear to be abandoning their belief in his innocence.

I think they were pretty successful at treating these issues delicately. They focused on the cruelty of the death penalty, without putting too much emphasis on why Jake shouldn't receive it. It was more of a "this is too horrifying for anyone" message than "our client doesn't deserve it." They used some risky tactics, such as implying that Natasha wouldn't want him to die and saying that ending Jake's life wouldn't offer long-lasting satisfaction for anyone who wants to see him suffer, but they kept those points short and asked the jury to make the most humane decision possible.

The defense only had one witness at the sentencing hearing and that was one of Jake's current therapists. Her name is Margaret Weston and she specializes in therapy for inmates. (She did not testify at his trial.) Adam Cole questioned her about Jake's current treatment program and his progress. The defense wanted to point out that life in prison would provide effective rehabilitation. In one sense, that was kind of an odd point because a life term would be without parole, but I think it was more appropriate than bringing in Jake's close friends as character witnesses.

The prosecution didn't present any additional evidence in the sentencing hearing. They offered testimonies from Natasha's family and briefly explained why they were asking for the death penalty.

Kristin Hillshaw spoke first.

As I thought about what I wanted to say to you all today, I realized the dilemma I'm facing. I want you to understand what I'm feeling, but I don't want your pity. I want you to make the fairest decision possible and that won't happen if you're consumed by feeling sorry for me. And sometimes I feel that my grief is all I have left now—the only thing that's my own, so I don't want to give any of that up or share it with anyone else. However, I've decided that I can't ask for your help, if I don't let you in, so that's what I'm going to try to do today because I truly need your help.

My pain is sharp and permeating. I would not wish it on anyone else. I honestly hope that none of you here have experienced a loss like this or will experience it in the future. But I have to ask you a favor. I have to ask you to think of one of the people you love the most in this world and then imagine yourself going home today and finding out that you can never see that person again. Never. The last time you saw them is truly the last. The last words you said to them, the last meal you shared, the last outfit you saw them wearing—that's it, that's what you are left with as the final good-bye and the final memory. You don't get a warning and you can form as many questions in your head as you want, but you'll never get the answers.

This is of course what I am living with. It's real for me and I can't tell you how badly I wish that I was one of you, sitting in your chair and trying to imagine my little sister being taken away, only to realize that's all I was doing—imagining it. I would feel a lump in my throat, as I would think to myself, "Oh God, that's terrible." I would go see Nate, give her a huge, tight hug, tell her how much I love her, and pray to God immediately to thank Him for not taking her out of my life. More than anything, I wish that was my reality.

I need you to see this whole terrible, painful situation from my standpoint, so that you can figure out what would help me the most. What would help me go on? I'm so glad that it's your job instead of mine because I'm not strong enough to do it. I don't know what should happen to Jake.

I am very confused. I look over at Jake ... um. I look at him, and I ... excuse me. I look at Jake, and I don't know what to think or feel. Everything just surges into my brain and into my heart all at once. This is the man my sister loved, the man she laughed with and cried with, the man who hurt her and made her fear for her life every day, and the man who killed her. Should I hate him? Should I feel sorry for him? Should I pray for his soul? I'm angry, sad, scared— everything.

I look at his hands and imagine my sister's skin under them. I look at his mouth and I can see her face in front of it. I imagine her body being in the space directly beside and under and around him, as he kissed her, yelled at her, slapped her, told her he loved her, punched her, made love to her, and murdered her. He did all of those things and we know it. We all know it, Jake!

There's another reason I'm glad I don't have your responsibility-- you have to think about what Jake did. You cannot decide the appropriate punishment without thinking about him and his crime. Of course, I think about what he did all the time, but I wouldn't be able to measure its worth and then place a value on my sister's life. Maybe I'm wrong, but that's how I see this process. Exactly how bad an act was it? What's the price for this loss?

As Natasha's older sister, I always thought I could protect her and teach her. I learned how to just arm myself with this confidence that I would always give her the right answers and guide her. That confidence began to fade when Jake became abusive. And now it's gone. So, I don't have the right answers anymore. I didn't know how to help Nate by saving her life and I don't know how to help her now. Please help me figure it out.

Thank you.

Kristin spoke slowly and softly when she was speaking about the jury's role. Her voice was shaky throughout the statement, but she became very upset when she was talking about Jake. When she addressed him directly, she lost her composure and cried loudly for several minutes.

Jake turned his head towards Kristin when she first said his name, but looked straight ahead or down at his lap for the rest of time she spoke. He was crying during parts of it, covering his face with one hand.

Natasha's mother's name is Elizabeth Sands-Hillshaw. She prepared a statement, which Annia Valdez read for her.

A lot of things in my life have changed since September 19th, 1997. Some are probably temporary changes and some will definitely continue to exist for the rest of my life. I will only mention a few examples. I hate the man who killed my daughter and I can't even think about forgiving him, I can't bear to be around my friends who have children, and I long for my daughter Natasha every single moment of every single day. The first two things may be different over time. The last one will not.

My other daughter spoke to you about Jake. She told you that she doesn't know what to feel about him. I do not have that problem. I have never felt as much anger for someone as I do for him. If I looked at Jake's hands right now, I wouldn't picture Natasha smiling or embracing him. I would see her struggling with him and begging to live. Then I would see the limp, lifeless body that I actually saw right before midnight on September 19th, when I had to identify her body.

Jake Grazen has, or had, a lot of problems--depending on whether you believe he is now cured. I personally don't care about that because I don't view his violence and his murder, or his "mistakes," as he calls them, as part of the growing process. What is he growing into if those are stepping stones? Regardless, he has been through a lot of terrible, terrible things and I do sympathize with him for that. He and I have something in common.

He had a mother and siblings who he loved very much. Then he lost them. He will never get them back, just as I will never get Natasha back, and I completely understand his pain and confusion about that. Why did such a terrible tragedy happen? Why did he lose so much?

Of course, there is an important difference between our losses. For me, the question "why did this happen?" is not applicable in the same way that it is for him. Natasha's death was not accidental. It happened because Jake made it happen.

For me, Jake's violence cannot be softened by anything that happened to him. My daughter's pain wasn't a justifiable retaliation for his past abuse. Her death is not the price tag for his losses or struggles. I do not accept that.

Part of me is tempted to end my statement here, without revealing my opinion of the correct sentence. Sometimes that seems like the easy way out because I could escape judgment from others and avoid facing my true feelings about this. The down side, of not advocating for my daughter in the way I need to, is worse though.

I've prayed about this decision every day and God has given me the answer. I do not believe that Jacob Grazen should die for killing my daughter. His death would not make anything better, easier, or just. I respect the prosecution's decision and understand their legal obligation to ask for the death penalty, but I can't agree with it.

I believe that life imprisonment is the appropriate punishment and I think that intensive therapy should be a required part of his incarceration. Thank you for listening.

Annia Valdez gave a very brief request for the death penalty.

In Arizona's criminal law statutes, the death penalty has been established for the most serious crimes. First degree murder is such a crime. If the state did not ask for this penalty, we would be treating the murder of Natasha Hillshaw as an exception to this very clear legal standard. I can't think of a reason that justifies such an exception. Is this crime a less severe case because the defendant killed his ex-wife instead of a cop or a government official? Of course it isn't.

This is not about judging Mr. Grazen's life as deserving of death. It's not about the morality of the death penalty and it's not even about what Natasha Hillshaw would want or what her family wants.

This is simply about following the law.
Thank you.

It's rare to hear such a short sentencing request from a prosecutor. They usually stress the feelings of the victim's family and reiterate the details of the crime. I think her choice made sense and I probably would have done the same thing in her situation. If the state law wasn't as clear-cut on the death penalty, it would have been a different story, but this gave her the chance to present it as the only choice the jury had, if they wanted to follow the law. It was also effective to let the victim impact statements stand on their own, without commenting on them. I think that choice helped highlight the emotions.

I didn't focus on post-trial reactions from the attorneys, in my columns or TV appearances, but I saw some of the coverage on it. Nothing too surprising. Each attorney seemed exhausted and not interested in spending much time with the media. There were press conferences for both sides, the night the verdict was announced and then no comments for about a week. John Whitten has appeared on a few programs and Annia Valdez has said that she may give some interviews at some point, but needs a little break from the trial. Adam Cole and Mary Solnik have given several print interviews.

So far, Samuel Hadwick has been pretty thrifty with his interviews. He is devastated by the events of this case. He was very soft-spoken and withdrawn at the press conference, leaving early after becoming visibly upset. He has explained that re-hashing the details of the case makes it difficult for him to just accept the verdict and move on. I ran into him during a radio call-in show for my network and he told me that it's been the most difficult loss of his career. He said, "I cannot even think about getting through another trial until I face my turmoil on this."

The jurors who have spoken out about the case, generally have positive things to say about the lawyers' performances. They talk about how they were rarely bored, how impressed they were with the attorneys' skill level, and say that the arguments were easy to follow. Sometimes it feels like you're listening to a review of a new movie, which is disturbing, but that's the reality of high-profile cases. People do become fascinated and get caught up in the hype.

The jurors' collective reason for the verdict is "the amount of evidence." One juror expressed disappointment in the witnesses, saying it was difficult to establish credibility. Several jurors felt the lawyers contradicted each other, so they were confused about who to believe. They said this made it difficult for them to define reasonable doubt and determine which witnesses were reliable. I find these comments really unsettling. I think their focus was in the wrong place. It's one thing to interpret a piece of evidence in the same way as a particular lawyer, if they considered all the evidence and happened to draw conclusions that matched the argument, but their post-trial comments make it sound like they went into the jury room and said, "Ok, who's right?"

Most jurors seemed eager to speak out and several are considering book and movie deals. The death penalty decision is the one subject that seems to stifle their enthusiasm. The comments have been that it's something they can't control. They try to act comfortable with their decision, but it's clearly not how they feel. They are upset about it.

I had to take a vacation as soon as I finished my work on this case. I rode the same emotional roller coaster as everyone else involved and I needed some down time. I am glad to have been a part of this case. I learned a lot, as I always do, from the people involved in the trial—especially the attorneys and Natasha's family. These people are in my thoughts, and I deeply admire and respect their strength, as they struggle to heal.

Mitchell Garrison

Mitchell Garrison was a defense witness in this trial. He is an attorney in Phoenix, at the same firm where Jacob Grazen worked. He specializes in tax law.

April 10, 1998

When I agreed to take part in this project, it was under the condition that I could explain myself in my own way. A disclaimer would be a good lawyerly term to use here. I am not a particularly good writer, when it comes to this type of thing. Technical reports and proposals are my forte, while addressing such a personal, complicated topic as this, is not. The only way I can really do it, is in my own simple, straightforward style. The same way I speak.

I'm not going to ask anyone to believe that Jake Grazen is innocent as a favor to me and I don't want people to think I'm just saying, "Hey, I worked with him, he's a nice guy and I'm sure he didn't kill his ex-wife." I spend enough time at work trying to persuade people to think about something in the same way that I do, so I'm not going to do that here. I just want to take the opportunity to explain what I know about Jake.

Night after night on the news, we see clips of Jake Grazen. We've seen him put his head between his knees when the verdict was read at his trial and we've seen his look of terror after the sentencing verdict was read. To me, this isn't an act for the camera. I know him and I can see his pain.

Jake is someone I worked with, confided in, and socialized with, and I truly feel for him. A grave error has been made. I don't understand those who have hailed it as a revolutionary decision. My friend is paying the price of a terribly misguided attempt at justice.

I have known Jake for about 7 years, but I only really got to know him during the past 2 and a half years. We both attended ASU College of Law at Tempe. In fact, we shared the same concentration, so had the same classes, but there was virtually no socializing at that time. It was a rigorous program in a competitive field and neither of us did anything besides study. It wasn't until we wound up working at the same firm that we became good friends. He had an internship with the firm, then started working here full-time when he graduated. I joined about a year and a half later, after working at a friend's practice in San Antonio. The work was slightly confusing to me, because I had straddled the border between civil and criminal law for a while. Jake helped me get acquainted with the details of the job, and introduced me to everyone, so the transition was easier.

My impression of Jake in law school was slightly negative, at least in comparison to the way I feel about him now. I'm not revealing any secrets here—Jake knows all about this. I thought he was cold, conceited, and introverted. I had heard that he was extremely outgoing as an undergrad, so I didn't know if that lifestyle had bored him, or if "outgoing" was synonymous for gaining a reputation you wanted to lose. I tried to limit my judgments and take the atmosphere of law school into account. The pressure can turn anyone from Prince Charming to a cold fish. Socialization is not a priority and neither is a friendly image. The constant, intense competition can result in arrogance. You learn to act like you know everything and have every confidence in the world, covering up your insecurities with bravado.

I didn't give much weight to those initial impressions of Jake and when we met again at the firm, he contradicted them instantly, with a warm demeanor and terrific sense of humor. I got along with him really well from the beginning, as did our other colleagues.

Jake's high-profile status always seemed strange to me. This guy I worked with, a friend, was a celebrity. It didn't seem to fit and I would forget that he was a model.

For a while, I didn't know how significant it was because I never saw that part of his life.

As we got closer, I saw the pressure he felt. I learned about things like image, impressing people, schmoozing, looking good. I think it conflicted with his position at the firm, because he was a little embarrassed. We teased him occasionally, when he had photos in a magazine or something, but everyone respected him.

Jake would tell me about his general life plan, during lunches or drinks after work. It was pretty straightforward: He wanted to live an affluent lifestyle with Natalie. He hadn't been excited about marriage and kids until he met her, so his definition of success changed.

I saw Jake's struggles from 2 angles. He was my friend and I could see that he was hurting, and he was my co-worker, trying to survive professionally. When the stories of violence came out, he found himself in devastating, humiliating circumstances. I wanted him to get help and save his marriage, and I didn't want to watch him lose his career. He started taking time off "to straighten things out," but I didn't think that was going far enough.

The assault arrest was obviously public knowledge and he didn't know how to handle it. It was the turning point where his private life was completely exposed and his shame crushed him. He was a criminal. How could clients and co-workers, let alone his friends, respect and trust him? He couldn't just come up with an explanation to make it go away.

I was probably less sympathetic than I should have been. I hated to see Jake go through such a rough time, but I didn't see it as something that *happened* to him undeservedly. Natalie was the victim of turmoil, which Jake *caused*. Taking a casual, mild stance or not wanting to offend Jake weren't thoughts I considered. Once I knew what had really been going on with him, it seemed like everything that came out of his mouth was an excuse.

I did try to be understanding at first, in the sense of not judging him and being unconditionally supportive. That wasn't possible though, because I couldn't make exceptions in my values. If it's not okay for me to hurt my family, how can I listen to excuses of why it's okay for Jake to be abusive? I *have* to judge his behavior as wrong.

I wanted him to take responsibility for his abuse. I expected that from him because he'd had a strong character up until that point. So, when he began creating excuse after excuse for his behavior, I was really disgusted with him. He tried to soften up the brutality of his violence with elaborate theories about not having control of his life. He talked about his fear of failure, his desire to be perfect, and his confusion about Natalie's needs, as if these were acceptable catalysts for violence. I told him, "She *needs* to be safe and you *need* to stop making excuses and get help." He didn't like that.

He couldn't believe I'd betrayed him, I was the last person he'd ever expected to judge him, and he was completely offended by the suggestion of therapy. I saw his reaction as melodramatic and annoying. One night we had dinner and my parting line was, "I am not betraying you Jake, I am trying to be your friend by telling you the truth. It's not Natalie's fault, my fault, or the system's fault that you are abusive."

Jake was in and out of therapy and he would inform me each time he went, implying that I needed to back off. It was a game. Sometimes he would apologize for his previous hostility (many incidents of that), saying he had the clarity of seeing "the error in his ways," since he was in therapy. He always had a hint of sarcasm in his voice.

When Jake was arrested for murder, I had to answer some tough questions. Of course you don't want to believe that a friend could commit such an act, but lying to yourself will not help matters. Jake was a batterer, he had threatened to kill Natalie before, and there were times when I was afraid that he would kill her. He was capable of it, so if I hadn't considered the evidence, I would have thought that he probably killed her. However, I had to examine the details of the night she died.

I was not with Jake and Natalie when she died, but I do believe his account of events, because it fits with what I do know. At about 4:30 that day, Jake got a call from her, which I took initially. He was in a meeting with a client in the conference room and I was in his office looking for a file, so I picked up his phone to take a message. Natalie was crying and she sounded intoxicated, slurring her words. I called him out of the meeting and he talked to her briefly. When he hung up, he told me he was going to meet her at his house after he finished up with his client. He left the office a few minutes after 5:00.

When I pulled into my driveway that night, my wife was running to my car with the cordless phone. Jake was crying and screaming. I couldn't understand anything he was saying, so I handed the phone back to Shelley and drove to his house.

His yard was filled with police cars and the garage was blocked off. I knew it was a crime scene and that

Natalie was dead. My stomach dropped as I watched Jake talk to a detective. He was trying to cooperate, but he kept losing control. When he saw that I was there, he got even more upset. He looked terrified, as he said, "Oh my God, Mitchell. She's dead. Oh my God, what am I going to do?" Of course, I had no answer for him.

As I watched him fall apart, I thought of how he and Natalie's lives had spiraled down over the past several months. Violence, alcohol abuse, depression, and finally, tragedy. Maybe I was naïve, but I was truly unprepared for it. I thought that eventually Jake would stay in therapy, Natalie would get help for her depression, and they would learn how to have a healthy friendship.

Hindsight shows me the clues about how severe Natalie's depression was. She called me the Monday before she died, saying she needed to talk. She felt like the reconciliation wasn't going well, she felt guilty for initiating it, and she was really confused. She was drinking heavily again and taking a lot of anti-depressants, but felt like nothing was working. I listened and tried to gently voice my concerns, but she ended the conversation abruptly.

The prosecuting attorneys in this case essentially asked the jury to throw out my testimony. When they cross-examined me, they stressed the fact that I cannot say, with 100% certainty, that Natalie committed suicide. I personally think it was a little far-fetched, since this was true for every other witness. No one was claiming to have witnessed her death (other than Jake of course).

Those who believe Jake is guilty, say that the evidence is clear. This isn't true unless you don't consider the explanation for it. Jake's gun had both his and Natalie's fresh prints on it because he tried to get it away from her. Her blood was on his hands because he held her after she died. There is no supporting evidence that Jake shot her in the mouth to make it look like suicide.

As for domestic violence being an irrelevant issue in this case, I disagree with that statement. It's a part of their history and explains elements of Natalie's depression. However, the existence of violence isn't proof of murder. The jury came up with a verdict that fits the best with public opinion. They now have the support of domestic violence shelters, but they slaughtered the principles of justice to get it.

To Natalie's family, I would like to express my deepest sympathy and sorrow. I do not mean to offend them with my opinion of her death. I do not dispute or minimize any of the pain she went through with Jake, but I have to honestly share my reasons for believing she took her own life.

To Jake, I don't know where to begin. How will I say goodbye to him? How will I continue practicing law in a system that allows something like this to happen?

Melissa Foster

Melissa Foster recently graduated from the University of Arizona College of Law and is working for a private law firm in Phoenix. During the Grazen trial, she was a law student intern, working for the defense team.

May 3, 1998

Working on the Grazen case was an honor. It was frightening, difficult, and devastating. But I was there to learn and I am grateful for the amazing education I walked away with.

I became involved with the case by luck and coincidence. Two weeks before the tragedy, my internship advisor placed me in Adam Cole's office. I was supposed to analyze the research techniques they used, by studying how evidence collection fits in with courtroom strategies. He planned on involving me in a few current cases, but it would mostly be organizing files and sitting in on trials.

Then they got Jake Grazen's case. Adam asked me to shift all my attention to that, which delighted me. I didn't want my internship to be so boring that I would dread becoming an attorney. He speaks rapidly and sounds nervous, but it's just his tone. He told me, "There's plenty of work on this, we just need you to be flexible and ready to fill in anywhere."

The publicity of the case was daunting and when I found out I had known the victim, I was even more

320

overwhelmed. We were in a summer term Psychology class together, a couple of years prior. I skipped more than Natalie did, but I remember seeing her with Jake, as he picked her up from class occasionally. It was a short class, I only spoke with her a few times, and I didn't see her after that time, but it was still a strange feeling to know that our client was accused of killing her.

Despite that, I didn't ever question whether or not I wanted to be involved with this case. I did. In law school, everything is a competition and you have to snatch up opportunities before someone else does and appreciate every experience. My advisor was concerned about the impact of a high-profile murder case on me, so he teamed up with Adam and Sam to talk to me about what was ahead.

I listened to their warnings, but didn't want to show any signs of anxiety. Here were these 3 men who were entrusting me with crucial work. Cole and Hadwick had long held the reputation of excellent attorneys who rarely lose. I didn't want them to regret their choice.

Adam described how I would be directly associated with the defendant. The victim's family and friends would see me as a predator. Jake's name would become synonymous with battering, he explained, and I would appear to approve of it. We talked about how my own feelings towards Jake would confuse and haunt me as I got to know him. Sam told me, "You won't be able to decide whether you want to like him or keep your distance."

All these points turned out to ring true. I received long, cold stares in the courtroom and heard a rainbow of accusatory comments and obscenities everywhere else. I was on the unpopular side of the case. As for my relationship with Jake, I wrestled with anxiety for a long time. I didn't want to be superficially friendly to him, but I didn't want to show him my discomfort either.

I had nightmares about the 11th hour confession. I don't know what I would have done if Jake had pulled me aside one day and said, "By the way, I did it." And I was green enough to worry about that. Adam called it the guilt issue and advised me, "Just deal with your feelings directly, then focus on giving your client a fair, adequate, and thorough defense." He predicted, "Your head will be saturated with this question for your first few years as a defense attorney, then your devotion to defending your clients' rights will block it out."

Sam talked to me about this too. He reminded me that I am not exempt from the presumption of innocence rule. "You can't ask a jury and judge to adhere to it and ignore it yourself. If you make guesses about your client's guilt, you're treating him with prejudice."

In the Grazen case, I started out with witness screening and sorting. The lead attorneys gave me outlines and I would compile lists of potential witnesses. I would then contact the ones they approved of, to set up interviews. I attended most interviews, with an attorney and made the follow-up calls with witnesses we decided to use. We also had to look at the prosecution's witness list, to predict the direction they would take. That shaped our decisions about witnesses, especially with expert testimony.

Our intent was not to portray Jake positively and Natalie negatively. It wasn't a contest of character, but we had to examine the details of their relationship in order to disprove the prosecution's theory of natural progression from violence to murder. We had to discuss the gaps in their relationship and Natalie's depression.

A few reporters have written that we couldn't make up our mind about how to present Jake's personality. Annia Valdez agreed with this, adding that we confused the jury with invalid theories. I don't agree with either criticism. We presented Jake's personality honestly and it's up to the jury to decide which arguments are valid.

Despite the warnings, I didn't realize exactly how much defense attorneys are despised, until I experienced the cold shoulders and rude treatment firsthand. I was the enemy. At the least, I was working for a batterer and at the most, I was working for a murderer. I tried the "comes with the territory"/ "just my job" type of mantra, but I cared too much about the work to become apathetic. And I cared about the reactions, but it's something I just had to deal with. I can't pick the parts of my work that I'm proud of to take credit for and deny responsibility for the difficult parts.

It wasn't personal. Some of the animosity was just shoved onto anyone connected with the case. Our jobs were deemed evil and we became the all-purpose venting source. Some people were pissed off because their soap operas were interrupted. Others started out with a mild interest in the trial and got sick of it.

I wanted to tiptoe around the toughest issues in this case, by feeding myself the "it's just a job" mantra and by keeping my distance from Jake. This resulted in anger and resentment. I didn't want to get close to him, I didn't want to hear his side of the story, and I sure as Hell didn't want to feel sorry for him.

The most helpful thing Adam Cole did for me, was introduce me to his wife, Patricia Sangria. She's a criminal psychiatrist who works with various criminal lawyers. I got that "everything's going to be okay" feeling when she walked into the room. She was an advisor to the Grazen case and provided me with countless hours of encouragement, support, and fresh perspective, not to mention a much-needed dose of estrogen in my work environment.

I worked on the case for several months before talking with Jake extensively. I was nervous and oddly curious. His entire life had been exposed to the nation and he was treated like a serial killer and a movie star simultaneously. Protesters threw objects at him as he walked out of the courthouse and women sent letters to him at the jail, professing their love and telling him they didn't care whether he killed his wife or not.

I expected him to be either cocky and charming or depressed. He was calm and forthright instead. He wasn't walking on egg shells or kissing everyone's ass. He asserted himself, but was always polite.

Jake is very honest about everything. He doesn't necessarily offer information about personal issues, but he will answer anything he's asked, without hesitating or trying to polish up his answers.

Patricia talked to me about distancing myself from Jake. She told me to use my professional boundaries as a rigid structure for every conversation. "It will feel cold at times, but it's the only thing to rescue you from the guilt of sympathizing with him. And if you reach out to him, you cannot reverse the damage. He's not your friend. He *does* need someone to listen to him and support him, but that's what therapy is for."

Every member of the defense team took a few days off after the sentencing hearing. Sam, Adam, and Patricia all called me every couple of days to make sure I was okay. I didn't take any phone calls for about a week solid because I was a miserable person to be around. I had to promise my boyfriend that I would never behave that way again! I was emotionally tested during the trial, then the conviction and death penalty verdict were devastating blows. I failed and couldn't just brush it off as a professional loss.

I've spent a lot of time thinking about Natalie's suicide. She was so desolate that she couldn't bear another day. She decided to take her own life, knowing that she would leave many people behind who loved her deeply. I think about her family and how nothing in the world can make up for the loss of a child.

The jury fulfilled the prosecution's request to punish Jake for every time he abused Natalie. Then a second jury helped Annia Valdez follow through on her vow to "make sure that Arizona cracks down on domestic violence," by granting the death penalty. Killing a popular, respected man who abused his wife sent exactly the kind of message she wanted.

There is an automatic appeal for death sentences in Arizona and I'm in touch with the attorneys who are working on Jake's case. I was asked to participate, but I decided that it would be too much for me right now.

Author's Name Withheld
Former Victim of Domestic Violence

The following was originally written on August 3, 1995, and the names have been changed for confidentiality.

I was 23. I had a lot of friends, a good job, and a great family to support me in everything I did. I was happy, but I thought time was kind of running out on me. Ever since I was little, I knew I wanted a family. I wanted a big wedding, kids, and my marriage had to last forever. I'd been in several relationships, but nothing had worked out. I had faith that I would get what I wanted, but I was getting a little nervous about it.

So, when I actually met the man who I thought was "the one," it was like God reached down and tapped me on the shoulder. It wasn't love at first sight, but we got to know each other really well and I became spellbound. Here was this older man (he was 36 when we met), and I thought he was so smart and distinguished. He made me feel smart too, because he respected me and we could talk about anything.

When he showed a romantic interest in me, I felt so special. We dated for 7 months, got engaged, and got married 2 months later. My wedding day was everything I'd dreamed it would be. Everyone said things like, I was the happiest bride they'd ever seen and I was glowing.

Things were great for about a year and my head was in the clouds. We argued once in a while, but there was nothing physical and he didn't say any of the terrible things that he said later on. He usually treated me really well and I looked forward to every minute we spent together.

Ron called himself an "old-fashioned gentleman" because he wanted a wife at home and he felt strongly that working was his duty. He said he believed a man and his wife were equal and that we should divide things right down the middle. I would do all the household chores and he would handle the financial stuff and the house maintenance. He wanted to have the protective role and I would have the nurturing role. He made it sound so romantic.

When I got pregnant, the trouble started. My first pregnancy was rough and he didn't like it when I was lying in bed instead of fixing dinner and scrubbing floors. I was so tired though, so I didn't rush to please him. He started calling me lazy and worthless, which made me cry hysterically because my hormones were so wild. Then he began throwing things around the house, breaking stuff, like dishes my grandmother had given me. He chose to do things that would upset me the most. He wanted to punish me and teach me a lesson. He slapped me in the face a few times and pushed me, but it really didn't go beyond that until I had my daughter.

She cried a lot and it aggravated him. He would rage and the more I tried to calm him down, the worse he got. He would say how terrible a mother I was, because I couldn't make her stop crying. I didn't lose the weight fast enough for him, so he would tell me how fat and disgusting I looked. He wouldn't let me join a gym because it meant spending money and being outside of the house.

He didn't let me use a babysitter ever and he didn't want to share any child-raising duties, except for holding them once in a while. When they were old enough to do fun things, he would occasionally take them out. No diapers, feeding, or getting up in the night with them.

There were good periods, when he stopped hurting me for a while and said he really wanted to be a good father. I didn't want to raise any more children in a violent home, but he really wanted to have 3 for some reason and I had no chance at talking him out of it. (He didn't abuse the kids, but of course it wasn't healthy for them to see and hear him hurt me.) After our third child was born, the abuse was steady and brutal.

I took the kids and left a few times, but he always found us. He was a threat to my family and friends too, because he would terrorize anyone who took us in. I was putting my kids at risk by being with Ron and I have spent a lot of time hating myself for that. People have said that I should not have had children with a violent man, but when I look at my kids, it's impossible for me to feel that way.

Usually, when I think about what it was like to live that life, I feel sick to my stomach. I hated myself then and I hate the memories of it all now. However, I have grown by facing my past and getting consistent support to become a stronger version of the person I was back then.

What I can't seem to explain to people, is that I don't know "why." That's what everyone wants to know. Why did I stay? Why did I love him after he hurt me and my kids? I didn't sit down with a pro and con list and make rational decisions. I can't even say for sure that I *did* still love him after he started hurting me. I didn't have any money of my own, he always found us when we left and hurt me worse than the time before, so I never thought I was making the right choice. I didn't feel like there was one.

Counselors say that all the focus has to be on the abuser, when you're trying to fix a violent relationship. If you say the victim did something wrong to make him violent, you're making excuses for him. I agree with that, but if anyone had told me, "focus on Ron," during the worst parts of the violence, I wouldn't have wanted anything to do with that advice or the person giving it. Thinking about whose fault it was, would be like stopping in the middle of a house fire to ask how the fire got started. I didn't care.

Before I went through it, I never gave domestic violence a second thought and I probably wouldn't have even known what those words meant if someone said them to me. I didn't fear it, or plan what to do if it happened to me. When it did happen, I didn't think about Ron controlling me or being hateful to all women, or anything like that. I just felt that he hated me and wanted to hurt me.

I don't feel comfortable giving advice to a woman who is in a violent relationship. Support can be really helpful—I know that firsthand, but receiving advice is too close to being told what to do by your abuser. I don't feel like I'm a strong woman for getting through it and I don't feel lucky to have inside knowledge about being a battered woman. I do pray that victims can learn all their options and gain the strength to find a safe life.

In the battered women's support group that I'm in, we had to fill out a question sheet about how we wanted people to treat us. I guess it was an exercise to get us thinking about our needs. The only thing I wrote down was "respect." When Ron was hurting me, I couldn't respect myself. I obviously didn't get respect from him, so I didn't want to open up to anyone because I thought they'd just pity me and talk down to me. The therapists who really helped me were the ones who just listened to me, without trying to fit in suggestions. That made me feel like they accepted what I had been through, which was huge.

I don't feel that my life is forever scarred because I was a victim of domestic violence. It happened, it was terrifying, and I survived it. I don't know if my ex-husband will ever get help and I honestly don't care. I'm grateful that I found my way to safety and that my kids are no longer exposed to violence. Now I can focus on having a much better life.

Author's name withheld
Client, New Beginnings Center

New Beginnings Center is located in Phoenix and offers individual therapy, group sessions, and other programs for men who batter.

November 17, 1997

I can't speak for any other man. I can't say if Jake Grazen did or did not kill his ex-wife. It's not my business. However, I can talk about what it's like to hurt a woman you love. It's hard for me to remember the bad times, but if it helps anyone else, I want to do it.

I went through a lot of hard times when I was a kid. A lot of things happened to me that I didn't tell anyone about. I thought I was a bad person. (Adults told me I was worthless and I believed them.) There was always fighting in my house. My dad drank. He hurt my mom and she was very timid and quiet. She didn't seem to love us. I have 2 older brothers and my sister is 2 years younger than me. My mom left, then my dad did too.

My hardest times were after they left. I had to go to different foster homes. I ran away a lot and tried to live on the streets because the homes were not right. I saw couples fight and a lot of foster parents drank or did drugs. Sometimes they gave me beer and pot. I got beat up and adults forced sex on me. It happened a lot.

When I was 14, I got into a home that was safe. I got to see my brothers and my sister sometimes. I went to a school I liked and started fixing cars. The bad things were gone and I forgot everything.

I finished high school and moved out West. I drove with a friend and we got different jobs all over. (We'd land in a town for a while and work, then move on when we felt like it.) When I was in Reno I met a girl named Vanessa and we started dating. I worked at a garage and she was a waitress at a casino. We moved in together when she told me she was pregnant. I thought I was in love then. I was young, but I felt ready to settle down. When I got home from work one day, there was a note from her. It said she wasn't pregnant and she had to leave. All her things were gone and she'd taken some of my money and stuff with her too.

I was really sad and confused. I thought I must have done something wrong to make her leave, but I didn't know what. I tried to forget about her, but I couldn't really get over what happened. I felt like a loser and I was mad at Vanessa for making me feel that way. Then I was mad at other women. I thought they were all alike.

I moved to Vallejo, California to forget what happened in Reno. I got a job I didn't like and the money wasn't too good. I thought I was too good for it. I knew about cars and was good at my work. I had different owners and bosses all the time and most of them didn't know much about cars or running a business. They wanted to rip off their customers and under pay their help, so the customers were upset and rude to me.

I decided I could do better. I stayed there for a little while, but took on second and third jobs to save money for business school. For about a year after Vanessa left, I didn't want anything to do with women. I couldn't even stand to look at them when I went out to bars and places like that. I didn't go out very often because of that. I would have angry thoughts about the women I saw and if they tried talking to me, I would just leave.

When I finally dated another woman, it was around the time I had better luck with work too. Maybe I thought that was a good luck sign or something. I found a better job at another auto-body shop and met Kasey in one of my classes. She pursued me for about 2 months and I finally agreed to go out with her.

Everything seemed okay at first. We were together for about 6 months before the fights started. I hadn't told her about Vanessa or about all the stuff I went through as a kid. Whenever she asked me something personal, I was defensive. I thought she had some hidden reason for wanting to know about me, which made me angry and suspicious.

She was a secretary for an insurance company and I thought she was fooling around with her boss. Whenever he called her at the house, I got mad. When she had late meetings, I got mad. I even hated seeing her work papers or files around the house. I burned them. I thought she was using me until he left his wife or she found someone else.

After a while, I didn't let her use the phone at all. She didn't have any friends because of me. She lost her job because I wouldn't let her leave the house. Now I can see that I made her life impossible, but at the time I was just angry with her and felt like my reasons were always good.

I thought I was being nice to her when I took her out to dinner or bought her new clothes, but it was all for selfish reasons. I liked to show her off, but I got angry when men looked at her and took it out on her. I thought she was attracting attention on purpose and looking for someone better than me.

I loved Kasey most of the time and hated her just some of the time. Mainly I hated myself. I couldn't understand why Kasey would ever fall in love with someone like me. I'm not smart or good-looking and I can never erase all the bad stuff that's happened to me. Since I thought I was a bad person, I didn't see that hurting her was wrong. I actually thought it was something I was supposed to do.

All my feelings seemed jumbled up at the time. I wasn't able to sort them out and hitting her seemed like the simple way of solving things. It gave me the results I wanted. Later I saw how wrong it was, but at the time all I could see was that I made someone listen to me and do what I wanted. That made me feel like I was fixing everything. People had hurt me and I was getting revenge.

A lot of men talk about therapy like it's something they wanted to do. They're usually lying. You don't wake up one day and think, "hey, this is wrong." You don't think there's a problem and when anyone tells you there is, you push them away. You block out their words. Something big has to happen to get you in for help.

I got help because I got arrested for putting Kasey in the hospital. I wouldn't be telling the truth if I said I felt bad when I saw what I did to her. It was just one more time. I blamed her for making me do it and I was more angry than usual because I got arrested. People had found out about our business. I didn't like that and, in my mind, it was all her fault.

The arrest wasn't a wakeup call or anything like that. The judge ordered me to do batterer's treatment and that is the only reason I did it.

I have learned about my own behavior over time. At first, I hated group therapy. I wasn't one of those weirdos that lashed out at everyone for their own problems, so I wanted no part of it. Individual therapy wasn't any better. I had sessions where I didn't say a word the entire time and that probably wouldn't have changed if the counselors hadn't asked my probation officer to revoke me.

Finally, I listened. I dropped my attitude and looked at all the ways I'd ruined my life and Kasey's.

I don't think a batterer is ever completely better. You have to stay with therapy and groups because the violent urges don't just leave forever. I learned that I can't just put everything in the past without looking back. Not everyone feels this way. "Forgive and forget" is a popular slogan for former batterers. For me, it's scarier to believe my past actions are dead than to accept them as part of my history because denial and blocking caused me so many problems to begin with.

Whether Jake killed his ex-wife or not, he is a batterer. This country has got to take that seriously and stop treating him like a hero. He can get help and change his life, which I believe he has to do. I've been there, but now I'm delivered. I'm a born-again Christian and I've turned my life around because of Jesus. I know I'm forgiven and that keeps me in line. Jake needs that and I pray that he gets it.

The Letters

Kristin Hillshaw wrote the following note about her sister's letters. Select letters have been published, in this book only, at Kristin's request.

When I was going through my sister's belongings, about a week after her death, I found a large, thick mailing envelope. When I opened it up, I saw that she had written countless pages of thoughts. She plainly expressed her angry questions and desperate confusion. Some pages are letters and some are just dated, like journal entries.

As I've mentioned in the interviews I've given, I believe that Nate knew what was coming. She felt strongly that Jake would one day kill her and she expressed that to me on many occasions. I think she wanted to make a record of her experiences and prove to the world exactly what Jake was. She knew there would be a time when she wouldn't be able to answer the questions we all have, so she left us an explanation in writing.

I decided to publicize some of these letters, in limited release to this project only, in order to honor my sister's simple desire to tell the truth. People need to know what she went through for so many years and listen to her true feelings. I think it's the least anyone can do. We're still alive and we have the time. Let's grant her this favor.

Kristin Hillshaw
December 17, 1997

January 25, 1993

"I wanted to know if dreams could lie. You said they would try and I said 'Let them, you just let them.'" (Shawn Colvin)

I know I'm young. I know that to anyone looking at my life, all the stupid little fights with Jake, and the worries I have about my friends and the ways my life is changing seem normal. But it doesn't to me. It doesn't feel like a phase or a part of college. I feel old. I feel like everything is getting away from me.

Part of it seems so far out of my hands that I want to forget about everything. I want to grab onto the stereo-types about people my age and disappear into the crowd of "typical" college students. Drink, drink, drink. But in the fun way. Eleven plastic cupsful of cheap beer on a night of dancing. Not half a bottle of Jim Beam in your bathrobe, with a counter full of make-up for the scratches. Do whatever kind of drugs are available and socially acceptable, but with your closest friends in the bathroom of a club or a guy you hardly know it the back seat of his car. Not sleeping pills in the middle of the night, wondering how many it would take, staring at a mostly empty bottle of scotch and imagining the bite of the gulp and the grit of the powder.

Eat too much junk food and too little real food because you're too busy partying or studying to eat. Not the worst version of "the Karen Carpenter story" you can imagine, as you binge and purge after your

341

boyfriend tells you you're too chunky to fuck. Chain smoke because it looks cool, not because you'll have the nicotine fit to end all fits if you don't.

You act irresponsibly because you can. You're making mistakes that don't really matter and you can excuse it all by citing stress and pressure. But it's not the real kind of stress, just grades and whether or not to go out with the guy in your biology class.

Unfortunately, I live the real kind of stress so none of this works for me. I can't choose the cool lifestyle. Everyone else can, for some goddamned reason, but I can't! Everything boils down to the "dirty little secret" we keep hearing about on the mini-series of the week. Gee, maybe if I'm lucky my favorite actress will be in one about me some day. To some it's a secret, to some it's an obvious fact, but it doesn't matter because I will deny it.

I'll refuse help and pretend to be stubborn, just because it's an old habit by now. I pretend to want to protect Jake, but actually, I have no idea what I want.

The secret. I can't even come up with the word that seems appropriate. Nothing really describes what I'm going through. "The violence." Too formal. "The abuse." Melodramatic. "The man I love beats the shit out of me" is the closest to accuracy. It's crass enough to fit the way I feel about it: humiliated and unclean.

I used to have certain expectations from the world. I thought most people were ethical and cared about what happened to the people around them. For a while, I was shocked every time I saw something that disproved that belief, like when I walked in on my roommate giving her best friend's boyfriend a blow job. Now it's almost like I expect people to constantly betray and hurt each other. I never thought I'd be with someone who hurts me and since I am, my previous view of the world has been dissolved.

March 2, 1993

I talked to Sarah on the phone last night and the sound of her voice took me back to high school. First, I felt happiness, then sadness, then anger. I long for the "innocent" times, but then I feel so stupid. I'm just torturing myself by even thinking about the times before Jake. And I shouldn't associate times that don't include him with happiness. I shouldn't look at life without him as a fantasy. That's sick.

I'm afraid that I'll get to the point where I don't even want to be friends with Sarah anymore, simply because she represents my past.

When I apologized to her, for not confiding in her earlier, I felt like I wasn't being truthful. I told her I was trying to protect her, saying something like, "You shouldn't have to think about all my crap. You're in college, you've got plenty of your own stress." That's true, but the real reason I didn't want her to know about all the shit that's gone on is I don't want to admit how pathetic I am.

When people find out, I feel like they've cracked the façade. It reminds me of going away to Girl Scout camp as a kid. It was for 2 weeks and I was surprised at how great it was. I only wrote one letter home, because I was so busy swimming, doing crafts, and making friends. The letter said how happy I was, so my parents were shocked to find me miserable when they picked me up from camp. Poison ivy and my first crush and heartbreak over a boy left me teary-eyed the whole ride home.

The contrast between the happiness I felt before Jake was abusive and the shame I have now is huge. Sarah has all these letters from me, describing how great my life was. I was really happy out here. I met great friends, I was excited about my classes. Meeting Jake topped it all off. I had dated other guys casually, which was a lot of fun, but falling in love with this gorgeous, funny, intelligent man was the best thing I'd ever experienced.

All those feelings were discounted when he hit me for the first time.

May 8, 1993

The more I try to stop arguing with Laura, Kristin, and Josh, the worse it gets. I resent that they know. I feel exposed and I don't want to be the one that's in the middle of a circle of normal people. They watch me struggle with my self-esteem, the pretense, protecting myself, and trying to protect them. They want to be able to deal with that for me and I want to take away their fear.

Josh told me the other day that he's scared for me and I was trying to explain that the physical pain isn't the worst of it. It's feeling like nothing I do will make

Jake accept me, feeling pathetic about that, and knowing that I have no control.

It's not that I've stopped dreading the abuse, but mostly I dread the thoughts I have when he's doing it. I feel inadequate and I think about how he will never love me the way I need him to.

July 27, 1993

I'm jealous of Ryan's fiancée because she is with someone who will always treat her the way she deserves to be treated. He will love her unconditionally and respect her as an individual, not as a carbon copy of his own personality. He believes she is important and special because of her own goals and thoughts, not because she can regurgitate his. Jake claims to want an independent woman who can "think for herself," but he actually needs her to be dependent on him and think the same way he does.

Knowing that there are men out there like Ryan and Josh is comforting, but it's also sad. Every woman deserves that kind of happiness. I hate self-pity, so I try not to think this way, but why don't *I* fucking deserve it?

February 11, 1994

Dear Kristin,

I had been dreading the conversation I had with you and Mom the other day. The engagement was a secret because I couldn't handle everyone's reactions.

I know it's not good news. It's so upsetting that my engagement is a source of tension. I feel cheated when I think of what being in love is supposed to be like. And the truth is, I don't feel like I'm in love anymore. It's more like my love for Jake was a one-way ticket to this state of confinement.

October 14, 1994

Some mornings I wake up and think I've forgotten how to speak. I plan out things in my head, to say to Jake to calm him down and to Laura or Kris to reassure them that I'm okay, and then I can't say anything. It's like those dreams where you're staring at the back of your potential rescuer's head, but when you try to scream for help, nothing happens.

Sometimes the wall between me and the rest of the world is a relief because I don't have to worry about the reactions. I don't have to lie, I don't have to deal with patronizing looks, and I don't have to feel guilty about the misdirected pity.

I don't want to tell anyone the details of my pain because there's nothing they can do about it. I don't want to hurt anyone else any more than I already have.

July 18, 1995

I'm hoping I can make the leap from going to therapy because everyone else wants me to and going because I want to. That seems a long way off though.

I don't want to talk about what I have to go home to. I don't want anyone to try to talk me out of a decision that I hate but am going to stick with any way. I don't want to defend myself anymore. I'm too tired and even *I* don't believe half of my little speeches any more.

I do feel awful every time I drop out. Like the lamest break-up line ever— "it's not you, it's me." I feel helpless and depressed in therapy because it's a sharp reminder of the healthy choices I should be making.

My life is one big public service announcement and I'm not following the message. I'm the example of how *not* to live your life.

Some people believe I'm responsible for the way Jake treats me and that I'm letting it happen. I believe that too, but the accusations don't help me.

It's confusing and aggravating to live in a bubble where everyone is watching my every move and offering their opinions freely. I don't get to do that to anyone else. The contradictions give me a headache. I'm to blame for Jake controlling me, but I don't deserve to be hit. How do those ideas coexist? If it's my fault, I deserve it.

Sometimes I get a flashback to the "old me" and I feel sick. I didn't have all this anger before. I would never have pushed people away like I do now. Now I am apathetic most of the time and when I do feel something, it's bitterness.

I want to turn things around, I want to get out of this mess. I feel like everything is moving super slow and it's painful to be aware of every detail. I wish my life would speed up or I could close my eyes to everything. In the past, I felt the exact opposite, wishing time would go on and on when I was with my friends or with Jake when we first met.

November 14, 1995

Infidelity. How do people get shaped into someone who cheats or someone who doesn't? And why can't we just match up cheaters together so the rest of us don't have to deal with the pain? It's like when you sign up for housing at college and check the non-smoking box. Then your smoke-allergic roommate looks at you with perplexed, watery eyes as you light up one night because you're "really stressed out." You don't want to be with someone who cheats or smokes, but it's fine for you to do it.

I am so sick of hearing about how many relationships have survived affairs and about all the intricate reasons behind cheating. I can't take responsibility for Jake's desire to screw other women. It's one more victim-blaming rally. The person who gets lied to and cheated on is at fault for not doing enough, not listening to the cheater's needs, or not being supportive enough. What a load of crap.

If you stay in a marriage post-affair, you're approving of it and if you leave, you don't care enough about the commitment to work at it.

I can't understand either side of an adulterous affair. The married partner is looking for something the marriage can't offer, according to the theories and studies. I don't know what that is. If it's freedom and superficiality, why was the idea of making a legal commitment appealing in the first place? For the person who has sex with married people, whether they are married themselves or not, I don't get that either. If marriage and commitment is obsolete in your world, does that mean you just don't care about the person you're betraying? I guess the answer is a resounding no, or else, how could you do it? These are the questions I have for Sheila. Do you expect to be married some day and just hope another woman doesn't do what you're doing? Or would that be okay as long as you were still sleeping around?

Sometimes I look at women like Sheila, who go out every weekend and hook up with a different guy, and think how cool it would be to simply not give a shit about consequences. No guilt, no anxiety. But of course, I don't really know if that's true. It's hard for me to believe that they really have no emotional attachment to the men they fuck and if they don't, I wouldn't think the physical pleasure would feel like enough.

I get so incensed with Jake's paranoia about my socializing. That word is a joke for me. I can't do it anymore. I'm not allowed. I can't even have friends, basically. So, if he really believes I would ever have an affair, he's completely out of his mind. He would kill me if I did and we both know that.

The closest I've ever come to cheating was when I dated this guy from my math class during my freshman year, for like 2 weeks, before finding out that he had a girlfriend in Dallas. I went to confession and cried so hard that the priest couldn't understand me. It was like I was confessing to a murder.

February 7, 1997

As I look over these notes and letters, I realize that even though I'm constantly telling myself that I don't expect things to change, I really do have that hope buried inside me. I look at what an experience *should* be, like the engagement and the marriage and being in love, and while I know I can never have the happiness, I still want it.

I filed for divorce today and I was hoping to feel relief and a sense of freedom. I feel neither. I'm trying not to let him get to me at all any more. I'm trying to believe in myself again and treat myself well.

I've always believed in taking marriage seriously, so now I feel like I've betrayed my own values. I can't legitimately say I have no other choice, but I can't continue to put myself through this.

I'm trying to distance myself from my memories of the worst times, but it doesn't work. The fear seems to follow me everywhere and I don't feel safe. Maybe I need that so I won't change my mind.

When I find myself looking at couples I don't know and wondering what their relationship is like, I think of the transition between thinking that physical violence would never happen to you, to being right in it. The realization that it is actually happening and that there's nothing you can do to stop it, is terrifying. It's something you can never envision. When you walk across an empty parking lot alone at night, you can think to yourself, "I would have a nervous breakdown if I got into my car and felt a hand on my shoulder," but even as you have a glimmer of panic when you hear trees rustling, you know it won't happen to you. Your life will never go beyond the perspective of listening to Oprah's hysterical guests tell their horror stories, while you sit on your couch, sipping a Diet Coke and thinking, "Gee, how terrible."

April 20, 1997

Dear Jake,

I feel like I can say some good things about our relationship, for the first time in a long while. You've made the right decision, by not fighting me on the divorce, and I know you'll see that soon. It takes a lot for us to admit that we can't make our marriage work, since we both hate admitting failure. But we're proving that we respect each other and care enough to stop hurting each other.

Trying to be friends seems like a reasonable task, but I'm very nervous about it. It seems comparable to coming out of an alcohol rehab. center and deciding to drink one glass of Chardonnay a day. I love you and I would still have you in my life if I could have the security of knowing you'll never try to control me or hurt me again, but I don't think that's realistic. You're still the same person and you haven't gotten the help you keep claiming to want, so what would stop you from stalking me, hassling me to take you back, and threatening me? Ideally, I would move away and start a life that is solely my own. That's what I deserve, Jake. But I also deserve to live anywhere I want. I deserve to finally see my friends. I shouldn't have to continue to shape my life around you.

I take the blame for some of our past problems, but not the way you blame me. I believe I was at fault for staying with you and that's where my responsibility ended. I can't take the blame for your anger, insecurity, control issues, or rages. That was all you.

I'm constantly praying that you will get help. That's the only way I will know you are sorry. You didn't love me enough or feel guilty enough about hurting me, to get help when we were together. That's bad enough, but if you can just go on now as if nothing ever happened, it'll sting so much worse.

I know you're not going to live out the rest of your life alone. You will fall in love again and if you don't face up to your demons before that happens, you will ruin another life. You cannot hurt another woman the way you hurt me, Jake. Neither of you will survive it.

I know you want my forgiveness. I know that you have always regretted your violence, manipulation, all of it. But I do not know how to forgive you. I lied so many times to you, when we were together, by saying I forgave you. I never could. I am going to try to do it now, but it's going to be hard. You've got to understand that.

I look back at all the times I told my friends about the positive aspects of our relationship and I feel sick. I was devaluing myself more and more, every time I said that you didn't mean it, that I did things to encourage you, or that our love was more important than the "bad times." I spent so many years creating layers of detailed excuses that I started to believe them. Now I need to let go of your issues and reasons for hurting me, as I try like Hell to get on with my own life.

September 12, 1997

Dear God,

Please forgive me for all my sins and accept my humble efforts to be worthy of your love.

I'm sorry for being fearful. I didn't mean to doubt you, but I knew Jake could kill me and I was afraid that he would.

I understand your will now. I know you have always loved me and protected me. I know that I have chosen my own fate by not being able to sustain my marriage.

Thank you for your forgiveness and everlasting love. I am ready and willing to accept your plans for me.

Amen.

Gift
Local Author
#2

CPSIA information can be obtained
at www.ICGtesting.com
Printed in the USA
FFHW011103261118
49637857-54010FF

9 781644 383032